GONE
FOR
GOUDA

St. Martin's Paperbacks titles
by Korina Moss

CHEDDAR OFF DEAD
GONE FOR GOUDA

GONE FOR GOUDA

A Cheese Shop Mystery

BY

KORINA MOSS

St. Martin's Paperbacks

First published in the United States by St. Martin's Paperbacks, an imprint of St. Martin's Publishing Group.

GONE FOR GOUDA

Copyright © 2022 by Korina Moss.

All rights reserved.

For information, address St. Martin's Publishing Group, 120 Broadway, New York, NY 10271.

www.stmartins.com

ISBN: 978-1-250-79521-2

Our books may be purchased in bulk for promotional, educational, or business use. Please contact your local bookseller or the Macmillan Corporate and Premium Sales Department at 1-800-221-7945, ext. 5442, or by email at MacmillanSpecialMarkets@macmillan.com.

Printed in the United States of America

St. Martin's Paperbacks edition / October 2022

10 9 8 7 6 5 4 3 2 1

For Mom and Dad

ACKNOWLEDGMENTS

My gratitude goes to Madeline Houpt for being an insightful editor, a great cheerleader, and the most pun-filled person I know; to my terrific agent Jill Marsal, to Danielle Christopher and Alan Ayers who designed and illustrated, respectively, another gorgeous book cover; to copy editor John Simko, for skillfully teaching me how much I don't know about the English language; to my supportive publicity and marketing team, Sarah Haeckel and Allison Zeigler; to my production editor John Rounds for herding the cats and shepherding this book to completion; and to everybody at St. Martin's who had a hand in bringing this book to life. I am so proud to be a St. Martin's author.

I owe a huge debt of thanks to Caitlin Lonning, whose advice and enthusiasm for *Gone for Gouda* made a considerable impact. This would not be the book it is without her expertise.

A special thanks to Robin Grenier, for coming up with just the right name for an important character in this book.

I'm thankful for all the mystery authors who have befriended me—their kinship has allowed me to traverse this author journey with much more grace and confidence than I would've otherwise had. I humbly thank

Julie Anne Lindsey (Bree Baker), Carolyn Haines, and Liz Mugavero (Cate Conte) for their endorsement of my series. I'm grateful for Sisters in Crime, Mystery Writers of America, and my Writers Who Kill colleagues for providing an invaluable sense of community.

A special shout-out goes to Rosalie Spielman, a kick-ass author and friend, who by the grace of God—or rather, the incomparable Barb Goffman—crossed paths with me last year. I'm glad I don't have to do this author thing without her.

I am so grateful to my wonderful readers who are already invested in my Cheese Shop Mystery series, to the bloggers and podcasters who've told their fans about my books, and to my friends who've been loud and proud in their support of me—it means the world to me. I must especially mention my fabulous Aunt Judy and her extraordinary peeps.

I've saved the final thanks for my family, especially my siblings—Kim, Kari, Kelly, Kris, and Ron—and their spouses, my nieces and nephews and their families, and of course my amazing son, for being supportive in every way. Being able to share this adventure makes it all the sweeter.

#TeamCheese!

The great thing about cheese is
that it never goes out of season.

Willa Bauer

CHAPTER 1

❧

"Bavarian beer cheese."

I slid the ramekin of my version of German Obatzda across the sampling counter to the middle-aged couple the way a bartender might offer up a brew. Since I was a cheesemonger, however, the cheese-to-stout ratio favored the cheese heavily.

"It's a different take on American beer cheese," I continued. "The Germans came up with the recipe as a way to use up their soft cheese before it went bad. It's mixed with butter and seasonings. The orange hue is from the paprika. You can make it with a combination of Camembert, brie, cream cheese . . . or you can go more authentic and use a strong Bavarian cheese. I mixed the two—Camembert and Romadur—for this one. Spread some on that pretzel bread and see what you think."

The couple had come in looking for some elevated tailgating ideas, as the Cal vs. Stanford football game was approaching. I could see they were hesitant after putting a nose to the pungent concoction.

Archie, my loyal employee and friend, stood next to me behind the counter, watching the interaction. I'd been mentoring him since he began working in my shop last spring. "I don't blame you," he said to them. "I was a little scared to try it, too, after we made it. It's got some intense flavors in there, but it's delicious, believe me."

They must've decided to trust the affable nineteen-year-old, because they each plucked a bite-sized piece of the kosher salted pretzel bagels from the proffered basket and slathered on the dip, bravely popping it in their mouths. They nodded with satisfied smiles.

"That *is* good," the husband said, going back for more.

"There's a reason it's been around since the nineteen twenties," Archie said, handing them one of the recipe cards we'd typed up that morning.

I stepped back to let him take over the sale with Mrs. Schultz, who'd also been with me since we opened Curds & Whey seven months ago. She stood behind him at the checkout counter. Under her apron, she wore a blouse, a colorful string scarf, and a pleated skirt that showed off her good ankles. It was a trait she took pride in, being smack dab in her sixties, as she liked to say.

I'd told her and Archie the history of Obatzda while the three of us experimented that morning with several recipes until we came up with the current concoction, the best of the lot. Outside the shop windows, the brilliant red-orange leaves still clung to the crepe myrtle trees dotting the Pleasant Avenue sidewalk, making me yearn for hearty fall recipes. That was yet another thing I loved about cheese—it never went out of season.

While Archie cut and wrapped the cheeses the couple settled on buying, I noticed a twenty-something guy tentatively enter the shop, barely stepping across the threshold. He had a Clark Kent look about him, with his slicked-back hair and equally dark-framed glasses, and his shirt buttoned all the way to his Adam's apple. Just like Superman's alter ego, despite the outward humble appearance, he had attractive features and a fit physique.

I felt a chilly breeze follow him in as I approached to

greet him. I attributed it to a blip in the gorgeous October weather Yarrow Glen was having, which usually hung in the low seventies, but was dropping bit by bit as November neared. However, days later I would consider whether it had been a sign of things to come.

"Can I help you?" I asked him.

Contrary to his hesitant body language, his eyes scanned the shop intently. I followed his gaze, wondering what he thought he'd find while rooted to his spot by the open front door. Curds & Whey was made for exploring up close. Only then could one appreciate the variations in texture and color of the cheeses and dare to inhale the intensity of their fragrances. My store held wheels of aged cheeses in wax casings and wrapped wedges from all over the world stacked on distressed turned-leg tables, so they towered over jars of relishes, olives, and jams. More hard cheeses crowded reclaimed shelves lining the wall opposite the checkout and sampling counters where soft cheeses were displayed in refrigerated cases.

When his attention finally returned to me, he asked abruptly, "You work here?"

I looked down at my wheat-colored Curds & Whey apron I wore over a white cotton blouse and khakis that made it rather obvious that I worked there. Even my sleeves were rolled up. "Yes. I'm the owner, Willa Bauer. How can I help you?"

"Oh, you're Willa Bauer." He visibly relaxed. "We spoke on the phone. I'm Thomas Doolittle, Phoebe Winston's personal assistant." He spoke with a slight lisp and now made an effort to smile.

"Yes! Thomas. Nice to meet you." I offered my hand for a proper greeting. He pulled his hand out of his jeans pocket and finally stepped farther into the shop to shake mine. I noticed his other hand was clutching a tablet.

He leaned in and spoke quietly. "I-I'm sorry, but they're going to have to leave." He pointed to the beer cheese customers who were paying for their order.

"Excuse me?"

"Phoebe's here to look over the place before her Book and Cook event tomorrow and we don't want anyone bothering her."

"They're customers of mine, not fans of hers."

"Everyone wants a piece of Phoebe, even if they're not a fan."

"I'm sorry, but my shop is for my customers, so—"

"Thomas, don't be silly." None other than Phoebe Winston, herself, swept in.

I recognized the striking twenty-eight-year-old from my research skimming through the celebrity gossip pages, but anybody would've known she was *somebody*. Normal people didn't have glowing skin and perfect posture and that ineffable *something* about them. Her presence filled the room. The beer cheese customers stared at her, sensing it too.

Mrs. Schultz and I had heard the name 'Phoebe Winston,' but didn't know much more than that until the company whose vegan cheese we carry contacted us to host a promotional event for her new cookbook/autobiography/ self-help book *Authentically Me: My Journey to Kindness, Authenticity, and a Vegan Life*. However, the same couldn't be said of Archie. He had watched her season of *Fire It Up* six years ago, a reality competition show that blended *Big Brother* with *Chopped*. The program, which showed contestants living together and cooking against each other in a bid for the final prize, was on television three times a week, but viewers could watch their every move 24/7 via the show's app. Afterward, she became the new reality show 'It girl.' Archie had confided that Phoebe Winston had been his first teenage crush. Thus, I disregarded the fact that the beer cheese couple now seemed invisible to him, as he stared past them at Phoebe. Mrs. Schultz finished the transaction, and the couple left with thanks and one last look behind them.

Phoebe nodded almost imperceptibly at her assistant Thomas, who duly closed the door after the couple left. Except for extreme weather, it always remained open during shop hours to make customers feel more welcome to come in, but I'd make an exception for Phoebe Winston. Having a celebrity like her give a talk and a cooking demonstration in my little shop was a huge stroke of luck. She had a rising lifestyle brand and an almost cultlike following on social media.

It would've taken me hours to put together the stylish, deliberately casual look that Phoebe Winston had—a short white blazer over a thin matching sweater, which she wore tucked into her wide-legged rose gold slacks that perfectly skimmed her tall frame. I would've looked like a sweating marshmallow in all those layers. Her thick blond hair was just as impeccably understated, parted in the middle and flipping in at the bottom just below her shoulders.

I self-consciously pressed my short hair behind my ears and ruffled my bangs in hopes that I could cover the premature gray strands that kept popping up like neon against my otherwise jet-black hair. For heaven's sake—I was only thirty-three. When I lamented about it recently on the phone to my mother, she told me she never worried about her hair turning gray, that she'd earned it with all those long days on the farm. If you ask me, that's a lousy reward for hard work.

Before this very moment, I was fine with my sufficiently satisfactory appearance. My blue eyes sometimes garnered compliments and my bangs covered my oversized forehead. I didn't mind my heart-shaped face or my perky nose. I'd been five-foot-two since the seventh grade, so except for having a hard time reaching upper shelves, I never thought much about my height either. I came by my cottage cheese thighs honestly, and despite my diet being mostly made up of cheese, I still managed to have a waist. But now, standing before the beautiful, statuesque Phoebe Winston, I couldn't help feeling a little crabby about my draw in the gene pool lottery.

With her perfect chin pushed in the air maybe higher than it needed to be, she stood waiting to be addressed. I obliged.

"Phoebe, hi. I'm Willa Bauer. It's so nice to meet you."

Her multiple rings pinched my hand as she shook it. "We're already on a first-name basis. How nice." Behind her unnaturally white smile, I got the feeling maybe she thought it wasn't.

A white fluffy head, no bigger than a softball, with floppy little ears popped out of the oversized handbag hanging from her arm. Oh no—Phoebe's famous dog. I should've known. He was melt-on-the-spot adorable, but this was one thing I couldn't overlook.

"He's precious, but I'm so sorry, we can't allow him in here. Health department regulations," I said.

The dog barked—a high-pitched yip—as if to protest on cue.

"I know," I said to him. "You're so cute. I'm sorry."

Archie broke from his trance and went over to soothe the dog with puppy talk. I'd seen him do the same with his own Chihuahua, who was smitten with him. It seemed to work just as well with Phoebe's Maltese, and with its owner for that matter.

"You must be a dog person," she said to Archie. "He likes you." She took the well-groomed dog out of her bag with a single hand and tucked him in the crook of her arm. He almost looked like a stuffed toy with his shiny black eyes and button nose against the white fluff that was the rest of him.

"Hi Buttercup," Archie cooed at him.

"You know his name?" Phoebe seemed pleased.

"Of course!" Suddenly realizing he'd given himself away as a superfan, he continued shyly, "I-I've seen him on your Instagram. I can bring him outside for you."

She handed Archie the dog, who immediately licked his face. "And what's your name?" she asked.

"I'm Archie."

"So nice to meet you, Archie."

It was definitely a warmer hello than I'd gotten. It even sounded a bit flirtatious. Archie's face was generously sprinkled with freckles, except where the port-wine stain was located across his left cheek. A light pink blush now overtook his pale complexion.

"Do you mind putting him in the car?" she asked him.

I was surprised by her acquiescence. Archie was a miracle worker.

"I can—" Thomas began.

"Thomas, can you give Archie the key?" Phoebe spoke over him.

Thomas silently handed Archie the key fob from his pocket.

"Is that the car?" Archie indicated the white Range Rover he viewed out the front window blocking the near side of the street. "You're bound to attract attention double-parked like that. You want me to pull it into a space?"

"Good idea, Archie. Thank you. See Tom-Tom? That's what initiative looks like," she said.

Thomas looked down at his spotless white Nikes, seemingly embarrassed.

She turned her attention back to Archie. "You can put Buttercup in his bed in the back seat. While you're there, would you be a doll and bring in the boxes of signed books in the trunk? I need your brawn."

I had to press my lips closed when I caught Mrs. Schultz's eye. I knew she was giggling internally. I was too. There was a plethora of positive adjectives to describe Archie, but *brawny* was most definitely not on that list. He was lanky with rangy limbs, which his T-shirt, camo cargo shorts, and Curds & Whey apron didn't hide. However, Phoebe's flattery seemed to work on him—it was obvious he was smitten.

"You bet." Archie practically skipped out the door with the tiny dog.

I introduced Mrs. Schultz, who, after a few pleasantries, surprised me by also being taken in by the charismatic Phoebe Winston. Upon learning that Mrs. Schultz was a retired high school drama teacher, they were belting out a duet of the refrain from "There's No Business Like Show Business" in no time. With Mrs. Schultz's cropped curls and toothy smile, the song highlighted a resemblance to Ethel Merman I'd never noticed before.

Afterward Phoebe said to her, "Can I ask a huge favor of you? There's no water for Buttercup in the car and I don't want him getting too warm in there."

"Sure, I can bring him some water," Mrs. Schultz replied.

"Bottled, if you don't mind."

"Oh, okay, sure."

"In a ceramic bowl. We don't use plastic." Phoebe scrunched her nose at the word *plastic*.

"No problem." Mrs. Schultz hurried to the back of the shop and through the swinging door to the stockroom to fulfill Phoebe's request.

Closing the front door hadn't done much good. Chet from the meadery wandered in. His tousled shoulder-length hair sometimes covered the sharp angles of his face and soulful eyes that looked like they might be hiding deep thoughts. He stopped short upon seeing Phoebe. She seemed to have that effect on people.

"Do I know you?" she said to him.

"Uh—I'm here for Willa," he answered uncomfortably.

"Hey, Chet. Don't tell me I was supposed to put together a cheese platter for Roman," I said. I supplied Chet's boss—and the owner of Golden Glen Meadery—with cheese for his mead-tasting events. Roman and I were also close friends, inching our way to possibly more.

"I don't know about any cheese platter," Chet said to my relief.

I caught a glimpse of Phoebe's silent direction to Thomas in the form of a scowl before she plastered on the same smile that had disappeared the moment Mrs. Schultz had gone to the stockroom.

Thomas cleared his throat and addressed Chet. "I'm sorry, but we need to keep the shop clear of fans right now so we can prepare for tomorrow evening's event."

"Fans?" Chet said, his eyes questioning the three of us. "Sorry, I don't know what you're talking about." He turned to me and added, "Although I *am* a fan of yours, Willa."

I chuckled. "Thank you, Chet. He works at the meadery across the street," I explained to Phoebe and her assistant. "You should stop by there when you're done here. I can introduce you to Roman. Have you ever tried mead? It's an alcoholic drink made with honey. Oh wait, so does that make it not vegan because of the bees?"

"I don't have time for it, anyway. Tom-Tom, the lists." Phoebe snapped her fingers and Thomas threw back the cover to his iPad as crisply as an army private clicks his heels at attention to his sergeant. She looked impatiently at Chet to leave.

He ignored her, addressing me, "I was supposed to meet Ginger when I got off from work, but she's not outside." Ginger, his girlfriend, worked at the bookstore café a few doors down from Curds & Whey. "My phone has zero battery, so I probably missed her text. I thought maybe you'd seen her."

"Sorry, I haven't. Maybe she's still working. Is the café closed already?"

"Are you talking about Ginger O'Donnell?" Phoebe interjected, much to my surprise.

"That's right," Chet said.

"Ginger's an old friend of mine. We went to culinary school together. I knew she moved here afterward, but I wasn't if she still lived here. I was hoping to see her. Can you be a doll and let her know I'm in town?"

"Sure. Who are you?" Chet dared to ask.

Thomas huffed, "This is Phoebe Winston!"

Chet snapped his fingers. "Oh, yeah, the one on Willa's flyers. Ginger's never mentioned you, but I'll tell her."

"Let her know I texted her last week if she's still at the same number. It's been a few years."

"Sure thing. See ya, Willa."

"Good luck finding Ginger," I answered.

On his way out, he held the door open for Archie to enter, struggling with a heavy box emblazoned with the publisher's logo.

"Where do you want these, Willa?" Archie asked, an obvious strain in his voice.

"On the floor behind the register is fine," I said.

Momentarily I heard the box of books meet the floor with a thud. Mrs. Schultz came out from the back, carrying a small ceramic bowl and a bottle of spring water, as instructed. She and Archie went back outside together. Thomas shut the door behind them as soon as their shoes hit the sidewalk. Phoebe's full attention returned to my shop.

"Now onto the matter at hand." She looked around, but I couldn't discern how she felt about what she saw.

My shop's aesthetic was inspired by my brief time

working at a fromagerie outside of Lyon where my passion for cheese blossomed. I wanted to bring the color, warmth, and romance of France into my shop. The textured orange-gold walls resembled rich wallpaper above raised panel wainscoting the color of light butterscotch. It was offset by one full antique oak-paneled wall behind the checkout and sampling counters. I hoped the publicity of having Phoebe Winston would generate enough sales for me to afford the crimson Aubusson area rugs I'd had my eye on, but still couldn't justify buying. My hardwood floors sufficed for now.

"This is very . . . quaint," she said.

I wasn't sure it was meant as a compliment, but I thanked her anyway. "Let me show you where we'll be doing the event tomorrow."

I led her to the rear of the shop where we'd be holding her event in the kitchenette area. The pale teal cabinets added a splash of color to the white quartz countertops and matching island. The long farm table perpendicular to the island was used for cheesemaking students to sit and enjoy their creations with the proper accompaniments. During shop hours, it held displays of beautiful cheeseboards, spreaders, and novelty gifts for cheese lovers, including Phoebe's cookbooks.

"I'm thrilled you chose Curds and Whey to promote your newest book," I said when we reached the kitchenette.

"Ve-Cheez is partially sponsoring this book tour and you were one of the first shops to start carrying it. Plus, Sadler Culinary School had gotten in touch with me to contribute to their raffle, seeing as I'm their most famous graduate, so it made sense to combine the two."

My confidence plummeted knowing her decision to hold the event here had nothing to do with her being impressed by the quality of my shop. I supposed beggars couldn't be choosers. I'd have to capitalize on my fortunate location. "I have no doubt this is going to be a great event."

"Thank goodness for your confidence, because it looks like we've got quite a bit to do to make this workable." She continued to survey the space I was proud of having designed myself.

"Let me first show you what I had in mind," I said. "You can prepare the recipes here at the island. The farm table will be pushed against this back wall, and we'll set up the folding chairs here to face you. We've had talks here before that were standing room only. It's always worked out great."

"I don't want my fans to stand. They tend to get too close. This is why we made it an after-hours ticketed event, so everyone would have a seat."

"Oh. Well, I have about fifteen folding chairs in the stockroom, plus the two farm-table benches we can use for the back rows." I knew we didn't have enough chairs for the event, but customers never minded standing before.

"Willa, you've read my book, haven't you? So you know what we need to do now."

"Of course. Sure." Truth be told, I skipped the *intentions*, *integrity*, and *authenticity* mumbo jumbo and went straight to the vegan cheese recipes.

"Let's set our intention and make it happen. Thomas." The finger snapping recurred. "Find a rental place for appropriate seating and send Willa the information ASAP." She then assessed the kitchenette's island. "Thomas, what's wrong here?"

He looked up from his tablet. "There's no demonstration mirror. Phoebe needs one set up behind her so the audience can see what she's making," he said to me.

Phoebe smiled like a teacher after her star pupil answered a question correctly from the whiteboard. "We can't have people hovering," she added.

"Uh . . . I'm not sure how I'd get something like that installed, especially on such short notice."

"That's what Thomas is for. Right, Tom-Tom?"

"We'll make it happen," he said.

I'd have to have a serious discussion with *Tom-Tom* later. Unless he was a magician, he was over-promising.

"Let's talk about the food," she said.

"I got Thomas's list weeks ago. I bought everything fresh this morning." Finally! I had something well in hand.

She sighed and shot another glance at her assistant.

"I'll send you an updated recipe list later today," Thomas said. Phoebe cast him a look of approval, which seemed to feed his soul.

"What do you mean 'updated'?" I asked with a sinking feeling.

"My food needs to match my creative energy," Phoebe answered. "We merely sent those recipes so you would get an idea of what we'd be doing. I have to *feel* the food. You can understand that. I can tell by looking at your shop that you're a creative, yourself."

I never trusted anyone who used the word *creative* as a noun. I didn't care about *feeling* her food, only about buying it.

Thomas spoke as he tapped his tablet. "I'll email you the names of the recipes and you can use her new book to find the ingredients." Phoebe cleared her throat, which spurred on Thomas again. "You'll also need to have everything measured out and ready to go before she arrives for the event."

My mind was reeling with things still to be done. I'd been naïve to think I had everything handled, having never hosted something of this caliber. Thomas must've seen the look of panic I was certain was apparent on my face.

"Some of the ingredients are bound to overlap," he said, obviously trying to make me feel better.

Phoebe patted his arm to halt his reassurances. "I have no doubt Willa is more than capable of managing a shopping list and measuring out a few ingredients," she said.

Of course I'd do whatever she asked. I knew I'd only break even from the event itself if I sold plenty of Phoebe's books and the Ve-Cheez we carried, but it was the publicity from having her here that would put my little shop on the map. Thus, for the foreseeable future, her signed books would be featured in the front-window displays along with the event announcement, and Archie made sure our website featured Phoebe's appearance. We had to make this count.

As Archie had told me, becoming vegan was only the jumping off point of her career. Being an *authenticity influencer*, whatever that meant, was her rising brand. In short, she saw herself on track to become the next Oprah. Seeing how her charisma affected people, perhaps she would be.

Still, I couldn't help but worry that every new demand was costing me money. I could practically hear the incessant dings of an old-fashioned cash register, as cartoon dollar signs circled above my head.

"I completely understand your reservations," she said, placing a hand over mine, as if offering condolences for my finances. "It's my publisher. They're the experts and I just follow whatever they say to do. Thomas makes sure of that. I have to toe the line with him around."

Thomas puffed up with pride. She certainly had him fooled, but I knew who was running the show. Phoebe's modus operandi—to compliment you into doing what she wanted—was apparent to me.

"Will I be able to get in touch with you in case I have

questions? Will you be staying at the Inn at Yarrow Glenn?" I asked her.

"I've rented a house outside the town center. I need my privacy, otherwise I get fans and paparazzi following my every move. You can contact Thomas. He'll be staying at the inn. I trust him implicitly to know exactly what I need." She smiled at him again, which made me gag a little. If she blew any more smoke up Tom-Tom's butt, he'd have it coming out of his ears.

Mrs. Schultz came in, followed by Archie with another box of books. He set them down atop the first box.

"All set," he said, shaking out his arms. "Your car is in front of Lou's Market." Archie handed her back the key.

"Thank you, doll." She smiled at Archie. He was a goner.

"Buttercup is resting comfortably in the back seat," Mrs. Schultz declared, seeming happy to please her.

Not Mrs. Schultz too!

"Boy, Willa, you really hit the jackpot with these two," Phoebe said.

She certainly liked to hand out fake compliments, but this time she happened upon the truth.

She headed to the front door. "I think our work here is done," she said.

And mine's just beginning.

Thomas flipped his tablet closed. "I'll be in touch," he told me.

"Oh, one more thing," Phoebe said. "I'll need to borrow Archie for tomorrow."

If I was surprised, Thomas appeared even more so.

"I'm afraid that's not possible," I said. "I'll need the extra hand to set up, especially after all these new demand—er, developments."

"You worry too much. Thomas will help you. He's

a whiz at this." She appealed directly to Archie now. "I could really use your assistance hauling tomorrow's books and signage, and especially with Buttercup. He's simply enamored with you, and he doesn't take to everybody." She pointedly looked at Thomas, then returned her focus to Archie. "You'd be a huge help to me at the house. Surely Willa doesn't want me arriving late and frazzled."

I could see right through her, but Archie looked like a puppy who'd just been given a tennis ball and told he could play outside. I didn't want to squash what was probably to Archie an opportunity of a lifetime, spending time in the company of Phoebe Winston.

"What time do you need him?" I asked.

Phoebe took out her phone and tapped on it. Then she handed it to Archie. "Put your number in and I'll call you."

"I can take his information," Thomas said, opening his tablet and inserting himself between the two of them.

"I'll be in touch with him *directly*." Phoebe stared down Thomas until he closed his tablet and moved to the other side of her like a scolded child. She returned her attention to Archie, her tone once again light. "The car will be at the inn. You can get the key from Thomas. I'll text you my address when I'm ready for you to come. I can count on you to be discreet, can't I? Only Thomas knows where I'm staying."

Archie merely nodded. His normally Tigger-like personality rarely left him at a loss for words. He was definitely under her spell.

"I knew from the moment I met you that you were an authentic soul," Phoebe said to him. Then to me, "We'll see you tomorrow, then. I have no doubt everything will be to our specifications so we can pull off a perfect event for my fans. All we have to do is . . ." She waited for me to finish her sentence.

". . . Make some phone calls?" I ventured.

"Set our intention," she corrected. She wagged a perfectly manicured finger at me, "You need to read my book again, Willa."

I'll add it to my to-do list.

Phoebe Winston sailed out with Thomas in tow just as she'd swept in—like a tornado. And I was Dorothy, caught in the vortex.

CHAPTER 2

I let Mrs. Schultz and Archie go home a little early. Tomorrow was going to be a long day, with Phoebe's event being held after hours upon her insistence. My list of things still to do was as long as a CVS receipt, yet just before closing I found myself flipping through both of Phoebe's cookbooks to replicate one of her vegan recipes. I felt guilty having such little experience with the vegan cheese I was selling. I wanted to be able to give an honest firsthand account of it, even if I only had one recipe under my belt.

Her debut cookbook had recipes based on the *Fire It Up* challenges, so only one section was vegan themed, and the recipes seemed a bit complex. Who knew I could make stinging nettle loaves three ways? (Or one way, for that matter.) I ended up choosing a simpler appetizer from her most recent book, made with Ve-Cheez's cream cheez and their vegan mozzarella, combined with chives, shallots, and garlic. The fun part was rolling the *cheez*-ball bites in a coating of finely crushed pecans mixed with spices. I left them chilling in the fridge while I washed the mixing bowls and utensils.

My best friend and next-door neighbor, Baz, pushed through the swinging door and wheeled his handmade demonstration mirror from the stockroom where he'd been working on it for the past hour. It looked like a portable chalkboard for a seven-foot teacher. I clapped excitedly and left the dishes to dry in order to get a better look at it.

"Baz, you're a genius."

"Told you I could put something together," he said, puffing up so he reached his full five-foot-eight stature.

"I had no doubt," I replied, which was the truth. Not only was Baz the local self-contracted handyman for Carl's Hardware, he was also skilled at woodworking. The cheeseboard he'd made for me last spring engraved with *Favorite Cheesemonger* under my name, which hung proudly on the wall of my shop, was just a small example of his talent. "It's just missing one minor yet humongously major detail."

"I know—the mirror. As soon as Carl opens up the store tomorrow, I'll get a sheet of that flexible mirror material and see if that works well enough."

"You're not sure if it will work? Don't tell me that."

"It'll be fine. Don't worry so much."

"Easy for you to say."

"Not so easy for me to say, 'cause when Willa's stressed, everybody's stressed."

I was going to protest, but he wasn't exactly wrong. That was the great thing about being best friends with Baz—we didn't hold back with each other. Over the months of our friendship, he'd become the little brother I'd lost, or close to it anyway. Nobody could replace Grayson. Our easy banter patched a small part of that wound, though.

"Okay, I'll relax," I promised.

"Good."

"As soon as tomorrow's over."

He shook his head in resignation.

"Know what'll help ease my anxiety?" I asked almost rhetorically.

"Cheese," he answered without hesitation.

He knew me too well. I took the small plate of vegan nut-covered *cheez* balls out of the refrigerator while he washed his hands. "I think they should be firm enough to eat. They'd be cute with little pretzel sticks in them as edible toothpicks, but since it's just us, you can use your fingers. I might have some leftover pieces of pretzel bagels if you want."

He dried his hands and reached for one. "What are they?"

"Vegan *cheez* balls with—"

He retracted his hand. "Never mind."

"You're not even going to try it?"

"Listen, you got me to eat cheese other than cheddar, all right? Be happy with that."

"Fine. Baby steps. But it won't kill you to eat something healthy."

"You never know. My body might go into shock."

I took a bite of one, not letting on that I, too, was feeling a bit dubious. The crunch of the pecans was a nice contrast to the creamy center imbued with the warm spices of chili powder, cinnamon, and nutmeg.

Baz waited for my assessment.

"It's not going to convert me, but if I had a dairy allergy or wanted to go vegan—"

". . . or was on a desert island, starving . . ."

I ignored his teasing. "This would make the cut. I'll leave the rest in the fridge for Mrs. Schultz and Archie to try tomorrow."

Baz laughed. I wasn't fooling him. What could I say? I grew up on a dairy farm, selling and eating cheese with an 'se' all my life.

I noticed the time and ambled to the front of the shop to close and lock the door. "I have other things to concentrate on right now anyway . . . like Phoebe Winston."

"Is she here?" A. J. Stringer, the editor of the *Glen Ga-zette*, had walked in just as I reached the front door.

"Hello to you, too, A. J."

"Yeah, okay. Hi, Willa." No matter the season, A. J. was rarely seen wearing anything other than one of those green Salvation Army jackets with multiple pockets over a T-shirt and a pair of worn jeans. Even for a potential interview with Phoebe Winston, the thirtyish editor hadn't upgraded his outfit, or by the looks of it, tried to give his curly black hair any other style besides a fresh-out-of-bed look. His hand rested on the strap of the worn canvas messenger bag he wore across his torso. "So is she here?" He quickly scanned the shop and gave Baz a nod when he came to the front to join us.

"Sorry, she was in earlier. You missed her," I informed him.

He sighed heavily. "Too bad. I was hoping to get an interview with her for tomorrow's paper. I wouldn't mind another publicity boon for the *Gazette*."

"Something a little more positive this time would be good," Baz said.

Last spring's murder of a magazine critic pushed the *Glen Gazette* out of the shadows of the larger city papers by supplying insider details of the crime to the Associated Press, but it wasn't the kind of publicity anybody in Yarrow Glen wanted—except maybe for A. J. Perhaps he had felt the rush of hard-hitting news for the first time in his brief career.

"I invited Deandra to Phoebe's Book and Cook event tomorrow," I told him, referring to one of his longtime writers. Despite the rough start she and I had when we'd first met over questions about a dead body, she'd become an ally, always fitting anything special Curds & Whey was doing into the next issue.

"I know," he replied. "But I want to get an in-depth interview with Phoebe, one-on-one. Her publisher didn't return any of my calls. You don't happen to have her direct number?"

"Sorry, I don't. But her assistant is staying at the inn. You could try him. His name's Thomas Doolittle."

"Thanks for the tip." A. J. bounded out of the store. I locked the door behind him—closing time.

His request reminded me to check my phone, which left me disappointed. "Thomas hasn't sent me the recipes yet that Phoebe wants to use. Tomorrow's going to be one busy day."

"Why don't you take your own advice?" Baz said.

"What do you mean?"

"Let's go find Thomas at the inn so you can get those recipes from him. While we're there, we can grab some food at The Cellar."

"Have I told you lately you're a genius?"

Baz checked the nonexistent watch on his wrist. "It's been over ten minutes. You're slacking."

Our growing appetites propelled me to complete the shop-closing duties in record time with Baz's help. We walked the two blocks up Pleasant Avenue across Main Street to the historic Inn at Yarrow Glen. The turn-of-the-century inn was tucked between rows of evergreens. An inviting porch and an identical exterior second-floor balcony wrapped around the entire white, symmetrical structure. Bordeaux-colored blooms overflowed from two large urns flanking the door, providing bursts of color.

We stepped into the modest lobby. There was a beautiful spindle staircase to the right, but the crackling logs ablaze in the arched fireplace caught my attention. Around it was a sitting area comprised of a Chesterfield sofa and two wing chairs on either side of what looked like an antique walnut coffee table. The highly polished wood floor was covered with a dark print rug. A matching runner led to the ornate reception desk at the rear of the lobby.

We were starving by the time we got to the inn, so Thomas was going to have to wait. With a quick wave to skirt Constance, the extremely chatty front desk receptionist, we took the short hallway off to the left of the quaint lobby. At the end was a red door with a tattered paper list of acoustic bands taped to it that would be playing each weekend after eight. There was no sign for the pub, which wasn't a problem for its clientele. Although the inn had changed hands many times, The Cellar, which originally held the inn's wine, continued to be the top hangout among locals.

Descending the steps to The Cellar always gave me the feeling of going to some secret society. The stone walls and floor gave it a somewhat gothic feel that was highlighted by the wrought-iron ring chandeliers that hung from the ceiling.

A booth tucked into one of the nooks in the wall became free, so we grabbed it. It was the coziest place to sit and drowned out some of the ambient noise. Baz handed me one of the narrow menus kept on the table, as if we were going to order anything other than their Cellar Reuben. We'd been obsessed with it ever since they'd added it to their seasonal menu last month, thanks to my suggestion to use raclette cheese instead of an everyday Swiss. The pungent raclette is warmed until melty, then scraped from its wheel and draped onto pastrami, sauerkraut, and a crispy hash-brown patty, which is all packed within a sourdough *batard*. Even for food lovers like us, the sandwich was too big to eat by ourselves.

I handed the menu back to him and checked my phone again for Thomas's email about the recipes.

"This is a big deal for you, huh? This event?" Baz said, ignoring the menu as well.

"Phoebe Winston's the next big thing, if you believe the celebrity magazines and social media. Archie told me all about her." I filled him in on her reality TV stint.

"Did she win *Fire It Up*?"

"Runner-up, but she gained instant fame. The cookbook she put out with recipes based on the reality show challenges they did was a bestseller. But then there was a video someone took of her being nasty to one of her fans at a restaurant, which started a domino effect of people posting other stories of her bad behavior. Just like that, her fifteen minutes were up."

"So how did she rally?"

"She laid low until people stopped talking about her, then she posted a live Instagram story at an animal shelter that ended up going viral. She had this immediate bond with a dog who went right up to her and wouldn't leave her side. Kismet, she said it was."

"That's an interesting name for a dog."

"No, the dog's name is Buttercup. She said meeting the dog was kismet, like destiny."

"They say dogs are a good indicator of someone's character."

"Maybe that's why people decided to give her another chance."

"Ah, I see. She saw the error of her ways?" Baz said with more than a hint of cynicism.

"I think she was going for the heart-of-gold-underneath-the-rough-exterior bit."

"I've seen pictures of her. Her exterior's not too rough either."

"I'm sure her beauty doesn't hurt her brand. From what I read, it all happened at the same time she was hired as the face of a start-up vegan cheese company. She was probably the only high-profile celebrity they could afford, but it's worked out in her favor and for the company too. This second book has vegan recipes

highlighting the Ve-Cheez brand, but it's also an autobi-
ography and self-help book. She's definitely using her
cooking background to branch out."

"That makes sense. Cooking's her bread and butter."
Baz laughed harder at his pun than I did.

"I read that her next venture is authenticity retreats."

"What the huckleberry is an authenticity retreat?"

"I don't remember exactly. Let me see where I read
it." I went into my phone to bring up one of the articles
I'd found about Phoebe. "Here's the blurb I read about
Phoebe's retreat. It says here she'll *show retreat partici-
pants how to tap into their most authentic selves so they
can start living a life that's aligned with their beliefs. Being true to who you are is the most important thing anyone can do for themselves.*'"

"No offense, but how does a cheese shop fit in with
that?"

"No offense taken. I wondered the same thing, but Ve-
Cheez is helping to sponsor the book tour, so that ex-
plains it I guess."

"It still seems weird that Read More Bookstore's not
the one doing the book signing. I know it sells second-
hand books, but Ginger even sells some vegan stuff at the
café."

"It made even less sense after Phoebe said she knows
Ginger. Wouldn't you do your event at the café your old
friend works at?"

"She knows Ginger?"

"Yeah. Phoebe mentioned it earlier when Chet was at
the shop and Ginger's name came up."

"Chet," Baz grumbled.

"You have a problem with Chet? Since when?"

"No problem."

"Is it because he's dating Ginger?"

Baz guffawed and issued a denial. "I barely know
Ginger."

"What do you mean you barely know her? You get your daily thirty grams of sugar from her every morning when you buy your fancy iced coffee drink."

"Yeah, well." Baz wouldn't look me in the eye.

"Wait a second. It's not the fancy coffee drinks you like so much . . . it's Ginger, isn't it?"

Baz changed the subject. "I'm gonna order at the bar. The servers look busy." He scooched to the edge of the booth.

"Ba-az." I gave him a look that usually elicited more information.

"What are you having?" he asked, ignoring my appeal.

"Don't you want to split the Reuben like we always do?"

"With the crispy fries?" he confirmed.

"Of course." I glanced at the bar to see what the order line looked like and did a double take. "Isn't that them at the bar?"

From the back, the woman seated at one of the stools had the same petite figure and thick auburn hair scooped in front of one shoulder that Ginger had. I was sure the man standing next to her was Chet—his athletic build and surfer-style blond hair were easily recognizable.

Baz looked too. "Yup." He slid back into the booth but combed the top of his brownish-blond hair with his fingers. "I think I'll just wait for our server."

I looked around for one. Instead, I spotted Thomas on his own at a table, tipping a beer bottle to his lips. "There's Thomas."

"Which one is he?"

"Over there. The one with the glasses and his shirt buttoned all the way up."

"Taking up a whole table by himself? He's gonna get kicked to a bar stool if it gets any more crowded."

"I'm going to ask him for that email." I scooted out of the booth and approached his table. "Hey, Thomas."

He stared back at me through the thick black frames of his glasses as if we'd never met.

"Willa from the cheese shop," I reminded him. It didn't bode well if he'd forgotten me already.

"Oh, yeah. Sorry, I got a lot on my mind."

"You're not the only one. I never received the recipes Phoebe will be using. I'm going to need to go to the market first thing tomorrow. I'd appreciate the list tonight."

"Sorry, I'll email it to you now." His phone sat on the table and he tapped it to life.

It was then I noticed an army green jacket on the other chair at the table. I recognized it immediately.

"So A. J. found you," I said.

"Hm?" His focus was still on his phone.

"A. J. That's his jacket, isn't it?"

He put his phone away. "Oh yeah. You know him? Nice guy. He's getting a second round for us."

"I told him you were here when he was looking to interview Phoebe earlier."

Thomas's one-beer-in vibe vanished. "What do you mean? Is he some kind of reporter?"

"Yeah, for our local paper, the *Glen Gazette*."

"Willa." A. J. was behind me holding two mugs of beer and looking as if he'd like to pour one of them over my head.

"I'm outta here." Thomas's chair scraped the floor as he quickly rose and headed for the stairs.

"Thanks a lot," A. J. groused. He deposited the mugs on the table without care, the beer sloshing over the rims.

"Sorry, I didn't know you were undercover," I said.

He ran up the stairs after Thomas.

"Oops," I said to myself. I returned to the booth and checked my phone. "Great."

"What's the matter? He still didn't send it?" Baz said.

"No, he did. He sent six recipes. Six! She's only making

two, but we're supposed to prep all of them? I don't even have enough bowls for all those ingredients."

"So prep two and those are the ones she'll have to make."

"I couldn't do that."

"Why not? She can manage."

"You haven't met Phoebe Winston. Besides, I want everything to go perfectly. I'll make it work." I put my phone away. "You want me to go order?" We looked over at the bar again. "Ooh, Chet left. You go. Chat her up."

"He's probably just in the restroom."

"So here's your chance."

"We just went over this, Wil. They're dating."

"Do you know if they're together-together?"

"If she's into him, she's not gonna go for me."

"Why not? You're not that different from him."

He raised his eyebrows at me and stared me down.

"You're both nice guys, you're both the same age, and you're both blond . . . sort of. See? Not so different," I said.

"Yeah, we're totally twinning, except he's six inches taller and has a six-pack instead of a beer gut."

"Don't sell yourself short. Oh, sorry, maybe that was the wrong phrase to use. But you know what I mean."

"Does the love interest of the main character in an action movie ever decide she wants the sidekick instead? I don't stand a chance. Besides, they've been together for three months."

"How come everyone but me always knows what's going on around town?"

"You work all the time."

"Speaking of, get my half to go. I need to get back to the shop and look at these recipes to start making a grocery list."

Baz shook his head and scooched out of the booth, colliding into someone trying to hurry past.

"Sorry," they said in unison, before we recognized the taller man.

"Hey, Chet," I said.

Awkward.

"Hey, guys. Good to see ya. I finally found Ginger," Chet joked to me, laughing as he walked back toward the bar.

Baz thumped back down on the seat. "Not a chance."

CHAPTER 3

I should've been tired the next day after tossing all night, endlessly dreaming of searching the grocery aisles for recipe ingredients I couldn't find. But the anticipation of pulling off a flawless event kept my batteries charged, even through the afternoon slump. That and the Gouda I'd been snacking on. We'd just gotten in a shipment of Noord-Hollandse Gouda. The cheese earned its name from the Dutch town of Gouda, where it was originally developed. Nowadays, the name *Gouda* refers to the type of cheese, not the region, as it's made all over the world. However, the traditional Noord-Hollandse Gouda, made from the milk of Northern Holland dairy cows, couldn't be beat. I'd been breaking off pieces from a wedge of the double-aged and delighting in it turning from brittle to creamy when it hit my tongue.

Thomas showed up, as promised. To my surprise, he was quite helpful, procuring enough chairs for our ticket holders and rearranging the rear of my shop so we'd be able to accommodate them when they arrived. Mrs. Schultz took care of the shop while we met the delivery truck guy at the alley door.

"Thank you for finding chairs for me," I said to Thomas as we helped take the white folding chairs off the truck two by two and stacked them against the stockroom wall. "I couldn't find any place that would deliver them on such short notice. And on a Saturday nonetheless."

"You just have to mention that it's for Phoebe Winston. That's how you get results," he replied.

"How did you come to work for Phoebe anyway?"

"I was the office manager for Ve-Cheez. They wanted her to be their spokesperson after her Buttercup video went viral and she announced she was vegan." A smile played on his lips at the memory. "She came in for a meeting and . . . I guess she liked what she saw. She asked to get together for some advice from an 'insider' at Ve-Cheez, and within a week I quit my job and started working for her."

"Wow. Another moment of kismet, huh?" No wonder he didn't like it when Phoebe asked for Archie's help. He must've had flashbacks to his own hiring.

The delivery guy returned from his truck and held out a portable card machine for me to swipe my credit card for payment. I heard myself squawk when I read the sky-high price of the chair rentals.

"Did you ask about price?" I called over to Thomas.

"They said something about adding a rush fee. I'll start setting these up in the shop." He carried a folding chair under each arm and pushed through the swinging door.

Apparently it wasn't the high-profile name that got results, it was the willingness to be extorted. But there was nothing I could do. I swiped my credit card through the machine.

"So is she here?" the delivery guy said.

"Who?"

"Phoebe Winston. Is she here? I wouldn't mind meeting her."

"And I wouldn't mind not being overcharged, but it looks like both of us are going to be disappointed today." I signed the screen and the guy plodded out the alley door, grumbling.

Thomas seemed to have the chair situation in hand, so I moved on to the grocery bags of food I bought at Lou's market as soon as they had opened at nine a.m. The next hour, at least, was going to be spent chopping, separating, and measuring. I stared inside the few cabinets I had in my shop's kitchenette, wondering how I thought I'd ever have enough matching bowls to put everything in. I was going to have to make do with mismatched ones from my own kitchen upstairs and hope I had enough.

My betta fish, Loretta, seemed to be studying me from her fishbowl on the counter. I'd decided to bring her down to the shop today since I'd be working so late. She and I watched a lot of Food Network's *Chopped* together, so I could sense her judgment as I struggled with how to prep so much food.

"I'm no Ted Allen, Loretta—don't I know it. He gets everything all set for the contestants in big perfectly placed baskets and I can't even come up with matching bowls."

"Did someone say matching bowls?"

I turned around to see Roman, the owner of Golden Glen Meadery and the guy who zapped me with endorphins anytime he walked into a room loaded with charm and a chill gait. Everything about him said laid back—from his simple V-neck T-shirts, jeans, and cowboy boots to his close-shaven beard. He carried in a cardboard palette of glass bowls and set them on the kitchenette's island. His crooked smile widened when he saw my reaction.

"Where did you get those?" My surprise quickly turned to glee when a quick count indicated there would be more than enough.

"After we talked on the phone last night, I thought of my friend who's opening a restaurant soon, so I called to see if you could borrow them. We'll have to return them."

"Of course. No problem. Thank her for me."

"Him," he corrected.

Even better. If there was anything I knew about Roman, it was that he had lots of female friends, so I'd assumed this one was a woman. "Everybody's been so helpful. You and Baz have been making sure I have everything. Mrs. Schultz has been holding down the fort all day while I prep. Oh, and this is Thomas, Phoebe Winston's personal assistant."

Thomas looked up from the chairs he was placing in even rows.

"This is Roman from the meadery across the street," I said.

"You mentioned that place yesterday. I'd love to check it out," Thomas said. He came over and he and Roman shook hands in hello. He was a lot more pleasant without Phoebe around.

"Come by anytime," Roman told him. Then to me, "Where's Archie?"

"Phoebe requested his help," I said.

Thomas's aura immediately shifted. "More chairs," he said, explaining his departure.

I made sure he was through the swinging door before I said to Roman, "I think he got his feelings hurt that Phoebe asked Archie to do Thomas's job. They seem to have kind of a weird relationship. She calls him *Tom-Tom.*"

Thomas came through the door with two more chairs, so I zipped my mouth. My focus returned to the bowls.

"I really appreciate you getting these for me. When I vented about it on the phone last night, I didn't expect you to go on a hunt for bowls."

"I know you didn't. Just because you don't like to ask for help doesn't mean I don't like helping. It's worth it to see that smile. Yeah, that one."

I couldn't help it. He made me smile. And blush.

"I better get back so Chet can call it a day." He glanced

toward the front of the shop. "Looks like you've got quite a crowd. You might need a velvet rope and a bouncer. Talk soon?"

"Of course." I watched Roman leave the shop and weave his way through the cluster of people at the front. Normally, I'd be delighted by this many customers, but I didn't see cheese in anybody's hands. I looked at the clock again. "I wonder if all these people couldn't get tickets before they sold out and are hoping to come to the event tonight. I hate turning people away."

"You're going to have to tell them there are no walk-ups," Thomas said. "Phoebe has a strict policy against that."

He returned to the stockroom for more chairs. *Coward.*

I approached the register, where Mrs. Schultz appeared uncharacteristically flustered as she brought the laptop out from under the counter.

The first woman in line had sky-high heels, a pencil skirt, and perfectly slicked hair that brought to mind that iconic Robert Palmer video. I instantly recognized her as the hostess from Apricot Grille. We'd had a couple of run-ins last spring when I was trying to prove her boyfriend Derrick, the manager, had killed Guy Lippinger.

"Can I help?" I asked.

"I'm here about the tickets to see Phoebe Winston," she said curtly.

"You're Angela, the hostess from Apricot Grille, right?" My parents always said unpleasant news was better received by a friend than a stranger. I'd have to make up for the times I'd avoided her at the restaurant since our uncomfortable encounters last spring. "I'm Willa. I don't think we ever officially got a chance to meet."

"I'm the manager of the restaurant now that Derrick's gone"—she paused to cast a blaming glare at me before continuing—"and yes, I know who you are."

So much for going the friendly route.

"I'm afraid we're all sold out," I told her.

"I already have a ticket," she corrected me.

"She wants a refund," Mrs. Schultz explained.

"We all want refunds," a tall brunette standing behind Angela said. The ten other people now in the shop nodded in concurrence.

The phone rang and I directed Mrs. Schultz to answer it while I went behind the counter to figure out what was going on. I opened the laptop and went to our website where our list of ticket holders was kept.

Lou from the market two doors down pushed his way in, clutching a broom, his lips pressed together in a tight line. His green apron hung loosely on his thin frame. He ran his free hand over his salt-and-pepper hair.

"Is this because of Phoebe Winston?" he growled. He stared down the people in my shop, his bushy eyebrows dropping lower over his eyes. "You people can't double-park in the street. You're blocking my customers."

"I'll sort it out, Lou. Sorry."

He harrumphed and left as abruptly as he'd entered.

I couldn't get our website to open. All that appeared were error messages. It looked like it had crashed. I stepped next to Mrs. Schultz, who was trying to manage the customer on the phone.

"Yes, just a moment. Can you hold, please?" She pressed the hold button. "Another customer wants a refund," she whispered to me.

"What's going on?" I asked.

Mrs. Schultz had no reply.

The tall woman behind Angela spoke up again, "Haven't you seen the internet?"

When I still looked befuddled, Angela slapped this afternoon's *Glen Gazette* onto the counter. "Phoebe Winston's a fraud. She's not a vegan. She's certainly not authentic."

I'd been too busy prepping for Phoebe's event to go outside and take one of the free newspapers from the sidewalk dispenser. I looked at it now. On the front page was a photo of Phoebe Winston. It wasn't the publicity headshot I'd given Deandra to announce our Book and Cook event. This was a candid shot, in color. It was unmistakably Phoebe, and it looked like she was eating something with her hands. I turned the paper over the fold. Three more photos of Phoebe, this time zoomed in. The food she was gnawing on looked like ribs. In case it wasn't obvious enough, a bag was next to her with Mac's Big Mouth BBQ written on it above the restaurant's logo.

Mac's was the most popular barbeque place in the area, and for good reason. It was the best. As far as I knew, they didn't serve anything vegan. It was all meat. Even the veggies and beans were infused with lard. If she was eating from Mac's, the vegan queen was about to be dethroned.

CHAPTER 4

I politely asked everyone to contact us through our website, where I assured them they'd be refunded as soon as possible. I almost wished Lou was still here to help shoo them out with his broom. Eventually, they decided to trust me and left. I shut the door and flipped the sign to Closed.

Mrs. Schultz was staring at the newspaper photos.

"Is this what I think it is?" she said.

I went back to my laptop. "I'm looking online. I want to know where those photos came from."

"They can be doctored, right?"

"Of course they can be. It could be someone with a vendetta against her. I can't believe A. J. would publish a smear job story right before our event." My shock at seeing the photos turned to anger that A. J. would trample a considerable opportunity for my shop to benefit himself.

Mrs. Schultz stood by my side as I typed Phoebe's name in the search bar. The incriminating photos came up on several national websites. I clicked on the first one and quickly skimmed the story.

"It looks like the original story is from the *Glen Gazette*," I told her, surprised for the second time in a matter of minutes.

"Does that mean A. J. took the pictures?" she asked.

"I have no idea."

"Would every outlet run these without proof they're authentic?"

"Have you been introduced to twenty-first-century journalism?"

"You're right. Stupid question."

"It says in the story the photos were checked and found to be authentic . . . which means it *must* be true," I said sarcastically.

"Checked by whom?"

"I'd like to know that too." I looked out the front window where the group was now milling about. "Those people believe they're real."

"I thought Archie said she had loyal followers."

"There's nothing people love more than to build up celebrities just to take them down. She's been through it before."

"Did you take care of it?" Thomas left his chair duty to join us. "Why are there still people waiting outside? Didn't you talk to them?"

"They want refunds for the event," I explained. Another look told me that maybe they wanted more than that. They appeared angry.

"Refunds?"

I reluctantly turned my laptop screen to show him the photos. He adjusted his dark-rimmed glasses and leaned in, only to recoil a moment later.

"Listen, I'm sure the pictures aren't re—" I started to say.

"I've got to get to Phoebe," he announced hastily, before running out the front door and through the throng of people.

"What are we supposed to do now?" Mrs. Schultz asked. "Are we still doing the Book and Cook?"

"That's an excellent question. I don't have any way of getting in touch with Phoebe directly."

"What about Archie?"

"Archie! Of course." I tapped his name on my cell phone, and he answered before the second ring.

"Willa. I was just about to call you. I don't know what to do. Phoebe got a phone call that really upset her. Then she told me to take Buttercup for a walk, so I did, but now she's locked the doors and won't let me back in the house. She says she needs to be alone, but I have to make sure she's ready in time for her appearance."

I didn't like the distress in his voice. This wasn't something he needed to handle on his own. "Do you have the car keys?"

"Yeah, they're still in the car."

"Just come back to the shop. I know what's going on . . . or at least some of what's going on. I'll explain when you get here."

Mrs. Schultz and I paced the shop waiting for Archie. She fiddled with the strings of her scarf, a nervous habit I recognized, as the crowd congregating out front grew. I stood in the front corner and peeked out the window.

"Oh great. There's A. J. Stringer. It looks like he's interviewing people," I said. A journalist was the last person I needed to talk to right now.

As soon as I dashed to the door to lock it, it opened, making both Mrs. Schultz and me jump. It was Baz.

"What's going on out there?" he said.

"Oh, just my biggest event going down the drain, that's all." I heard the tremble in my voice. Until now, I'd tried to keep myself from fully absorbing the repercussions of what was happening by allowing a sliver of hope that this would somehow all work out. Admitting it out loud extinguished any optimism I had left.

The quick *whoop whoop* of a siren sounded. A black-and-white cruiser double-parked where Phoebe's Range Rover had been yesterday. Was that just twenty-four hours ago? Two officers emerged. I recognized one of them as Officer Shepherd, a dark-haired guy with a buzz cut about my age—early thirties. Having spent his life in Yarrow Glen, most everyone in town knew him as Shep. I thought of him as the golden retriever of cops—friendly to everyone and good at doing whatever was asked of him. Lou immediately approached him.

"Leave it to Lou to call the police," I said, although I found myself relieved to see them. People scurried to their illegally parked cars before they'd get ticketed.

The door opened again and this time it was Archie, holding Buttercup.

"What's going on out there? Are they here to see Phoebe already?" he said, worry once again coloring his voice.

This time I locked the door.

"Mrs. Schultz, do you mind putting the dog in my office while I explain what's going on to Archie and Baz?"

"Of course not," Mrs. Schultz said. Archie handed over Buttercup.

I showed Archie and Baz the photos of Phoebe as I went through the story again.

"Whoa. No wonder Phoebe was so upset," Archie said. "That's got to be what the phone call was about."

"What did she say on the phone? Did she deny it?" I asked him.

"I didn't know what they were talking about, but I knew she was hearing something bad. By the look on her face, I thought maybe someone had died, but then she kind of did like a nervous giggle, which seemed weird coming from her. She doesn't seem the type to get nervous . . . or giggle. She told me to go take the dog outside, so I did. It was obvious she didn't want me to hear their conversation."

"And then when you got back? Was she angry?"

"I never got to see her again. She locked the doors and wouldn't let me in. I called her, but she didn't say much.

She just wanted me to go away. She might've been crying. It was hard to tell over the phone."

Mrs. Schultz joined us again sans Buttercup.

"You think those photos are real?" Baz asked.

"At first I didn't think they could be, but the way Thomas reacted and now Phoebe . . . I'm beginning to think they are. Thomas didn't even question them. Even after the short amount of time I spent with Phoebe yesterday, I'm pretty sure I know her enough that if the photos were faked, she'd be screaming up a storm," I said.

"So then she really did eat Mac's Big Mouth Barbeque." Mrs. Schultz stared at the photos. Like the rest of us, I was sure she was trying to reconcile her disbelief in what she was seeing with her own eyes.

"At least if her career was going to take a dive off the vegan wagon, she picked the best place to do it with," Baz said.

"I hate to ask, but does this mean the event is off?" Archie asked timidly.

"I'm going to try to get in touch with Thomas. Let's see if this is salvageable." I called his number, but it rang until it reached his voicemail. I hung up and tried again. Still no answer. I left him a message to call me ASAP. "No answer," I said needlessly to the others. "I'm not sure how we're expected to get in touch with her."

"What about her publisher or the Ve-Cheez people?" Mrs. Schultz suggested.

"No offense, but you think they're going to take the time to talk to you guys? They gotta be doing major damage control," Baz said.

"Baz is right," I put my phone back in my apron pocket.

"Phoebe called me this morning. I've got her number." Archie pulled his phone from one of the pockets of his cargo shorts. Their phone conversation was near the top of his list. He hit call and put it on speaker phone. We all waited in anticipation, but it clicked over to her voice-mail. Archie hung up. "What should we do now?" he said.

I felt something brush up against my bare ankles and when I looked down, I saw a white fluff ball, no higher than the rolled-up cuffs of my khakis.

"Buttercup. You're supposed to stay where we put you," I admonished gently. He was too cute to be seriously mad at.

"What are we going to do with him?" Archie said, scooping him up.

"We're going to return him to his owner. This has gotten out of hand. I need to talk to Phoebe. Can you show me how to get to her rental house?" I asked Archie.

"I can take us. I still have the car. It's the only way we'll get inside the gate anyway. It's got the clicker to open it."

"Why don't I follow so you have a ride home?" Baz said. "Feel like keeping me company, Mrs. Schultz?"

"What about the shop?" Mrs. Schultz said to me. "We haven't done the closing or set-up for the event if there is one."

"It'll have to wait. We'll know what's going on after we talk to Phoebe." I was probably holding out hope longer than I should have, but my parents' words scrolled through my mind: *An extra dose of optimism costs you nothing.*

"How do you know she'll let you in the house? She locked me out," Archie said.

"Don't worry about that. That woman doesn't intimidate me anymore. We worked hard to put this together and now *our* reputation is on the line too. Phoebe Winston's got a lot of explaining to do."

CHAPTER 5

We drove outside the center of town for a good ten minutes, then took a right onto a poorly marked road. I looked behind us to make sure Baz had made the turn too. Under different circumstances, I would've enjoyed the beautiful autumn colors from the passenger's seat of the Range Rover. The winding road followed a creek where the yellow cottonwood trees were especially brilliant at the water's edge. Just when I thought perhaps Archie had gotten lost, he slowed and pointed out a white stucco two-story house set behind a wrought-iron fence. He reached for the gate opener attached to the visor near my head. I stopped him.

"Maybe we should try her first just to let her know we're here," I said.

Archie rolled down his window and extended his arm to press the intercom button. I heard it buzz, but there was no reply. I noted the glass eye of a surveillance camera and wondered if she was silently watching us. He pressed the buzzer again. "Phoebe, it's Archie," he said into the box. Buttercup stood on Archie's lap and put his front paws on the door, as if to announce his arrival, too, but there was still no response.

"All right, let's go in," I conceded.

A tap of the clicker caused the gate to slowly open inward, allowing us entrance. I saw through my side mirror Baz's pickup follow us through before the gate automatically closed behind him.

We climbed out of the car with Buttercup at the same time Baz and Mrs. Schultz exited Baz's truck. The sun had lost much of its midday warmth as it inched closer to the mountains. It would be dark within the hour. Buttercup ran in circles in the yard until Archie retrieved him.

What I first thought was a simple contemporary home, dazzled up close with a limestone entryway and wood pillars at the front portico where we gathered.

"I hope we have better luck at the door." I rang the bell, willing her to answer.

"Maybe Baz and I should wait out here? I don't want her to feel ambushed," Mrs. Schultz said.

"You seemed to have a good rapport with her. Maybe she'd feel better with some friendly faces, considering what she's probably been reading online about herself."

She wasn't answering the bell. I pressed it again and heard it chime inside.

"I was afraid of this," Archie said, glumly.

"You think she's in?" Baz wondered.

"Where would she go?" I said.

"She could've skipped town and gone back home," he said.

"Without Buttercup?" Archie pulled the dog closer to his chest protectively.

There were only two front windows on the ground level. Baz stepped off the portico and squeezed between the bushes and the house to look inside one of them. He cupped his hands to the sides of his face and pressed his nose against it.

"Do you see her?" I asked.

"Nope." He walked to the middle of the front yard and faced the house. "There's a light on upstairs."

I rapped heavily on the door. "Phoebe! It's Willa and Archie. We've got Buttercup."

Archie shrugged. "I guess we're out of luck."

I impulsively tried the door handle. To everyone's surprise, it turned, and the front door opened.

"I tried it before I left. I know it was locked," Archie said.

"Maybe she unlocked it for us. Phoebe!" I called as we stepped into the foyer.

The house was silent. We walked through the hallway, which eventually widened to an open-concept living room and kitchen with a natural-wood-beamed ceiling. We were drawn to the floor-to-ceiling windows that offered a view of the limestone back patio and a meticulously landscaped yard within the same wrought-iron fencing as the front.

"Whoever got the pictures of her had a clear shot. The dining table's right in front of these sliding doors," Baz noted.

"There's nothing but woods back there," Mrs. Schultz said. "Maybe a good hiding spot for someone?"

"What if she's sleeping? I don't want to scare her," Archie said.

Buttercup wriggled out of his arms and made a beeline for the kitchen where the contents of a small trash bin littered the floor around it. The dog pawed at a Mac's Big Mouth BBQ bag and stuck his nose in one of their plastic containers.

"The garbage wasn't like that when I left," Archie said.

"Maybe she took off in a hurry," Baz speculated.

"Phoebe!" I called again. I hadn't considered that she would abandon us. I was still clinging to hope that we could somehow salvage this event, but it seemed more impossible by the minute.

Having been pushed away from the trash by Archie, Buttercup raced up the open staircase. Archie called after her, but his command didn't deter her. I was afraid the tiny dog would slip between the steps to the floor. We went up after her.

From the landing, open double doors led to a master bedroom big enough to do cartwheels in if one was so inclined. The closed curtains necessitated the bedroom light that was on, as well as the en suite bathroom light. The plush bed linens were rumpled, and a bottle of tequila, a third empty, sat on a dressing table. An empty trash can lay on its side. My self-centered concerns about the event evaporated. Something didn't feel right. I could tell the others sensed it too. Nobody moved much past the doorway.

"Stay here. Maybe she fell asleep in the tub after one too many tequilas," I said to them.

They nodded assent as I stepped farther into the room and knocked on the partially open bathroom door. "Phoebe?" I said in a hushed voice, not wanting to startle her too badly.

When she didn't answer, I stepped into the bathroom. It was practically the size of my living room. Except for the upper third of the walls painted a contrasting dark gray, the room was virtually encased in white marble. Phoebe's cosmetics littered the expansive vanity countertop, indicating she was still here.

A few more steps in, I saw a limp hand hanging over the rim of the bathtub. I recognized the multiple silver bands on her fingers. A square tumbler sat on the edge next to her wrist with a mouthful of tequila left in it. I let out a breath in relief. I'd started to think something terrible had happened to her.

"Phoebe," I said gently, hoping to rouse her from her drunken state.

As I approached the tub, I heard a faint splat and looked down to see water puddled around my Keds. My gaze went to the wet towels and a sodden silky robe piled in the corner. Forget propriety, I walked all the way in.

In an oversized tub, her arm and one knee were the only parts of her body above the water. The rest of her was beneath the surface. Phoebe Winston lay dead in her bathtub.

CHAPTER 6

We waited in the driveway under a harsh spotlight, as three forensics people dressed in white zippered jumpsuits walked in and out of the house. Officer Shepherd was with the first batch of police to arrive. He'd asked us some questions, then told us to "stand by," which we'd been doing for the better part of two hours now.

We exhausted our theories to one another about whether she'd taken something and purposely killed herself or if she'd drunkenly drowned accidentally. I wondered if anything the people in jumpsuits discovered could definitively say which one it was. We leaned against Baz's truck, walked in circles, and took turns sitting in the cab with Buttercup, who didn't like being left by himself.

The shock of finding Phoebe dead in her bathtub was beginning to wear off and I was suddenly aware of the chill. Mrs. Schultz was the only one dressed properly for the drop in evening temperatures, as she always biked home after work.

"You guys should wait in the car. It's getting cold. I'll see if I can find Shep and ask him if we can go now. They've probably forgotten about us."

I walked down the driveway, looking around the front lawn for Officer Shepherd when I spotted him talking to a tall man in a perfectly fitted suit that outlined his broad shoulders. The well-dressed man's back was to me, but I knew who it was instantly, the fluttering in my stomach alerting me at the same time recognition kicked in—Detective Heath.

We'd become acquainted during a murder investigation last spring. We were both new to Yarrow Glen and new to each other, so trust had been in short supply. As it turned out, he was a decent man and a good detective. I'd only seen him a few times around town since then, but one or the other of us was in a hurry each time, so our encounters never extended beyond small talk.

I approached him and heard him ask Officer Shepherd, "Who found the body?"

Shep pointed over Heath's shoulder, and he turned to see it was me.

"Willa." His dark eyes widened. It might've been the first time I'd seen him surprised.

Shep stepped away and Detective Heath and I were alone.

"Hi." My gaze lingered on him longer than I meant it to. I'd almost forgotten how handsome he was. The shadows from the spotlights only seemed to highlight his sculpted jawline.

"You're making a habit of this," he said.

I'd also neglected to remember how annoying he was.

"I hope not. I have other things I'd like to be doing with my time," I said.

He took out a miniature notebook from his suit pocket. I knew it would be like the doctor's office, being asked the same questions I'd just answered for the nurse. I also knew it was pointless to say I'd already spoken to Shep, so I went along with his questions and told him everything leading up to finding Phoebe Winston's body. When he exhausted those questions, he asked some Officer Shepherd hadn't.

"Did you notice anything out of sorts when you went inside?" he asked.

"Except for the dead woman in the bathtub, you mean?" I tried to picture something besides that scene. "Yeah, now that you mention it, there was trash out of the can."

"What do you mean?"

"In the kitchen. Some of the trash that should've been in the bin was on the floor. We were thinking maybe she'd been trying to hide the evidence deep in the garbage in case anybody came by."

"Evidence?"

"The Mac's Barbeque bags and containers. If she wanted to deny the pictures were real, she wouldn't want the bags to be discovered. That's got to be why she tried to go through a bottle of tequila by herself."

Detective Heath didn't confirm my suspicions. As per usual, he was tight-lipped.

"Will they be able to tell if it was suicide or if she drowned by accident?" I asked.

"We'll have to wait for forensics to do the toxicology report. That may give us some idea, but in cases like this, it can be difficult to ever say for sure. A lot of it depends on her mental state beforehand. Do you know who was the last person with her?"

"Probably Archie. He was there when she got the phone call about the photos and then she wanted to be left alone. He's already talked to Shep—Officer Shepherd," I corrected myself.

Heath nodded.

"Can we go now?" I asked.

"Detective Heath?" A woman in one of the white full-body suits called out to him as she walked our way from the house, pulling off the hood to reveal a neat ponytail fastened at the nape of her neck.

Heath put a wait-a-minute finger up and left me

without an answer. I watched him stride over to the woman. Her red lipstick was especially noticeable given her monochromatic outfit.

I moseyed over to Shep. "Who's that?"

"Ivy Reynolds. She's the coroner."

She seemed to be filling Heath in on what she'd discovered, information I doubted he would share with me.

"So can we go now?" I asked Shep.

"Sorry, I have to get the official okay from Detective Heath. Here he comes."

Heath strode over to me. "Where's Archie?"

"He's over by Baz's truck. Why?" I answered.

"Phoebe Winston's death wasn't an accident or suicide. It was murder."

CHAPTER 7

After the bombshell of Phoebe's murder and more questioning by Detective Heath, we all needed to decompress, so I suggested we go back to Curds & Whey. I had bags of food I'd bought for Phoebe's event that would go to waste now that Archie had officially announced its cancelation on our website, so I suggested dinner even though food was the last thing on our minds. Sometimes doing normal things in an abnormal situation helps to process it.

Baz moved the hand-hewn farm table and benches back to their original spot perpendicular to the kitchenette's island so we could eat around it. I sprinkled fish food into Loretta's bowl and found some canned chicken to mix with my mildest cheese for Buttercup's dinner. I agreed to allow him in the shop with us since it was after hours and Archie assured me Maltese dogs don't shed. Mrs. Schultz retrieved my grandmother's afghan from the couch in my office to use as a dog bed. He danced around the blanket on the floor until she repositioned it right next to the table, then he curled up in it. He looked so cozy, I resigned myself to not getting it back for some time.

I hurriedly tossed vegan tortellini into boiling water and threw out the packaging so Baz wouldn't guess it was stuffed with almond milk ricotta. I heated fresh cremini mushrooms, plus butternut squash and Granny Smith apples that Archie cubed, and poured apple cider into the skillet to keep everything steaming until tender. After combining the mixture with the cooked tortellini, I went rogue from the vegan recipe and sprinkled in a generous amount of my favorite smoked Gouda, which melted slightly on contact.

The first few minutes were spent in silence as we tucked into our autumn tortellini toss, but it was impossible to forget what we'd just experienced. Seeing my shop half readied for the event that never happened didn't help either.

"This morning when I was contemplating all the things that could go wrong tonight, this scenario never came to mind," I said to the others.

"It's not how any of us thought it would turn out," Mrs. Schultz agreed.

Archie sat across from me picking at his food. "The photos were shocking enough."

"Don't forget her angry fans," Baz added. "Do you think one of them killed her?"

"Because she lied about being vegan?" I thought about this. "Killing someone would be against what they stand for, wouldn't it—that all sentient creatures deserve to live?"

"Then who? Is the coroner absolutely sure it was murder?" Archie asked.

"I was able to talk to Shep just before we left. The coroner told him there were signs that she was held down and drowned," Baz told us. It helped to have a cop as a friend.

"That would explain the water all over the bathroom floor." I shuddered. "How awful."

"Maybe there'll be some DNA that will point the police in the right direction." Mrs. Schultz pushed her bowl away from her. The conversation had made me lose my appetite as well.

"DNA's only good if the murderer has a record," Baz reminded us. He forked a few more plump pieces of tortellini, his voracious appetite unhindered.

"Archie, what happened today? I know you told us about the phone call and afterward, but how was the rest of the day before that? What was Phoebe like?" I asked.

Archie put down his fork. He'd barely touched his food, which wasn't like him. Although he was built like a bean pole, he could usually eat as much as Baz.

"She wasn't anything like I thought she'd be," he began.

"How do you mean?"

"I know this will probably sound stupid . . ." He hesitated.

"What is it, Archie? We won't think it's stupid," I prompted.

"I hate to say this now that she's gone, but she made me uncomfortable. She kept coming on to me and it felt like she was using it as a weapon. Like one minute she was ordering me to pick up dog poop, and the next she was flirting with me. It just felt strange."

"You think she would've followed through had you flirted back?" Baz asked him.

"I don't know. She seemed to like that I was uncomfortable, like she wanted to embarrass me that way."

Thinking it over, it fit with what little I knew of her. "That could've been why Thomas seemed jealous when she wanted you and not him to help her at the house." It made me think perhaps she chose men she could manipulate with her sexuality, men she figured to be too shy or inexperienced to take her up on her flirtatious offers. Phoebe was only twenty-eight years old, but Archie wasn't even officially out of his teens. Thomas was closer to her age, but their relationship did seem . . . odd. "I wonder how Thomas took the news of Phoebe's death."

"He must be devastated. Do you think we should check on him?" Mrs. Schultz asked.

"Detective Heath's probably got him down at the station," Baz said.

"That's true. He could offer a lot of information about Phoebe. We need to give him Buttercup at some point," I said. "What are we going to do with him until then? I don't have any dog food or anything for him."

"I can keep him until you see Thomas," Archie offered, reaching down to pet the dog.

"You sure your mom won't mind?"

"Nah, she loves dogs. We've already got Batman, what's one more?" Batman was Archie's Chihuahua who came by his name by way of his perky oversized ears and black markings that made it appear he was wearing a mask.

"Thanks, Archie. We'll try to check on Thomas tomorrow."

"What else did you find out about Phoebe, Arch?" Baz asked.

"Not much. She didn't like to do much for herself or maybe she just liked ordering me around, like I was her butler or something. Like she had me open some fan mail she brought, but she sat right across from me when I opened it. She could've just done it herself."

"I'm sorry, Archie. I shouldn't have given in to her demand for you to help her."

"No, I wanted to. I thought it'd be cool, like maybe she'd tell me stories about *Fire It Up* or tell me about culinary school. I thought I could learn some stuff from her, the way I learn from you being a cheesemonger. I didn't know she'd be the way she was."

"You should've told her to kick rocks and left," Mrs. Schultz said. "Sorry, Willa."

"Not at all. I agree," I said.

"I couldn't have done that. I knew how important her event was to us." Archie picked up his fork, but only moved the tortellini around in his bowl.

"I want you to know, in the future if you ever feel uncomfortable or disrespected, you can leave the situation and I'll always support you."

"Okay. Thanks, Willa."

"That goes for you too, Mrs. Schultz."

"I appreciate that, but no worries here. Once I crossed the AARP bridge, I stopped taking guff from anybody," she said.

Archie smiled at her and forked some pasta. His appetite seemed to return. "There was one kind of weird thing that happened that I told Detective Heath about. When I was opening Phoebe's mail for her, there was one envelope with a picture of a guy in it. On the picture, he wrote 'Remember me?'"

"Was there a letter with it?" I asked.

"No. Just the picture, but she wasn't happy about it."

"Did she remember the guy?" Baz asked.

"She said it must be a fan, but she seemed shook by it."

"Sounds like a stalker," Baz said.

"I don't know. She didn't want to talk about it. She told me to throw it out."

"It was good you told Detective Heath about it. They'll find it and try to figure out who it is." I picked out the cubes of Gouda from my bowl and munched on the smoky morsels as we talked. Cheese always helped me to focus. "There wasn't much of an opening to get her alone and kill her. Someone had to have been watching the house. Do you remember what time you left?"

"It was right after you called me," Archie answered.

I checked my phone. "I called at three fifty-two. So in the hour, give or take, between when you left the house and when we went back, someone killed her."

"How did they get in? The gate was closed and the front door was locked before I left," Archie said. "The fence looked too tall to scale."

"There were those trees all along the back," Mrs. Schultz recalled. "Is it possible someone climbed one of them and then got over the fence that way?"

"Maybe they didn't have to climb anything. Maybe she knew who it was and let them in," Baz said.

"She wouldn't even talk to Archie, so it would have to be someone she knew really well," Mrs. Schultz pointed out. "Someone she was comfortable with."

"Like Thomas?" Baz suggested.

"Thomas? I wasn't thinking of him as a suspect," I said, considering him now.

"He was very enamored with her, though," Mrs. Schultz said.

"You know what they say about love and hate and fine lines," Baz reminded us.

"Now that you say it, he would be the obvious suspect. Maybe too obvious?"

"Well then who else? Who else would she have opened the gate for?" Baz said.

I thought about it. "What about Ginger? Phoebe told Chet they were old friends from culinary school and Phoebe wanted to see her while she was in town. Maybe she did see her and something happened between them."

"I don't think it was Ginger." Baz sounded defensive.

"Why not?"

He shrugged. "I just don't."

I didn't harp on it, since I myself was just guessing. "We all agree the timing's not a coincidence, right? It has to have something to do with the barbeque photos that were published?"

This time Baz agreed with me, as did Archie and Mrs. Schultz.

"In that case, maybe it was someone she was in business with," Baz suggested. "If the spokesperson of your company was revealed to be a scammer, that could tick you off."

"Enough to come to town, know where she's staying, and perfectly time it to kill her in the hour she was alone?" I shook my head. "That seems like a tall order. We know the pictures were taken when she was in that house, and she just arrived yesterday, so the photos had to have been taken last night. Who would know where she was and that she was alone?"

We all looked at one another, thinking the same name again. Thomas.

"He ran off to see Phoebe as soon as he saw the pictures," Mrs. Schultz said.

"He would've been going to the house at the same time Archie was coming back here," I added.

"How did he get there, though? I had the car," Archie pointed out.

"He could've Ubered. He was super anxious to get to her."

Baz pointed to my neglected leftovers, which I knew to be his way of asking if I was done. I pushed the bowl toward him. I considered telling him it was vegan except for the Gouda but decided to let him continue to snarf it down in blissful ignorance.

"Ubering yourself to commit a crime might not be the smartest thing," Baz countered through a mouthful of tortellini.

"He has a point. Would someone leave that kind of trace?" Mrs. Schultz took her bowl to the sink and checked on Buttercup, who was snoozing in his makeshift bed, before returning to the table.

"There are some stupid criminals out there," Archie replied.

"What if it wasn't planned? What if it was a crime of passion?" I liked my new theory. "Maybe he was as angry as her fans were. I mean, he must've believed in her too. Then to find out that she's not at all who she claimed to be after all this time he's been working his butt off to help grow her brand? That could make someone snap."

"We have to make sure Detective Heath knows everything we do about Thomas. Surely, he would be their number one suspect," Mrs. Schultz said.

"I hope so," Archie said. "Otherwise, as far as the police know, I was the last person to see Phoebe alive. Right now, I'm pretty sure I'm their number one suspect."

"Don't worry, Arch. We're not gonna let that happen," Baz said.

Baz and I looked at each other and I knew we were thinking the same thing. We'd have to make sure Detective Heath's suspicions were pointed in the right direction. Which direction that was, I had yet to figure out.

CHAPTER 8

Sundays were normally our easy days—we opened late and closed early, plus there was usually a steady stream of customers, which made the day fly by. It was just me and Mrs. Schultz today. I'd insisted Archie take the day off. I was still feeling low after everything that had transpired, so I could imagine it would be even worse for Archie.

Mrs. Schultz took a page from her days as a high school drama teacher to remedy her mood. She explained, "When we'd decide the wardrobe for the characters we were playing, we'd factor in the mood we were trying to set. I feel it's the same when I get dressed every day." She had on an especially bright blue flared dress, cinched at the waist. Her ballet flats were the same cerulean color, as were the flowers in her linen scarf. "Convince your mood to match your wardrobe, Willa!"

Unfortunately, which of my eight pairs of Keds to wear was the only variety I made in my daily work wardrobe. I didn't like to make decisions on what to wear. However, my boring white and beige color scheme wasn't doing much for any of us.

"Does Loretta count?" I kidded. I'd chosen to bring my fish, showy in iridescent red and blue, to the shop again for some mood brightening too. Plus, she really seemed to enjoy the extra activity around her.

"Anything that works."

Mrs. Schultz was onto something—the happy colors were indeed a mood booster.

Cheese samples, however, were something I took delight in deciding. Today, I chose to showcase the seven categories of Gouda, which are classified by age. I first cubed a young Gouda, so labeled because it's ready to be consumed within four weeks of production. The light yellow cheese is creamy and mild, and delicious eaten on its own. As I took samples from the various Gouda, Mrs. Schultz lined them up on a cheese board, exhibiting how each category of Gouda is aged longer and is increasingly firmer and darker than the last. The flavor, of course, also changes, increasing in sharpness. At the end of the spectrum is extra-aged Gouda, matured between twelve months and four years. I cut this hard, golden, full-flavored cheese into much smaller bites, as it's preferable for enhancing soups and sauces than eating on its own.

I left Mrs. Schultz to finish arranging the cheese board, as I had to tackle the refunds on our website for everyone who'd bought a ticket for Phoebe's event. I was glad when I finally finished and could spend time with our customers. I showed those who were interested in our Gouda samples how the wax coverings could also help them decipher the maturity of the cheeses. The younger Gouda have yellow, orange, or red wax rinds and the more mature Gouda have black rinds.

During a lull after lunch, we began collecting the dozens of chairs to return to the rental gougers. The only thing worse than overpaying for the use of folding chairs was overpaying *not* to use them. Roman stopped by to take back the glass bowls he'd lent me, and he helped us schlep the final rows of chairs to the stockroom. Part of his charm was that he was always ready with a helping hand.

He'd heard about Phoebe's scandal and subsequent death and asked how I was doing. I filled him in on what happened last night and that I'd been the one to find her. He immediately wrapped me in a hug, which fought back the dread of having to think about it again.

"I'm okay," I assured him, as he released me. "Please don't tell anyone about it. I don't want to get into trouble with Detective Heath by talking about it before the police do." Word made its way around town fast enough without me helping it along.

"No worries. I'd be happy for your name to stay far away from this murder for as long as possible," he said. He was obviously recalling how entwined we were with the last one.

"Thanks. I was going to stop by the inn and check on Thomas, but I was afraid I might run into Detective Heath or A. J."

"It's smart of you to lay low. I'm sure you've got enough to worry about. I know you were excited about the extra business her event was going to generate. I feel for you." Roman's meadery was still fairly new compared to most shops in Yarrow Glen, so he keenly understood the touch-and-go nature of the first year in business. Any setback was a big deal.

"It worked out a lot worse for her than it did for me. It's hard for me to complain under the circumstances."

The rental guys came to get their chairs, so Roman took the borrowed bowls and went back to his own store. We both had plenty of work to do, but I was reluctant to see him go, not that I'd admit that to him.

I was relieved when the rest of the day continued to go smoothly and I didn't have to dodge A. J. I found myself peeking out the front windows often, paranoia creeping in whenever I saw people taking photos outside Curds & Whey. Was my shop going to be associated with another murder? I may have just been overly sensitive to it today. It was tourist season, after all, and my French-inspired cheese shop was adorable to behold. The outside of the shop was encased in wide cream-colored molding with *Curds & Whey* in a sweeping font above the matching teal door. The large plate-glass windows on either side of the door allowed any passersby to get a glimpse of what my shop offered.

I tinkered with the window display of aged cheeses in wheels and wedges. On the top tier of open shelves were brightly painted milk jugs and metal sheep and cow sculptures beside some books featuring cheese. I realized I still had Phoebe's first cookbook on display, and I snatched it off the shelf.

Out the window, I noticed a chubby, curly haired brunette bustling down the sidewalk. I soon recognized her as Olive Berns, the fiftyish woman in charge of fundraising at Sadler Culinary School. I'd met her once before when we'd discussed the raffle the school was holding to raise money for scholarships. She'd been aflutter with excitement about their most famous alumna, Phoebe Winston, coming back to town and agreeing to donate her time as a prize for their fundraiser.

This time, however, she entered with a funereal look on her face.

"Willa." She shook her head and squeezed her eyes shut.

For a moment, I was afraid she was going to cry. I briefly wondered if her all-black ensemble was mourning attire. I turned to Mrs. Schultz for what to do, but she looked just as alarmed about it as I did.

Olive Berns snapped open her eyelids. "It's so tragic. Suicide. It's all so shocking."

She must've not heard about the actual cause of death

yet. Maybe Detective Heath wanted to keep it under wraps for a while. I'd keep mum about it too.

"It's terrible," I agreed. Whatever the cause of death, it was indeed terrible.

"I don't believe those ridiculous photos for a minute. She was a top student at Sadler Culinary. There was no reason she needed to lie about her vegan status. I certainly hope someone is held accountable."

"Me too," I said. In fact, I was hoping Detective Heath was working on that very thing.

"She's spotlighted in all of our brochures, and we were hoping to do some more fundraising in the future with her help. Now we not only have to deal with her death, but this huge scandal. This really puts us in a bind."

"I'm sure the school will manage. There are worse things, after all." *Like being murdered.*

"You're right. The more pressing issue is the raffle we just held," she went on, still remarkably tone deaf. "Everyone contributed with the belief that if they won, they'd have a chance to join Phoebe during her cooking demonstration at your event. Now that it didn't happen, we can't keep the money without a prize."

"I suppose you're right, but these are unusual circumstances. There was nothing you could've done about it."

"People don't seem to care. I've already been getting emails and phone calls about it and I'm handing out refunds left and right. The woman who won the raffle asked for her money back, so now we have to pick another winner from those who contributed, but that means we have to offer some kind of replacement prize."

"I'm sure you'll think of something."

"That's where you come in. Could we offer an amazing Curds and Whey basket instead?"

More money down the drain. Would I never stop hemorrhaging money for this non-event? But as I'd just reminded both of us, there were worse things.

"Of course. I'm happy to help."

"Thanks, Willa." She stood a bit taller. "It seems things are looking up. I just saw another one of our alumni when I stopped at the bookstore café down the street, and she agreed to give a vegan cooking class to include in the prize."

"Ginger O'Donnell, you mean?"

"Yes, that's her. You know her?"

"It's a small town."

"I had no idea she was living in Yarrow Glen. She's never donated to our alumni fund, so we lost track of her." Olive said this last bit with pursed lips. "I had high hopes she'd want to help since it involved Phoebe. When they were students at Sadler, you never saw one without the other."

"You worked there when they attended?"

"Oh, yes. I started as an administrative assistant at twenty-three and have been there for the last twenty-eight years. You do the math—I won't tell my age." She cracked a smile, which only lasted a moment.

"You said Phoebe and Ginger were close?"

"Very. They both started around the same age as full-time students. We get a lot of part-time students, so I think that's why they bonded right away. They complemented each other perfectly. Phoebe was dynamic. She always had that *thing* about her, even before she was a celebrity. There was a lot of jealousy from others, though. There was even an incident with one of the part-time students who accused her of stealing his recipes for their final-exam dishes. But there was no jealousy from Ginger. She wasn't the competitive type. She was well-liked, but she didn't mind staying in the background."

I'd noticed Phoebe tended to surround herself with people who let her be in charge.

"I normally would ask alumni who've had more success to contribute to the fundraising prize, but Phoebe's death has put me in a bind," Olive continued. She noticed our sample counter and sauntered over to it. She began stacking samples of Gouda on one of our cocktail napkins as if she were at a wedding reception and wasn't sure when dinner would be served. "I remembered Ginger's vegan café ambitions, so I knew she'd be able to cover the vegan aspect of the prize."

"I knew she baked some vegan snacks for the café, but I didn't know she was a vegan."

Olive nodded. "Oh yes. She must've had an influence on Phoebe, because Phoebe wasn't vegan back then. Still, the two of them always had their heads together, making plans."

"Hmm. I wonder why their plans didn't work out," I said.

Olive shrugged. "Phoebe got the reality show pretty soon after graduating, so maybe that was it. Everybody at school makes big plans. If you're a chef or a baker, you're dreaming about more than just cooking. It's your passion."

At that age, I was also making plans to open my own shop with my fiancé and my best friend. But while I was putting in the hours for my cheesemonger certification, they were falling in love. I remember at the time having fleeting murderous thoughts. Did Ginger feel the same way? Six years had passed since their school days, but while Ginger was still working in a café, Phoebe's star had been rising. Maybe jealousy had gotten the best of her after all?

"I've got to run. Get in touch with me when the basket's ready, okay? Thanks again!" Olive popped a piece of Gouda in her mouth and made *mmm* noises as she walked out of the shop with her afternoon snack, courtesy of Curds & Whey.

She had a little more pep to her step now that her raffle was salvaged. I guess Phoebe's death was just a speed bump for Olive Berns and the culinary school.

The remaining couple of hours went by without a hitch, but I was still relieved to be closing up shop. Just before locking the front door, I brought in the cow scarecrow I'd made that had been gracing our entrance for the past week. The barrel-shaped dairy cow was draped in brown and white felt with a pink udder. I named her Guernsey, after the breed she was supposed to represent. She may not have turned out to be the brilliant bovine I'd envisioned when I started putting her together, but it was my first attempt at crafting a scarecrow. My family's dairy farm had no need for scarecrows.

Mrs. Schultz and I hurried through our closing duties, so we could get to work on our harvest fair float. August through October were the busy tourist months for our neighboring vineyard towns, which coincided with the peak grape-harvest season. Yarrow Glen was the smallest of the towns and was rooted in dairy farming, so we'd only get the stragglers who'd venture away from the larger festivals. This year, the Yarrow Glen tourism committee was attempting to draw more visitors to town by holding a parade, which would culminate at the park with a small festival of our own, complete with a scarecrow contest.

Each business was tasked with partnering with one other and making a parade float together that represented their businesses. I felt lucky to have Mrs. Schultz, who was practiced at creating theater sets for the high school plays she used to produce. At least one of us was crafty. When Roman invited us to partner with his meadery, I accepted. It made sense—Curds & Whey's cheese was a part of Golden Glen Meadery's tasting events. But I had to admit, the natural pairing wasn't the only reason I was happy to be working with him. It was a nice way to spend time together without having to let on that I was happy for the excuse. Roman was charming and sweet, but his reputation for having dated most of the single women in Yarrow Glen left me unsure where I stood with him, which made me stay safely at arm's length from him.

Roman and I took turns providing dinner for the group on evenings we worked on the float. It was my turn tonight, so Mrs. Schultz offered to pick up the food. Reluctantly taking the cash I offered, she mounted her cherry-red bicycle to ride the three blocks to Let's Talk Tacos, a taco truck parked in a lot across from the *Glen Gazette*. It was a favorite in town.

I locked up and brought Guernsey and our float supplies out the alley door and around to the back of the building where our float was parked. The narrow lot between the building and the woods emptied out after hours, leaving only my used first-generation CR-V and Baz's Chevy pickup, so we had more space here than behind Roman's meadery. I happily dropped the straw cow as soon as I reached Chet's old boat trailer, which he was kind enough to let us use as the float's base. I wanted to figure out where Guernsey fit best on the float, but I was already feeling the scarecrow's itchy effects on my arms.

I stepped back to assess our creation so far, but something looked amiss. Didn't we already put the giant plastic mead bottle on the float? And the cardboard cheese wheel was missing, too. I stared at the diminished float, a mixture of confusion and frustration coursing through me.

"Hello, Willa." Deandra Patterson, a writer for the *Glen Gazette*, had come up behind me. She was a middle-aged woman with dull brown hair she wore short and tucked behind her ears. She tended toward long, flowy Boho skirts and sensible shoes. The bulging, oversized handbag she perpetually had hanging from her shoulder would likely net her a prize if she were an audience member on *Let's Make a Deal*. "Am I interrupting your creative process?" she asked.

"Hi, Deandra. No, I was just noticing that some of the pieces to our float are missing. Maybe we didn't attach them well enough and they flew away."

"I've been hearing from others about pranks going on with the floats—teenagers stealing some of the stuff and then ditching it elsewhere. What's gone missing? I'll keep an eye out for it."

"A giant bottle that looks like mead. I can see how that would be enticing to teenagers. And a cardboard cheese wheel. *Ugh*. It's not like we really have the time to make things once, much less twice."

"Sorry about that. I was thinking of writing a story on it, but I don't want to taint the harvest fair. Besides, we've already had enough bad publicity, what with the Phoebe Winston story."

"Listen, I'm not up to giving you any statement about that."

She held her hands up, palms out. "I'm just here for the scarecrows and floats. I'm covering everyone's progress for the harvest fair. A. J. won't let me near the Phoebe Winston story."

"Oh? Why's that?"

"He wants the headliner for himself. He wasn't too happy with the way I handled interviews the last time we had something more nefarious than teenage pranks." She was referring to the murder I'd been embroiled in last spring. She continued, "He didn't think I was aggressive enough, so he's handling this one by himself, which works just fine for me. I work for the *Gazette*, not TMZ."

"So you didn't have anything to do with the photos?"

"I'm sorry I even showed them to A. J."

"What do you mean? A. J. didn't take them?"

"No. A USB drive with the photos on it was left on my desk Friday night. We always stay late the nights we put the paper to bed."

"Who put it on your desk?"

"I have no idea. The office isn't locked except for overnight. I went out to grab some food and when I came back, it was on my desk and no one else was around."

"But why leave it on your desk and not A. J.'s? He's the editor."

She shrugged. "Detective Heath asked the same thing. Mine's closest to the front door and A. J.'s office is upstairs. Maybe they just wanted to leave it as quickly as possible before someone saw them."

I was glad to hear Detective Heath had already questioned her, which meant he must've questioned A. J. too. "How did A. J. react when you showed it to him?"

"He was excited. He called Chet to come in and check it out right away to make sure it was authentic."

"Chet from the meadery?"

"Yeah. He's our website manager. He seemed to think it hadn't been tampered with, so A. J. decided to run with it."

"That seems irresponsible."

"A. J. didn't know if whoever gave us the USB also gave copies to other news outlets. He didn't want to get scooped. But now after everything that's happened . . ." She shook her head. "I'll gladly stick to my scarecrow stories. So, uh, what exactly is yours?" She stared at my attempt at a straw bovine, then walked around it to try to make it out from another angle.

"It's a dairy cow," I told her when it was obvious she wasn't going to figure it out on her own.

She cocked her head. "Ohhh, I see it now. That's the face and the ears . . ."

"No, that's the udder."

"Oh. Well, I'll come back for a photo when you're done making it."

"Good idea." I was too embarrassed to tell her I *was* done making it.

We walked together down the alley and parted ways

at the shop's side door. I popped back inside to fetch Loretta, but my mind was on what Deandra said. If A. J. didn't take those pictures, then who did? And did that same person murder Phoebe? Taking down Phoebe Winston first could've been the killer's plan all along.

CHAPTER 9

While I was retrieving my fish, I grabbed some of my leftover groceries and a hunk of asadero cheese from one of the refrigerated cases. I cupped Loretta's fishbowl in one arm and the paper bag of food in the other and went back outside to the rear of the building where I climbed the stairs to my deck, which led to my second-floor apartment above Curds & Whey.

Most buildings on my street housed two shops tucked between alleys with a second-story office or a cozy apartment like mine above each. There were no interior stairs to my apartment, which probably saved me a couple of extra inches on my hips, not being able to give in to my late-night cheese cravings with a fully stocked shop. It was still convenient enough to supplement my sad pantry on occasion, however. The shop's kitchenette usually held more food, as it had the space to serve as the hangout when my friends and I gathered for meals.

My cozy two-bedroom, one-bathroom apartment was just the right size for me and Loretta, however. Over the summer, I taught myself a successful double-tap method for prying open the tall, arched windows of the room that served as my kitchen and living space. The *charm* of stuck windowsills and a slightly slanted hardwood floor was made worthwhile by the ease of getting to work and the view of the sunrise over the Sonoma Valley mountains offered by the east-facing windows and deck.

I turned on Food Network's *Chopped* for Loretta as soon as I set down her fishbowl, but I felt guilty for subjecting her to the surfer waves the transport caused. I could've left her overnight in the shop, but I wasn't sure how she'd do by herself. Ted Allen, the host of her favorite show, almost always kept her company when we were apart.

I washed up and changed into jeans and a T-shirt, then peeked out the living room window. No one was at the float yet, so I had time to create my last-minute inspiration—queso blanco. It would taste fabulous with the street tacos Mrs. Schultz would have upon her return.

I slowly heated the asadero cheese on the stovetop along with some half-and-half, while I chopped tomatoes, cilantro, and green chiles. The mild white cheese (from which queso blanco gets its name) has a springy consistency from stretching and kneading and melts well. It also comes with a fun fact: It originated in the same place as one of the most famous dog breeds—Chihuahua, Mexico.

I folded the diced ingredients into the thoroughly melted cheese, then looked through my cabinets. Jackpot! A bag of tortilla chips. I ran a crispy corn chip through the velvety smooth queso blanco and hurried to bring it to my mouth, so none of the thick sauce would escape the coated chip. I did a little dance after each warm, creamy bite. Was there anything in the world better than melted cheese?

I poured the queso blanco into a wide soup thermos and screwed the top closed to force myself to stop eating it. *Good food is best when shared* my mother always said, and she was right.

I zipped a sweatshirt over my Life is Gouda T-shirt

and said goodbye to Loretta before leaving. Usually she was captivated by Ted Allen, wiggling her long red tail like a flirty flamenco dancer's dress, but tonight she only did a single loop around her bowl and settled in behind her pineapple house. Maybe the activity of the shop had worn her out. She did seem to enjoy it there, greeting everyone who came over to admire her.

I walked out the door with a six-pack of bottled water and the thermos of queso. Before descending the steps, I plugged in the string of lights I'd wrapped around the railings and pillars of the small deck outside my door. It was close to dusk and the lights not only gave off a festive feel, they also aided the two weak streetlamps that illuminated the strip of blacktop.

I heard the tinkling of Mrs. Schultz's bicycle bell as she pedaled to the float. Roman and Chet trotted from the alley to catch up to her and the scent of tacos that surely followed in her path.

She dismounted and removed the taco bags from the basket between her handlebars as the guys helped me tote four folding chairs from under the deck for our dinner gathering. My excitement at the mouth-watering street tacos was only matched by seeing Roman.

"Let's Talk Tacos. Good choice," Roman said, unfolding the chairs. "Thanks for dinner."

Chet echoed the gratitude. He tucked his mid-length hair behind his ears and rubbed his palms together in anticipation.

Mrs. Schultz curled open the bags for easier access. "Carne asada in this one, carnitas in this one. I hope that's okay."

"Your choices go perfectly with my homemade queso blanco." I held up the thermos.

Luckily, the tacos were small enough to have several, so none of us would have to choose between the two kinds. We generously dribbled the queso on the shredded meat and pico de gallo filling within the warmed corn tortillas.

As we were silently scarfing down tacos, Roman's gaze wandered to the float. His brow furrowed as he surely noticed the missing pieces. I gave them the bad news about the theft.

"Deandra said we're not the only ones. You don't think they'll try to take the whole thing, do you? I don't want you losing your trailer because of this," I said to Chet.

"I don't think they will. My boat stays docked at the marina anyway. I can afford it now that I'm not living in Silicon Valley anymore."

"How long have you been in Yarrow Glen?" I asked Chet.

"A little over four years now. I got burnt out at my old job and needed a change. Some friends and I did a wine-tasting tour up this way once and this seemed like a really laid-back town, so when I finally had enough, I ditched everything and moved here."

"That takes a lot of guts," Mrs. Schultz commented.

"I don't know about that. I saved as much as I could and I made a smart real estate investment, so it wasn't much of a risk. I knew pretty early on I wasn't cut out for the rat race."

"Do you think you'll make Yarrow Glen your permanent home?"

"I used to toy with going to live on my boat, but now I think there might be something to keep me here."

I wondered if he was referring to Ginger. I guess it was serious between them. Poor Baz.

"Mr. Schultz always wanted a boat. It was one of his retirement dreams," Mrs. Schultz told us.

I put an arm around her. "I'm sorry he didn't get to enjoy his retirement. He was taken from you way too soon."

"I told myself I'd go boating on my own someday and enjoy it for him, but I haven't gotten around to it."

"Let me take you out on my boat sometime, Mrs. Schultz," Chet offered. "It's a bit of a drive to the marina, but it's worth it."

"Oh, I wasn't fishing for an invitation." Then she chuckled. "Don't mind the pun."

"I know you weren't, but I don't get out on the water much myself anymore. It'll be a good excuse for me to go."

"He took me out on it once. It's like a mini yacht. You'll love it, Mrs. Schultz," Roman said.

Chet laughed. "It's just a cabin cruiser, but I do think you'll like it. We'll all go."

"Let's do it. We can plan it when the harvest fair is done and we have a little more time on our hands. Whaddya say?" Roman smiled at Mrs. Schultz and then at me until I felt my face warming.

"I say yes!" Mrs. Schultz exclaimed.

"I'm in," I said, willing my hormones to get ahold of themselves.

Mrs. Schultz perked up and went in for a second taco from the bag on the ground. I was already excited at the prospect of spending a whole day with Roman.

"Have you talked to the police about the missing float parts?" Roman asked me, coming back to the matter at hand.

"I think they've got more important things to worry about at the moment, like Phoebe Winston."

"The whole thing seems crazy. The police came to talk to Chet today," Roman said.

Chet nodded as he downed half the street taco in one bite.

"Why did they want to talk to you?" I asked.

"About the photos," Chet said out of the corner of his full mouth.

"Oh right. Are you absolutely sure they were authentic?" I had to ask.

He swallowed and wiped a smear of queso from his lower lip. "They looked legit to me, but I also ran them through some programs to double check. Nothing came up to indicate they were altered in any way."

"I didn't even know there were programs that could pick that out. Deandra told me about the anonymous USB drive. There were no hints as to who left it on her desk?"

"No. Deandra brought it to A. J., and he brought it to me."

"Is there any chance A. J. took the pictures himself?"

"I don't know how. He told me he was bummed that he didn't get an interview with Phoebe because he never found out how to get in touch with her. How was he supposed to take pictures of her if he didn't even know where she was staying? Besides, if he had that kind of access to Phoebe Winston, he'd make sure he got the credit. I know that much about A. J."

"That makes sense, but she was murdered right after the photos came out."

"How was he supposed to know that would happen? Or any of us? I wouldn't have given the green light for him to publish them if I'd have known." Chet dropped his head, allowing his shaggy hair to fall in front of his face.

"I'm sorry, Chet. You couldn't have known. You're not responsible."

"The police must think the photos are related to the murder, though, or else they wouldn't have asked me so many questions," Chet said.

"It seems too coincidental not to be," I agreed. "Someone wanted to humiliate her. Was it the same person who wanted her dead? Or was it cause and effect?"

"A. J. didn't tell me to run those photos because he

wanted to humiliate her. It was nothing personal. It was just a story that landed on his desk. Literally," Chet insisted. "He's my friend. He'll chase a story, but he's not malicious."

"Don't get me wrong—I wasn't accusing him of anything. I'm just trying to put all the pieces together of what led up to the time she was killed."

The sound of crinkling paper brought our attention to our feet, where a small white fluff ball was nosing his way into our remaining tacos.

"Buttercup! Get away from the food!" Archie reprimanded, zooming our way on his skateboard. One hand clung to a laden reusable grocery bag.

I put the small dog in my lap. "You ought to put him on a leash so he doesn't get lost," I said to Archie.

"He's usually obedient, and Phoebe told me that collar he's wearing has a tracking device on it just in case he gets lost or stolen."

"You can't blame him for knowing good food when he smells it," Roman said.

"What are you doing here, Archie? You're supposed to be relaxing," I reminded him.

"With my mother in the house hovering over me after what happened yesterday? Impossible." Archie pulled another chair out from under the deck and brought it over to sit with us, placing the heavy bag on the ground. "More bad news—Buttercup and Batman don't get along. At all." He looked crestfallen.

"Who's Batman?" Chet asked.

"My Chihuahua. Someone else is going to have to take care of Buttercup. He can't stay at my house anymore. I brought his food and some toys for him."

I kissed Buttercup on the head. "I'd keep him, but he can't come into the shop. He'd be lonely by himself all day. He seems like such a sociable fella. Do you have a dog at home, Chet?"

Chet plucked out some pork from his third taco and fed it to the dog. "I never have, but I've watched other people's dogs and thought about getting one. I wouldn't mind taking him for a while, but I have to check with my landlord first."

"Great. Thanks. It might not be necessary if Thomas can take him. I'd better go see him tomorrow. I also need to find out if anyone else knew where Phoebe was staying besides him."

"I know one other person," Archie said glumly.

I put a supportive hand on his shoulder. "Anyone who might've killed her, I meant."

Mrs. Schultz was now offering Buttercup the remains of her steak taco. "What about the people who own the house and rented it to Phoebe?"

"Good thought, Mrs. Schultz. How can we find out who they are?"

"You're not thinking about getting involved in another murder investigation, are you?" Roman asked me. "I thought you said you wanted to stay away from this."

"I said I wanted to stay away from Heath and any publicity, not the investigation. Archie was the last known person to see Phoebe alive," I told him.

"I was with Phoebe all day until she found out about the pictures," Archie continued to fill him in.

"I get it. So Detective Heath thinks . . ." Roman finished his thought silently. Nobody wanted to say aloud the words *Archie* and *suspect* together.

"Detective Heath likes to get all the facts first, but *I'd* like Archie's name off his lips as soon as possible," I said. "And Chet, please don't mention any of this to A. J. This is just between us, not for the *Gazette*."

"I'm friends with A. J. but he can get his own stories. I'm just their layout guy. Everything I hear is off the record, don't worry," he said.

Roman's skeptical attitude shifted. "If Phoebe rented

the house through a website, we'd be able to find the names of the owners online."

"You're good for more than just mead making, Mr. Massey," I said to Roman, grateful he was willing to help Archie's cause.

"Wait until you find out my other talents." He winked at me, immediately upping my oxytocin levels again.

I didn't let his flirtation deter me for long. "I'll look for the house on some vacation home-rental sites and see what I come up with. They don't usually list the address, but I know what it looks like."

"Now how do you know? You said Archie was the one with her," Chet said.

Oops. I guess it'll be found out soon enough. "We went to talk to her after we saw the photos. I was the one who found the body."

"Willa has a knack for that, unfortunately," Roman said.

"That's just bad luck. Her talent lies in investigating," Mrs. Schultz spoke up.

"I only managed to do it once, but I wouldn't mind making it two for two. With everyone's help again, of course," I said.

"How do you do that?" Chet asked.

"We ask questions, bat around some theories. Like we're doing now. Maybe the owners of the rental home will know something."

"Maybe they have something to do with it," Roman speculated. "Maybe when the owners found out who they were renting to, they decided they'd get some paparazzi type shots of her and make some money selling them to the tabloids. Little did they know she'd give them a lot more than they bargained for by ordering from Mac's."

"The only hiccup with that theory is that they gave the photos away for free," I said. I let Buttercup jump off my lap to beg for more tacos.

"Willa's right. They weren't sold, they were anonymously left on Deandra's desk," Chet reiterated, while the dog licked any residual taco juices from his fingers.

"And there's another hole to blow in that theory," Archie said. "Phoebe told me Thomas rented the house for her under his name. She was a little paranoid about people finding out where she was staying. At least I thought she was being paranoid. I guess she had a reason to be."

"Okay, so maybe the owners didn't have anything to do with it, but somebody else knew where to find her." I thought about it some more. "Whoever it was could've seen her come to the shop the day before and followed her car back to the house," I said.

"How would we find that out?" Archie asked.

The rest of us were silent. We were stumped.

"I really appreciate you guys trying to help me, but I don't think there's much you can do." His shoulders slumped.

I was used to the upbeat Archie, not this dejected one. I had to convince Detective Heath to find a better suspect. Thomas and A. J. were at the top of my list. "We've only just begun. There are still several key people to talk to. We won't give up. And we don't know yet what Detective Heath has discovered."

"Willa's right." I knew Mrs. Schultz was just as anxious to make Archie feel better as I was. "Let's not think about it anymore tonight. We've got a float to create."

Everyone patted Archie on the back in solidarity and Roman handed him the bag of leftover tacos, which cheered him up.

"Hey, didn't this have more stuff last time we worked on it?" Archie nodded toward the float, as he took out a taco and drizzled copious amounts of queso on it.

"Yeah. Someone took it. A teenage prank, so I heard.

Since they've already hit us, we'll just keep our fingers crossed they won't do it again," I said.

"Have you ever considered getting a surveillance camera? You could attach it to your deck. It won't prevent anything from being stolen necessarily, but at least it'll show you who did it," Chet suggested.

"I looked into those cameras when I opened the shop," I said, "but the footage is usually too grainy from a distance, especially with bad lighting like this, unless you spend a lot of money on it. And right now I'm pretty lean after all the money I spent on Phoebe's—" I stopped mid-sentence. I faintly noticed everyone staring at me, but something tapped at my memory and it took me a few long seconds to figure out what it was.

"Willa?" Roman's voice bumped me out of my thoughts.

"The surveillance camera. Wasn't there one at the gate of Phoebe's house?" I asked Archie.

"That's right. And another by the front door," Archie said. "They were motion activated. She checked them a couple of times with her phone. I told you she was paranoid."

I smiled broadly. "Then you're home free, Archie. The camera footage will show the last person who visited Phoebe that day, and it won't be you."

For the first time, I was optimistic. We just had to keep our fingers crossed that the cameras recorded whoever went to her house after Archie left. I called Detective Heath and left him a message about the surveillance cameras, even though I was certain the police must've already considered it.

Archie gobbled up the remaining street tacos, sharing the scraps with Buttercup. His appetite was back, so he must've been feeling better.

The sun was sinking behind the mountains, dimming

the sky. We worked for over an hour under the glow of the streetlight and my deck party lights. I didn't even mind remaking my cardboard cheddar wheel now that I knew Archie was in the clear.

A beefy sedan slowly pulled in through the alley of the hardware store and haphazardly parked across several spaces. We all stopped to look. Although it wasn't flashing its red and blue lights, the police light bar inside the rear window gave its owner away.

"Detective Heath," I muttered before he even stepped out of the car.

My earlier optimism made me think he was here to tell Archie not to worry anymore. Once he emerged from the car and came closer, still in his tapered navy suit, I could see he wasn't here to deliver good news.

He looked at me briefly before his gaze slid to Archie. "I thought I might find you here. I need to ask you to come down to the station for some more questioning, please."

"Did you get my phone message?" I asked.

"We were already on it. We got what we needed," he said matter-of-factly.

"Then what do you need Archie for?"

"I'll talk to Archie privately."

"You can tell me here. I don't have anything to hide from my friends," Archie said.

Heath looked down at his shoes and then back to Archie. He squinted as if it physically pained him to speak. "According to the surveillance recordings, there were no other visitors to the house where Phoebe Winston was staying. It appears you were the last person with her. Archie, you're now officially considered a person of interest."

I watched Buttercup try to climb Archie's shins. He reached down to pick up the small dog and nestle him in his arms. I wished I could comfort Archie as easily. He handed Buttercup to me, picked up his skateboard, and started to walk away with Detective Heath.

"I'm going with you," Mrs. Schultz said. "At least until your mother can get there."

"You won't be allowed in the interview room with us, Mrs. Schultz," Detective Heath said.

"I don't care. He's not going to the police station alone."

Heath accepted it and walked with both of them to the car. "I'll call your mom," I called after him as they got into the car. I watched them drive away, determined more than ever to prove Archie's innocence.

CHAPTER 10

Roman and Chet offered to take care of the float cleanup and put Mrs. Schultz's bike in a safe place. I retreated upstairs to my apartment with Buttercup and used up my reserves of remaining calm during the difficult phone call to Archie's mother. I fell apart once the call ended.

It was comforting to have Buttercup with me. He'd already curled up next to me on the love seat, settling himself on a corner of my grandmother's knit throw blanket. I didn't mind. My shabby chic décor had pretty much turned to shabby-shabby over the last eight moves while I worked at various cheese shops across the country. I'd put some dry food and water in bowls for him, but he was too focused on the *Chopped* contestants on television trying to make a dish out of beef tongue and fruit cake to pay attention to his own nourishment.

I marveled at how those contestants stayed so calm under pressure, impressed with how they harnessed their ability to focus. I, too, felt the clock ticking away. The longer Archie was a suspect, the more difficult it would be to divert Heath's attention to someone else. There had to be a mistake with the surveillance cameras. Someone else had to have gone to the house after Archie left.

Thomas. He left my shop that day in a hurry to see Phoebe. It was just before I phoned Archie and told him to come back to the shop. Thomas had to have seen Phoebe at the house after Archie left. Why didn't the cameras record him?

I popped up off the love seat, sending Buttercup into a fit of barking.

"Sorry, little guy." I picked him up. "How about helping me talk to Thomas?"

I carried him with me as I left my apartment and raced down the stairs to my CR-V. The Cellar was only two blocks up the road, but I didn't have the patience for the walk. Once in my car, I barreled down the parking strip with Buttercup on my lap and turned into the alley by Carl's Hardware, where a figure in front of me forced me to slam on the breaks. My heart seemed to stop at the same time my car did. Baz stood in my headlights, wide-eyed but unharmed. *Thank goodness.*

He came over to my car window as I loosened my instinctive grip on Buttercup and calmed my racing heart.

"Holy huckleberry, Willa."

"I'm sorry, Baz. You okay?"

"Glad your brakes work better than my reflexes. What's the rush?"

"Hop in. I'll explain on the way."

CHAPTER 11

Baz and I entered the Inn at Yarrow Glen as we'd done two nights prior, except this time we had a furry companion. We saw Constance at the reception desk, chatting with the couple who were checking in, based on the luggage by their side.

The inn didn't need a concierge with Constance Yi on their payroll. The petite twenty-four-year-old native of Yarrow Glen not only was able to direct any guest where they wanted to go, she could also tell you the history and gossip of each place and its inhabitants in equal measure. And she would, whether you wanted to know or not. The couple seemed relieved that our presence interrupted Constance's monologue. They thanked her and hastily headed to the spindle staircase.

"I can bring your luggage up through our staff elevator and meet you at your room with it," she called after them.

"No, no. We can manage," the wife said, as the couple willingly heaved their suitcases up the steps in order to make their escape.

She shrugged and brought her attention to us. "Aw, he's so cute," she said, coming around the reception desk to pet Buttercup. She wore a crisp plum silk blouse neatly tucked into black trousers that skimmed her petite figure.

"Thank you. I didn't even shave today," Baz jokingly replied.

Constance laughed at him. "I meant the dog. But we don't allow dogs at the inn, unless he's a service dog."

"He's Phoebe Winston's dog," I told her, hoping that would be enough cachet to allow him to remain.

"I thought I recognized him. Can you believe it? Getting caught eating Mac's ribs? Then being murdered?"

I wasn't surprised that Constance knew about the murder—she was one of the first to know most of the happenings in town.

"That cute Detective Heath was around again to ask me questions about her personal assistant, Thomas Doolittle," she continued. "Then he went up to question him. Mr. Doolittle's been holed up alone in his room all day since. He keeps calling the desk to bring him more beer. I've certainly gotten my steps in today." She subconsciously fiddled with the luxe fitness tracker on her wrist.

"What room's he in? We need to talk to him about the dog," I said.

"Sorry, I'm not allowed to give out that information. Besides, he gave me firm instructions that he didn't want to speak with anyone. A. J. Stringer tried twice today." Her phone buzzed and one of the red lights blinked. She went around to the other side of the reception desk. "There he is again." She pushed the blinking button and picked up the receiver.

I leaned closer to see the handwritten numbers on the phone. There were only nine guest rooms at the inn. The button she'd pushed read *six*.

"Yes, Mr. Doolittle. I'll bring it right up." She hung up.

"Room number six?" I confirmed.

"How . . . ? Oh."

"Why don't we bring it up for you?"

We knocked on the door to room number six, hoping the beer Baz had in his hand would soften the blow that we were the ones at the door. We heard a voice from inside beckon us to come in. The doors of the historic inn still used old-fashioned skeleton keys, so the wooden knob turned in my grasp, and the door opened inward.

Thomas was lounging atop the rumpled quilt of his bed. The circumstances (and likely earlier beers) had mellowed his Clark Kent persona. The muscular physique that was hinted at underneath his buttoned-up shirt was more obvious in his white undershirt and jeans. His hair, which yesterday had been slicked into place as if he were having his grammar school picture taken, looked like he'd run his fingers through it a few times, but not a comb.

His face registered a myriad of emotions in just a few seconds. His surprise turned into a scowl until he saw Phoebe's dog. "Buttercuuup!"

He unsteadily leapt off the bed with outstretched arms to take the dog. The antique brass frame creaked under his weight as he returned to the bed, doting on Buttercup. He stuck his face in Buttercup's white fur as he trapped him in a crushing embrace. Buttercup froze in his arms, his round eyes pleading with us to set him free.

"We brought you another beer," I said.

Baz held the bottle and the pilsner glass out to Thomas as if they were ransom for the dog.

It worked. Thomas loosened his desperate grip on Buttercup in order to take the beer, and Buttercup scurried to the opposite corner of the bed. Thomas ignored the glass in Baz's hand and drank straight from the bottle.

He looked at the dog with an exaggerated frown. "My last connection to Phoebe."

Baz, still holding the empty pilsner, moved a wayward belt off a settee situated in front of the window so we could take a seat. Buttercup made a heroic leap off the bed and pawed at our ankles. I picked him up and he squeezed himself into the few inches of space between us.

"This is my friend Baz," I said to Thomas, realizing they'd never met.

They nodded at each other in greeting.

"We came to check on you. See how you're doing," I said.

"I'd be doing better if I could go home. That detective says I have to stick around. This whole thing's a nightmare." Thomas slouched against the headboard.

"We're really sorry about Phoebe. You two seemed very close."

"Nobody knew her like I did. And now she's gone. We didn't even get to celebrate our three-year anniversary." His voice was thick with misery.

"Were you two . . . romantically involved?" I was afraid to ask, but I had to.

"I meant our *work* anniversary."

"No one could blame you if there was more," Baz said, one guy to another.

"We flirted, sure. Well, *she* flirted . . . when she felt like it." He took a swig of beer. "I was hired when her star was on the rise again. She didn't want anything getting in the way. We never hooked up, but we had a special bond. There was no doubt about that."

He seemed to want to talk about her. "Tell us about her, Thomas," I said.

He cradled the beer to his chest. "She was dynamic, like no one I'd ever known. She could make you feel like you were the most important person on the planet." He smiled and tipped the bottle to his lips again. When he brought it down, his smile had vanished. "She could also make you feel like you were something she'd scraped off the bottom of her shoe. But it just made you want to work that much harder for her, you know?"

That wouldn't have been my response to that kind of treatment, but I nodded anyway.

"Did you know she was lying about being vegan?" Baz asked unceremoniously.

Thomas tensed and sat up fully, his stroll down memory lane interrupted. "Phoebe tried to give her fans what they wanted. She loved her fans."

Well, that was a non-answer.

"They wanted her to be vegan?" I asked.

"They wanted her to be nicer. It was a part of how she was going to resurrect herself. Have you been on social media since it happened? Yesterday, they wanted to burn her at the stake. Now that she's dead, they're holding vigils. They're so fickle. She just wanted to win their hearts again."

"Do you know if any of them were stalkers?" I asked.

"The police asked me that too. Do they think a stalker killed her?" He seemed to emerge from feeling sorry for himself long enough to contemplate this.

"Someone sent her a photograph and we're not sure what it means," I explained.

"The police didn't show me any photo. Her followers *were* rabid. They either loved her obsessively or trolled her relentlessly, but I didn't know about any of them stalking her. She would've told me. They all seemed to relish in her downfall, though." His face showed his disgust.

"What do you know about the barbeque photos?" Baz asked.

"What would I know about them?"

"You didn't seem too surprised when I showed them to you," I said carefully. "Did you bring the food from

Mac's Big Mouth Barbeque to her? She wouldn't have chanced having it delivered."

Thomas shook his head. "The whole thing must've been a setup. Nobody can prove the pictures were real." He hopped off the bed and paced the floor, agitated. Buttercup burrowed deeper between us. "I'm not going to allow her name to be dragged through the mud now that she's gone."

I didn't want him to shut down now. Proving whether Phoebe was a liar wasn't my biggest concern at the moment. "Those are so easily altered. I'm surprised anyone believed it," I said to appease him.

Baz balked and I elbowed him.

Agreeing with Thomas seemed to work. He sat back down on the bed, but kept his feet on the floor, seemingly ready to spring into anger mode at any moment.

"I can see why you felt you had to go see her as soon as I showed you the pictures." I continued to ease him back into friendly territory.

"I needed to make sure she was okay," he said.

"*Was* she okay?"

"I didn't get to see her." He took off his glasses and used the heels of his palms to rub his closed eyelids before slipping the frames back on.

"But you did go to her house, right?"

"I came back here to get the car, but it wasn't here. I remembered that I gave the keys to that guy from your shop that morning."

"Archie."

"Yeah, Archie. So I called an Uber. He dropped me off at the gate. I rang the buzzer, but she refused to answer. I called her. I texted her. Nothing. I walked around to see if there was another way in, but I couldn't find one, so I buzzed some more. She never answered, so I came back to the inn. I figured she'd get in touch when she was ready."

"You didn't know the code to get past the gate?"

"It was only on her phone. I was supposed to have the car with the clicker, so there'd be no reason for me to need any kind of code."

"Did you see Archie at all?"

"No. At first I thought that's why she wasn't answering, but then I realized the car was gone, so I thought they must've gone somewhere—maybe she'd already left town."

"You're saying you left the house without ever seeing her or talking to her?" Baz's question held a hefty dose of skepticism.

"You don't believe me? Why would I lie? You think I killed Phoebe?" Thomas was on his feet again.

"She was a pretty demanding boss," Baz pointed out.

"What's wrong with having high expectations?"

"Nothing," I interjected in an attempt to calm him. "No one would blame you if you were getting tired of it, though."

"Maybe you were getting tired of the games she was playing with you and your emotions? I know if a chick did that to me . . ." Baz left the rest unsaid.

"I-I didn't mind it. You have no idea what we had together." Thomas squinted at us. "Why are you really here?"

He was getting impatient with us. I had to think fast if I was going to get more out of him. "We don't know what to do with Buttercup. Constance just told us he can't stay here at the inn, so someone will have to watch him until you can take him."

"Until *I* can take him?"

A few minutes ago, he'd acted like the dog was his last lifeline. Now he looked at me as if I'd just asked him to take care of my first-born child. "You said he was your link to Phoebe."

"I know, but I'm going through a lot right now and he's so needy."

It didn't appear that Buttercup wanted to be with him either, so I didn't press the point.

"Okay, well, do you know of anyone who could take him? Someone from her family?" I suggested.

"She wasn't close to her family. She wouldn't want any of them to have him."

"Her publisher? A friend? I guess I can ask around."

"She paid two thousand dollars for that dog, you can't just hand him over to anybody."

"I thought she got him at a rescue. Kismet and all that?"

Thomas cringed and tapped his forehead with the throat of his beer bottle. Obviously, he'd let something slip.

"So she didn't get Buttercup from the rescue shelter?" I prompted.

"Listen, it wasn't her idea to lie about it. You have to know that. It was her assistant who came up with the plan. Jeremy. I wasn't even working for her when it all went down."

"Why don't you start from the beginning," I said gently.

He sighed. "All right. But this can't leave the room."

He waited, and Baz and I nodded a vague consent so he'd continue.

"She bought the dog hoping for some brownie points with the public. This was after she'd lost a bunch of opportunities because of her behavior and got cancelled by her fans."

Archie had told me about her public tantrums after she became famous. That kind of behavior might've made for good reality TV, but in real life it was unacceptable, and rightly so.

"She planned to call paparazzi to take 'candid' photos of her with Buttercup," he continued. "But Jeremy told her buying a purebred dog instead of rescuing one can be worse than not having one at all as far as the public is concerned. So . . ." He hesitated.

"So . . . ?" I prodded.

"So she lived with Buttercup in secret until the dog bonded with her, and then paid off the shelter to pretend she found him there."

"So the video that went viral was faked?"

"Yes. But she did love Buttercup," he added hurriedly. "What was the harm? They'd built her up for being a villain on the show then took her down for acting the same way in real life. This was their chance to build her back up again. They wanted a redemption story, ya know? So she wanted to give them one. She was going to start a pet rescue after that, but that would've been too much work and expense, so she came up with the idea to start her kindness brand. That's when she decided to become vegan, and as soon as that happened, she got the Ve-Cheez spokesperson gig, and she found me."

"Was she ever really vegan?"

"Of course she was."

Of course? I wondered if her other assistant would tell a different story. "Does Jeremy still work for her?" I asked.

"No. He cut out a couple months after she hired me."

"Do you know his last name or how to get in touch with him?"

Thomas shook his head. "I never knew his last name and he left without telling me. I did try calling him once afterward, but he wasn't at that number anymore."

"Was he fired?" An old employee with a grudge would make a good suspect.

Thomas shook his head. "Phoebe said he took another job."

"So he just disappeared and left you as Phoebe's new number one. How convenient for you," Baz said.

"Are you accusing me of something again?"

"No, he's not accusing you of anything," I assured Thomas, glaring at Baz.

"It sounds like you're trying to pin something on me. I'm done with this conversation. You can get out now." He went over to the door and put a hand on the knob.

"Hey, we brought you a beer." Baz lifted the empty glass he was still holding.

"Get out," Thomas repeated, opening the door.

I sensed he was done sharing. Baz left the glass and picked up Buttercup and we made our way to the door.

"Wait." Thomas shut the door again before we could leave. His alcohol-infused emotions swung as quickly as a pendulum once again. "What are you going to do with Buttercup?"

"Gee, I don't know, Thomas, since you weren't very helpful about it," I said, no longer trying to play nice.

"My hands are tied. You said so yourself, they won't let me keep him here. Don't you think I have enough to worry about? You try setting up job interviews when you're a suspect in murdering your last boss."

"He's got a point," Baz said.

Thomas looked satisfied with this small triumph.

Baz finished, "We don't want Buttercup taken care of by someone who might be a murderer."

Thomas grabbed the knob again and swung open the door. "Out!"

We skittered into the hallway, muttering condolences about Phoebe, but it was too late to douse the bridge we'd burned. He slammed the door behind us. We walked downstairs and into the chilly night air back to my car.

"Jeez, you'd think with a name like Doolittle, he'd care more about animals," Baz said, still clutching Buttercup.

I rolled my eyes at him. "You could've been a little gentler with the guy instead of getting him riled up."

"I don't like him. Phoebe's first assistant disappears

after he comes into the picture and now his boss is murdered. Don't tell me you believe him," he said.

"The surveillance cameras must've backed up his story that he never got inside the gate."

"He admitted to trying to find another way in. Would the cameras see that?" Baz said.

"Archie said the cameras were at the front gate and the front door only. It's possible he could've gotten in through the back without being seen."

"Whoever took the pictures the night before she was killed managed to do it without being seen," Baz said.

"Yeah, but the pictures could've been taken from far away with a telephoto lens. We saw the woods behind her house. Someone could've camped out in a tree. That's different than going to her door and finding a way in." I unlocked my car and we climbed in.

"If they think it's Archie, then there must've been no evidence of a break-in. Either a door was unlocked or Phoebe let the murderer in."

"Archie said the doors were locked *and* she was a little paranoid, so I doubt she unlocked the door for no reason. He couldn't even get back in after he went outside to walk Buttercup. The only way she'd let the killer in is if she knew them."

"I wonder how long Thomas was away from the surveillance camera. He must've already been to that house before yesterday, right?" Baz clicked on his seat belt.

"For sure. There's no way she moved her clothes and books and stuff in there by herself. He was her manservant." I put on my own seat belt and started the car but didn't move it, my mind preoccupied with the possibility of Thomas being the murderer. "He could've known exactly how to get into the house without going through the front gate. Maybe buzzing her was all an act for the sake of the surveillance camera. Would he have the nerve to kill her while his Uber's waiting out front?"

I pulled the car out of the inn's parking lot and took a left onto Main Street instead of continuing down Pleasant Ave. Buttercup remained in Baz's lap and looked out the window, his whole back end wagging along with his stubby tail.

"Where are you going?" Baz asked me.

"To the rental house. Let's see if you and I can find a way in."

CHAPTER 12

Between my memory and Baz's we only made one wrong turn before finding our way back to the secluded rental house we'd driven to the evening before. That poorly marked road was easy to miss and I wished we'd noted the address when we were there last so we could've stuck it in my GPS. I drove slowly, my high beams cutting through the darkness of the quiet, winding road until we came upon the house. I looked for a place to pull over since the road had no shoulder. Less than a hundred yards past it, there was a dirt patch with just enough room for my CR-V, leaving Baz to tangle with the bush pressed up against the passenger door as he exited the car.

I used a flashlight from my glovebox to navigate our way back up the lonely road to the house. The front portico light showed the rented Range Rover still in the driveway, as well as a police cruiser and a van clearly marked *Forensics*. The houselights glowed from within. We extinguished the light and walked around to the side of the house.

"They're still processing the house," Baz stated the obvious.

"I figured it would have the police tape around it, but I didn't think the forensics team would still be here."

"We should probably do this in the daylight anyway, don't you think?"

"Would you like to wait in the car with Buttercup? Oh, that's right, Buttercup's ahead of us. Even *he's* not afraid to walk outside the house."

In the darkness, I sensed Baz's scowl rather than saw it. The moon and the yard's landscaped up-lighting gave us enough contrast amid the shadows to make our way through the tall grass. We followed the wrought-iron fence around the perimeter of the backyard, through the trees that made up the woods, and back up the opposite side from where we'd started. We were stopped by a thicket of leafy bushes.

Buttercup yelped. He was stuck in the thick brush. I reached in but recoiled when sharp thorns pricked my hands. Buttercup barked again. His high-pitched yapping resonated through the backyard.

"Shhh. It's okay, it's okay," I whispered, trying to reassure him without being heard by anybody in the house. "We have to get him out of there, Baz."

Baz got on the ground on all fours.

"Be careful with him. Don't hurt him," I warned, needlessly.

He reached in from the bottom of the brush but came out empty-handed.

"Where'd he go?" Baz said.

We heard more of Buttercup's high-pitched barking, but this time it wasn't right next to us in the bushes. I dared to look over the brush and saw something moving inside the fence. Buttercup had gotten in!

"We have to get him," I whispered to Baz.

Baz stuck his head inside the thorny bush where he'd tried to reach for the dog before.

"Ouch!" He pulled himself out. "I can't get in."

"This must be how the murderer got in, though. The

heck with it. I'm going to chance it." I turned on my flashlight. The concentrated circle of light illuminated a small burrow amid the lustrous wine-red leaves. It was only big enough for something the size of a groundhog or a very small dog like Buttercup. I stuck the light farther inside the hole and felt around with my free hand. There were only more sharp spines biting my face and hands. The bush, probably a barberry now that I got a look at it, pressed against an intact fence. The only way in was the space between the spires, just big enough for Buttercup to have squeezed through.

The back patio light clicked on, bathing part of the yard in a bright glow. I fumbled to turn off my flashlight. We saw the silhouette of someone at the sliding glass door. Baz and I remained crouched, as still as garden gnomes, hoping we were sufficiently hidden by the brush. Buttercup silently ran in wide circles on the lawn, moving outside the beam of the light.

My thighs began to burn in their bended position, but that wasn't the worst of it. I suddenly had to pee. Hide-and-seek always did this to me as a kid, and apparently, I hadn't grown out of it.

The light clicked off. After a moment, the figure moved away from the door. We dared to stand, my shaky hamstrings barely cooperating.

"Buttercup," I yell-whispered.

I made kissy noises and Baz joined in until the dog came over. We moved away from the barberry bush, so he could come through the fence safely. I picked him up, and his little tongue licked me, as if he was happy to be back from his big adventure.

Baz took him from me and tried to check him over, which was nearly impossible in the darkness.

We looked back toward the house where we could see the figures moving around inside.

"There are a lot of windows in that house," I commented. "You can see practically everything at night from here."

"That worked out nicely for the person who wanted to get some photos of Phoebe."

"It sure did. The house itself is out of the way, but for someone who wanted privacy, all those uncovered windows don't offer much of it, do they?"

"From the front, you wouldn't know it. She must've not looked at the house pictures too carefully when she decided to rent it."

"Archie said Thomas rented her the house."

"Interesting choice."

Baz and I stared at the house a few minutes more, able to watch the people within and glad they were no longer focused on what was outdoors.

Once we got back to the car, we conjectured some more.

"It doesn't look like there was any way in unless you scaled the fence," Baz said.

"We didn't quite make it all the way around the house. It's possible Thomas planned something ahead of time."

"That's true. Maybe he left a ladder on the ground to use?"

I recalled the spear-shaped spires atop the fence made climbing over it dangerous, regardless. "But then how to get back out without the surveillance cameras noticing?"

"Yeah, and how would he get rid of the ladder after?"

"He didn't have a car to transport it."

Baz nodded in reluctant agreement. "That didn't net us much except for some cuts."

We turned on the overhead light and checked Buttercup over. He seemed no worse for wear. Baz and I, on the other hand, looked like we'd lost a wrestling match with some sharp paper. Why did the smallest cuts always seem to hurt the most?

Baz looked surprisingly comfortable with Buttercup curled on his lap, asleep.

"Buttercup seems to be pretty taken with you," I said.

"I was Bella's favorite too," he replied, referring to his childhood dog. "Animals love me. What can I say?"

"You know, we need a temporary home for Buttercup. Archie's dog doesn't get along with him," I said.

"Why do I get the feeling I'm going to be doing you a favor?"

"He likes being with people and he's not allowed in the cheese shop. Is it possible for him to hang out with you just for a day or two?"

"How did I get wrangled into this?"

"You just said Bella liked you best," I reminded him.

"Yeah, but I didn't take care of her."

"You're almost thirty years old. I think you can manage."

"I don't have any dog food."

"Archie dropped some off. It's in my apartment. I can give it to you when we get home. He brought toys for him too."

Baz looked down at the sleeping dog without answering.

"Just until I find out if Chet can take him?" I coaxed.

"Why would Chet take him?"

"He offered until we find a permanent home for him. He has to ask his landlord if it's all right."

"I can do it."

"You sure? The shop's closed tomorrow, so I suppose I could keep him another day. It's just that—"

"I only have a couple of appointments tomorrow. I can bring him with me."

"Great. Thanks." I wondered why Baz had a sudden change of heart. Was he feeling competitive with Chet?

I turned off the overhead light and started the car,

hoping we'd get home before he changed his mind, since he didn't seem too thrilled with his decision. This time I could clearly see Baz's scowl, but I also saw him massaging Buttercup's ear.

CHAPTER 13

I handed Baz Buttercup's bag of food and dog toys over the low railing of our attached decks. Buttercup looked more thrilled than Baz at the new arrangement.

I went into my apartment and texted Archie to let him know Buttercup was fine and ask how things went with Detective Heath. His response: *They didn't arrest me, so that's good news.*

I'd have to be grateful for small favors another day. It was time to talk to Heath and set this straight.

It was getting on nine o'clock. I wondered if Heath would still be at the police station. I took the car again, this time forcing myself to go slowly down the alley. I drove through our quiet block and took a left on Main Street, past the old town hall and into the parking lot shared by the church.

I made my way across the street to the safety complex that held both the fire and police departments. As soon as I stepped up to the glass front, I saw how dimly lit the lobby was inside, so it was no surprise when the doors didn't yield to my pulling on them. I tried all of them with no luck. I reluctantly walked back to the parking lot but couldn't bring myself to get in my car. I was unwilling to let this rest tonight. I looked at the safety complex again when I noticed a dark sedan pulling out of the lot adjacent to the building. Only police cars parked in that lot, but this wasn't a cruiser. It looked like the Dodge Charger Heath drove.

"Heath!" I called out without thought. Of course he couldn't hear me. The car went on without stopping. On impulse, I fumbled to get into my own car to follow him.

Luckily, the traffic was sparse and I managed to catch up to him just outside of the town center as the traffic light turned green. I followed him past a vineyard and onto a residential street. Beyond the sidewalks were modest homes with neat lawns, some with picket fences. It didn't strike me as Heath's kind of neighborhood, but then what did I really know about the man?

If it wasn't for the police light bar in his rear window glinting off my headlights occasionally, I'd have begun to wonder if I'd followed the right car. Wherever his house was, he seemed to be taking the long way home. Eventually, we left the neighborhood behind and he led me into a gas station. His car avoided the pumps and pulled over the yellow stripes of a no-parking zone in front of the convenience store. It continued to idle.

I wasn't about to wait for Heath to pick up whatever food mart item he might've been craving this time of night. I quickly pulled into a parking space and hopped out. His car's engine finally turned off and he emerged from his vehicle as if he'd expected me.

"What are you doing?" he said, abruptly.

To think I used to be annoyed at how overly polite he was.

"I need to talk to you. I followed you from the station."

"I know. I picked up on it a few miles out. I couldn't tell it was you, though."

"Oh, sorry. I didn't mean to scare you. Not that you would be scared. I just meant that I didn't intentionally follow you."

"You followed me by accident? How does that work?"

His stance relaxed and he stuck his hand in his trouser pocket.

"No. I mean, I wasn't watching you to follow you home. I just happened to see your car leave when I went to the station to talk to you."

"I'm off duty now, so can it wait until tomorrow?"

"It can't. Please, can we talk? I'll buy you a cherry slush. Jumbo size. Whatever it takes. I can't allow Archie to be a suspect. It's not only stupid, it's . . . it's . . . it's all my fault." My voice cracked against my will. I pushed down the lump in my throat that acted as a dam, the only thing keeping my tears from spilling over.

I couldn't bring myself to look at Heath, so I had no idea what was going on behind his dark eyes.

He put a hand on my arm to move me out of the way of the people coming and going in and out of the store.

"Let's not talk here," he said. "Follow me . . . intentionally."

This time he had a hint of amusement on his face. I nodded and followed him home.

His single-story house was on a quiet side street with few homes, situated on what appeared to be at least a couple of acres of land. I collected myself as I followed him through the front door.

As he clicked on the lights, I suddenly felt self-conscious being in his private space. He led me into an airy living room with soft recessed lighting and tall ceilings. It was overstated minimalist—if you misplaced your keys, you'd spot them immediately. What made it come to life were the large moody paintings of abstract figures that broke up the white walls. I wouldn't have figured Heath for an art collector.

"This is very neat for someone who wasn't expecting company," I said.

"That's only because I'm rarely home. But promise not to look in the sink."

I chuckled. "I won't." I didn't mean to lie when I glanced over his shoulder to the open kitchen, two steps up. It looked just as spotless and unused as the rest of his place.

"Do you need something? A drink?" he asked. "Sorry, I'm all out of cherry slush."

"See? You should've taken me up on it. Just a glass of water would be nice." Now that I was here, I was suddenly too nervous to speak with him. I needed a minute to gather my thoughts. In his home, I couldn't very well be as indignant as I had been on the way to the police station.

"Take a seat," he offered.

He left me in the living room. I stepped around the coffee table to the square-edged modern sofa, but my attention went to a narrow bookshelf in the back corner. *Let's see what Detective Heath reads in his spare time.*

My hand traced the hardbacks—Dashiell Hammett . . . Walter Mosley . . . Raymond Chandler . . . Mickey Spillane . . . I wondered if he saw himself as a noir hardboiled detective, same as the investigators in these novels. My gaze drifted to an upper shelf, empty except for a framed photo of a beautiful woman with long, silky black hair falling over one eye. The other twinkled with delight, as she laughed at whoever was behind the lens. I suspected it had been Heath.

I heard him clear his throat and I turned away from the photo. He was back with my water.

"I-I was interested to see what you read when you're home relaxing. Role models?"

"My sister sent me those books to fill the shelf. She's got a sense of humor."

I nodded, then looked back at the photo. "Is this her?"

"My sister? No." He paused. "That's Abby, my wife. She passed a couple of years ago. This is her artwork." He gestured to the paintings.

"Wow. She was very talented."

"Yes, she was . . . among other things." He held out the glass of water for me.

I accepted it and sat on the couch. "I'm sorry about her passing."

He sat down in the matching chair across from me, not the comfortable lounger that was probably his favorite. He looked at his shoes, the fingers of his right hand absently twirling the gold band on his left ring finger.

Within days of first meeting, I'd made a callous remark to Heath, thinking he was still married. Ever since, I'd wanted an opportunity to apologize, but it had never presented itself before now. I ran my hand over the sofa's soft velvet fabric while I composed in my mind the correct thing to say.

"So what did you follow me home at nine o'clock on a Sunday night to talk to me about?" he asked.

And just like that, the moment passed once again. Drats. I set my water on the teak coffee table between us and proceeded with what I'd come for. "Something has to be awry with the surveillance footage at Phoebe's rental house. Isn't it possible someone came in through the back door, unseen from the eye of the cameras?"

"Yes."

I wasn't expecting him to agree. "Oh. Well, great. Then the surveillance camera recording Archie as the last to leave the house means nothing."

"It doesn't mean nothing, but it doesn't mean everything either," he said.

"What about Thomas? He rented the house for Phoebe. He had to have been there and known the layout. Possibly even known a way in or had a ladder hidden to scale the fence at some weak link. He was there after Archie left, you know."

"We know. He was on camera, buzzing her outside the gate."

"And how long was he off camera for? Long enough to kill her?"

"How do you know he was off camera? Have you been questioning people again, Willa?"

"Not people, just Thomas. He's the obvious suspect, isn't he? She treated him like a servant, yet he was obsessed with her. He even seemed jealous when she wanted Archie to come to the house that day."

"Willa." He stared at me.

I knew he was going to chastise me like the last time I stuck my nose into an investigation and almost got killed.

"It's not the same as last time," I countered before he even made his argument. "It's Archie. I know he didn't do this. *You* know he didn't do this."

"I'm going to be honest. It doesn't look good for him. I need to find some evidence against someone else that can put into question the strong circumstantial evidence we have against him."

"So let me help you."

"Absolutely not. You can't interfere in a police investigation."

"I'll be honest with you too. I'm not going to interfere, but I *am* going to investigate. We can either work together on this or I can do it on my own, but I won't pretend I'm not getting involved." A wave of emotion hit me again thinking of Archie's predicament. "Heath, he wouldn't have been at Phoebe's house if it weren't for me. He's a suspect because of me." I cleared my throat, trying to get control of my shaky voice.

A loud sigh escaped Heath as his hand traced the line of his sculpted jaw, massaging it in thought. He stood and removed his suit jacket and tossed it on the unused lounger. He loosened his tie and unfastened the shirt button at his Adam's apple.

I sat back, not because I was comfortable, but because being close to Heath—the man, not the detective—

unsettled me. I could deal with him as the detective I butted heads with, but the handsome, honest man I knew so little about? I was never ready for his appearance. I attempted to inconspicuously rub my suddenly sweaty palms on my jeans. I took a sip of water and focused on the holster that wrapped over his shoulders and ended at a sheath by his left side so my mind would click back into thinking of him in detective mode.

He sat back down, thankfully unaware of my inner turmoil, and said, "What do you know?"

I set my surprise aside, allowing the comfortable part of our relationship to return as I told him Thomas's account of that evening. "Do you think he had time to kill her while he was off camera?"

"We're looking at all possibilities. We have the Uber records and the surveillance video," Heath said, non-committally. He wasn't going to throw me a bone.

"Okay then, what about that fan mail photo that Archie saw? Is there a way to find out who that guy is?"

Heath was quiet for a few moments before he said, "There was no photo."

"What do you mean? Archie said he opened her mail for her and someone sent her a photo of himself. She told me she wasn't staying at the inn because of paparazzi, but maybe it was really because she had a stalker."

"It's possible."

"You don't sound convinced. What's up?"

"Archie wasn't able to give us much of a description of the man in the photo."

"So? What are you saying? You think he's lying about a stupid photo?"

"It does move suspicion onto someone else—an anonymous person who's a mysterious stalker?"

"You're accusing him of making it up?"

"I'm not accusing him. We have to leave all possibilities on the table."

I thought better of the retort I wanted to spew but instead, reeled in my anger. I recalled how long he'd kept my name on the suspect list during the last murder investigation. He did things by the book, and I was going to have to accept it, especially since he was being more forthcoming this time. Small favors.

"How about the other photos that you *have* seen? Do you have any leads on who took those pictures of Phoebe eating the barbeque?"

"Not yet."

"I think they have to be connected, don't *you*? The photos and the murder?"

"We're checking alibis."

"I saw Thomas and A. J. both leaving The Cellar Friday night." I leaned forward again, pleased to have useful information to contribute.

"You saw them leaving? Together or separately?"

I half expected Heath to pull out his mini notepad—he was once again in full detective mode.

"I needed some recipes from Thomas, so Baz and I went to the inn and we saw him at The Cellar, but he was in a hurry to leave. A. J. was trying to get some information about Phoebe out of him and he went after Thomas."

"What time was that?"

"About six thirty. I think Thomas is your guy. I saw how Phoebe demeaned him when they were at my shop, like it was a regular occurrence. Maybe he'd had enough and he wanted *her* to be humiliated for a change. He wouldn't admit to us about getting her the food, but he had to have done it. Who else would she trust with that?" I played it out in my mind's eye. "He brought her the food, then went around back and took the photos. Or maybe he tipped off A. J. Did you know that Thomas was the one who rented the house for her? It was pretty convenient that it has all those big windows, don't you think?"

Heath nodded slowly, taking in what I said. "You're

not saying anything we haven't thought of. He may have set her up to be humiliated, but if he wanted her killed, why not do it that night?"

That was a good question. Perhaps Phoebe wasn't the only one he wanted to avenge.

"Maybe he wanted to set up Archie for it? He wasn't too happy that she chose him to help her at the house. Or maybe all he intended to do was humiliate her with the photos and then be there to comfort her, but it didn't go as planned."

"Or the person who took the photos isn't the same one who killed her."

"Come on, Heath."

"It's all well and good to have theories, Willa, but the burden of proof is on us. I can't arrest Thomas just because we *think* he did it."

"What does the Uber driver have to say? She was killed in the tub. Was Thomas wet when he got back in the car? What was his state of mind?"

"All good questions. We're taking statements from all involved parties."

"Well, when you do, will you tell me what the driver says or are you going to make me talk to him myself?"

"Are you blackmailing a police detective?"

"Uh . . ."

His smile appeared, catching me off guard as it had the few times he'd let it loose before, turning him into that regular guy again. I was relieved that he was just teasing me, but I was suddenly very conscious that we were in his home together.

I stood. "I'd better let you get to bed, er, you know, whatever you were going to do before I . . . you know."

"Stalked me?"

"Nooo."

His smile lit up again, this time accompanied by a laugh. "It's okay, Willa. I appreciate your insight on this."

He walked me to the door.

"Good, because I want you to know, I'm not letting up," I told him.

"Neither are we. We're going to find out who killed her."

CHAPTER 14

I was feeling more optimistic on Monday morning after having spoken with Detective Heath the night before. Or maybe it was because the second espresso was kicking in. My thoughts all morning kept circling back to last night and Heath. *Oof.* He was an enigma, even more so after seeing a glimpse of his home. Was I confusing his natural quiet intensity with chemistry? It was different than the sparks I had with Roman. Roman was fun and flirty, so much so that I considered it a personality trait rather than having much to do with me. And Heath was obviously still in love with his deceased wife. Maybe what I thought were butterflies when I was around either of them was just anxiousness, as both men made me feel uncertain.

A knock on the door cut into my internal debate about making a third espresso. I walked over to it and put my eye up to the peephole, but nobody was there. Another battery of raps sounded. From here, I could tell it was Baz's door someone was knocking on. I didn't hear him open his door, so I opened mine and stepped out onto my deck, immediately crossing my arms to ward off the October chill that greeted me. I spotted a woman with a pony-tail of thick auburn hair who was now halfway down his steps. She turned when she heard me. It was Ginger. Her deep-set eyes registered her surprise.

She ascended the steps back to Baz's side of the deck. There was only a railing in between, as Baz had removed the privacy trellis months ago that only got in the way of our frequent deck conversations. I could see why he was taken with Ginger. Her leggings and a nylon workout shirt didn't mask an inch of her fit figure. She was holding a clear tumbler with a muddy green drink inside and something loaf-shaped wrapped in waxed paper.

"I'm sorry. I forget the time when I've been out for a run. I didn't mean to wake you," she said as she scanned me up and down.

Wake me? How did she know I hadn't already been out for a run too? We were both wearing leggings, although my oversized University of Oregon sweatshirt covered everything to mid-thigh. Maybe it was the fuzzy slippers . . . or yesterday's mascara that had invariably settled on the puffy rings under my eyes. My hands self-consciously went from my eyes to my uncombed hair, sensing my ratty bedhead. I'm much less judgmental about my morning appearance when I'm focused on getting to my espresso machine.

"Do you know where Baz is?" Ginger's gaze landed on my door.

"He's probably out walking Buttercup," I responded quickly to dissuade her notion that he might be in my apartment.

"Who's Buttercup?"

"Phoebe Winston's dog. Baz is taking care of him for a while."

"Oh."

Was she being overly casual about my name drop or did mentioning Phoebe Winston really not affect her?

I took the narrow opening created. "I'm sorry about Phoebe." When her only response was a look of puzzlement, I said, "She said you two were good friends from culinary school."

"We were friends for the two years we went to Sadler, but we've barely been in touch since."

"Really? Phoebe mentioned that she'd reached out to you, hoping to reconnect while she was in town."

"Yeah, she did. I haven't kept in touch with anybody from school—yesterday was the first time I'd seen Olive Berns since I graduated. She asked me to do a vegan cooking demonstration for the alumni raffle."

"She mentioned that. She said when you were in school, you had hoped to open a vegan café?"

"Yeah. I grew up vegetarian, but during college was when I became passionate about veganism. That's why I ended up leaving UCLA and going to culinary school. My parents weren't too happy. I was supposed to follow in my older brother's footsteps and become an engineer. They never fail to remind me how well he's doing in his career just because I'm still working behind that counter at a bookstore café. And it's not even vegan, but I do have some of my vegan baked goods on the menu."

I recalled my own long journey in making my cheese shop dreams come true, and suddenly felt a kinship with her. "I spent years working in cheese shops before I was able to open my shop. You'll get there."

"Thanks."

We stood in awkward silence for a moment. Kinship or not, I still had Phoebe's murder to solve. "Olive said that you had plans to run the café with Phoebe?"

"I wouldn't say we had plans. We talked about it occasionally."

"Was there a particular reason it didn't happen?"

"She wasn't a vegan, so it didn't make sense to do it after all. Why are you so interested?"

Gulp. I had to think on my feet. Luckily, I already had two espressos. "I just wanted to let you know I'm here for any advice you might want, seeing as I'm a new business owner myself."

"Oh. Well, that's nice of you."

Suspicion seemed to be on the other foot, as I wasn't sure she believed my offer. I couldn't say I blamed her. What did I really have to go on to suspect her? Maybe she *was* just another determined woman trying to work toward her dream. I put my hand to my stomach, which suddenly felt unsettled. My mother always said a guilty conscience lives in your gut, not your brain. I wanted to tell Ginger that my offer was true if she hadn't killed Phoebe, but that probably wouldn't go over well either.

"Is that why you moved to Yarrow Glen?" I asked instead. "Our town's known for promoting small businesses."

"Uh-huh."

It was obvious I'd curtailed her chattiness. I attempted to remedy it.

"We don't have any vegan places yet," I said. "Is that what you have there?"

I indicated the glass tumbler of what looked like blended seaweed and the wrapped loaf she was holding.

"After my run, I stopped back home for my energy smoothie. I'm trying to get Sharice to let me add them to the beverage menu."

She stuck the drink under my nose. I got a whiff of sour cider vinegar mixed with something mossy. Sharice Greene, who owned the used bookstore and the attached café where Ginger worked, knew what she was doing keeping them off the menu.

"Mmmm," I said, smiling, nodding, and holding my breath until she took it away.

She lifted the loaf that was in her other hand. "I brought this for Baz to try. He never orders anything vegan at the café, always just his cold coffee drink. It's a lemon stinging nettles loaf."

"Stinging nettles?" My radar shot up.

"It's not a very popular ingredient here in the States, but when my great grandparents lived overseas, my grandmother used to cook with them. Her recipe journal was passed down to me and it's got a whole section on stinging nettles—pesto, mint soup, even a stinging nettles bread pudding. I thought since his mom is from England, maybe he'd appreciate it."

I saw three stinging nettles recipes in Phoebe's first cookbook, one of them a lemon stinging nettles loaf. Was that a coincidence? I shook myself from my thoughts.

"I'm certain he'll gobble it right up," I lied to be polite. Baz was not one to take risks with his palate.

"You're working on the float with my boyfriend Chet, right?" Ginger asked.

"Yup. My shop is partnering with the meadery."

"Don't mention this to him, okay? That I was here?"

"Oh, of course. No problem." I hadn't pegged Chet for the jealous type.

The sound of someone singing reached us and ended the exchange. We both remained silent, and I cocked my ear. I recognized the tune immediately—"Build Me Up Buttercup"—and the voice that went with it. Baz! He was at the "Buttercup, Baby" refrain when we caught him coming up the stairs, holding Buttercup aloft, singing to him. He clammed up and brought Buttercup into his chest.

"What are you two doing out here?" he said.

I had to give it to him—he played it cool. Baz didn't normally get embarrassed, but it was as close as I'd ever seen him.

Ginger did the inevitable cooing over the adorable dog before answering Baz's question. Neither of us mentioned the serenade. "Sharice and I cleared our schedules later to work on the float again. We were going to text you, but we realized neither of us have your number." Carl's Hardware, where Baz was the self-contracted handyman, was partnered with Read More Bookstore for the float making. "Are you available later this afternoon?"

"I can come after my last appointment. I'm not exactly sure when it'll be."

"That's okay. Whenever you can make it. Do you want to exchange numbers so you can text when you're done?"

"Sure."

"Oh, and I brought this for you." She showed him the wrapped stinging nettles loaf.

"Thanks!" Baz released Buttercup to the floor where the dog raced in circles around their legs as if chasing himself.

Baz took the breakfast loaf and they exchanged phones, tapping in their respective numbers. I stood awkwardly entrenched as the third wheel on my side of the deck.

They returned their phones to each other, and Ginger gave Buttercup one last scrunch. She threw a wave goodbye, which I might or might not have been included in, as she descended the stairs. I wasn't getting the warm fuzzies from Ginger.

I quietly hummed "Build Me Up Buttercup" while Ginger walked away.

"You could've given me a heads-up," he said after she rounded the corner out of earshot.

"I didn't realize it was you until it was too late. But I don't think you have anything to worry about." I pressed my lips together and raised my eyebrows.

"What?" Baz squinted at me.

"I didn't say anything." I affected innocence.

"Do we need to go over this again? She's seeing Chet."

"But she's bringing *you* a loaf cake that she doesn't want me to tell Chet about."

Baz ignored the implication.

"There's something else about Ginger I want to talk to you about," I began. Telling him that she might be included on my suspect list wasn't going to be as fun to talk about.

"I'm going to go in and cut a piece of this cake. I haven't eaten breakfast yet. Can you keep an eye on Bruiser for a minute?"

"Bruiser?"

"I decided not to call him Buttercup anymore. Not while I'm keeping him."

"Okay, I'll stop humming the song."

"It's not that, Well, it is kind of that—I can't get the song out of my head. More importantly, he's small, so he at least needs a tough name. I know what it's like being the shortest kid in elementary school with a weird name. Basil's not an easy name to go through childhood with."

"I don't think Buttercup's going to be going off to school anytime soon."

"That's not the point. He'll be happier being called Bruiser, trust me."

I chuckled. "What are you going to sing to him then?"

He ignored me again and went inside his apartment. Buttercup immediately began pawing at the door.

"It's okay, sweetie. Come here. I'll pet you," I told him.

He jumped into Baz's plastic deck chair, which was positioned next to the railing, and seemed satisfied by my attention. I unfolded my camping chair and sat in it, while I stuck my hand through the railing to pet him. I found myself humming the song without thought. *Drats. He's right.*

Most mornings, I lingered out here over my first creamy caffeinated cup of something warm in order to breathe in Sonoma Valley, both the air and the view. This morning it smelled of pine and eucalyptus. My compact deck only fit my camping chair and a side table, but it overlooked a protected patch of woods with a walking trail to the park. This time of year, the oaks flashed their yellow leaves and the rolling hills beyond blazed red and orange among the evergreens.

With Buttercup, aka Bruiser, now happily curled up in the chair, I left mine and walked to the edge of the deck to properly take in the view. The sun had already crept above the distant mountains, bleeding its brilliant colors in long brush strokes across the sky.

I thought about the stinging nettles recipes. Ginger said it wasn't a popular ingredient, so what were the chances Phoebe would happen to choose the same stinging nettles loaf cakes for her own cookbook that Ginger had the recipes for? Olive said Phoebe had been accused of stealing another student's recipes for her final class, so maybe this was a pattern. If Phoebe had used Ginger's recipes for her first cookbook, that could be the reason for the falling out. Could it be the reason Phoebe was killed?

As I continued to contemplate Ginger as a possible suspect, my gaze wandered to the parking strip and landed upon our float. "You've *got* to be kidding me."

The parade float bandits had struck again.

CHAPTER 15

I stared at our practically bare parade float in disbelief.

Baz emerged from his apartment with a hunk of the forest green loaf cake in his hand. "What's the matter?"

"It looks like stuff was taken from the float again." I walked down the stairs to get a closer look. Baz walked down his set of stairs and we met by the float. He held his loaf cake in one hand with Buttercup in the other, resting against his chest like a child. Guernsey sat alone on the float with a couple of Styrofoam cheese wedges. The newly made giant mead bottle and cheese wheel were gone again. "Unbelievable. How are we supposed to work on our floats? Have you guys had anything stolen?"

"We're good. Sharice said she saw some teenagers the other night carrying something that looked like it came from one of the floats. She saw them stick it in a dumpster. I guess it's not stealing if you don't keep it?"

"It's still vandalism. How are you keeping them from stealing your stuff?"

"We're using the bed of my pickup for the float, so nothing's on it yet 'cause I'm using my truck for work. The night before the parade, we'll have to secure everything to the truck. The timing's gonna be tight, but it looks like it turned out to be a good thing with all these thefts. Our papier-mâché books took a long time to make."

"You're doing papier-mâché? Jeez."

"Not me. I'm only good with wood. I built a bookshelf and I'm doing the sign. Sharice and Ginger are the crazy creative ones."

"That's right, Sharice is an artist. No wonder the bookstore always looks great." Sharice once told me she opened the used bookstore almost a decade ago as a way to supplement her career as an illustration artist.

Baz took a long look at the cake in his hand. The deep green color was not one usually associated with breakfast breads . . . or any baked good for that matter, unless it had been left out too long.

"You want to try it?" He held it out to me.

"No, no. She brought it for you."

Baz stuck it under his nose then looked at it again as if it was going to morph into something dangerous.

"Try it already!" I prodded.

He took a nibble. His nose wrinkled.

I laughed. "How much do you like this girl, Baz?"

He stared down the piece of cake, then chomped off a bigger piece. He squeezed his eyes shut like he was enduring a painful medical procedure.

"That much, huh?" I was convinced.

As soon as he swallowed, he swirled his tongue over his teeth to remove any lingering cake from his mouth.

I reached over and picked off a piece to try, expecting the worst, but tasting a zingy spring freshness. "You've got the taste buds of a toddler. It tastes like a lemon cake."

"It's not sweet," he complained.

"It's a healthy vegan breakfast loaf, not Fruit Loops. Listen, this might be something you're going to have to get used to if you ever get the nerve to tell her how you feel."

"Hey, if she wasn't seeing Chet, I'd ask her out. I'm not like you and Roman."

"What does that mean?"

"You guys have been circling each other for six months now like vultures over a landfill. Just admit you like each other and get on with it already."

"He likes everybody."

"Not the way he likes you."

"We're good friends. Like me and you."

"It's not like me and you at all. There's no sexual tension between us."

"Okay, you've got a point. All I meant is, he and I are just friends. That's good enough for now." I nodded at Buttercup in his arms. "Looks like he likes the loaf cake." I was happy to change the subject.

Baz looked down and noticed Buttercup's little pink tongue searching the cake and finding a piece to chomp onto.

He patted the fluffy head in approval. "You're a good wingman, Bruiser," he said to him. Then to me, "Don't tell."

"I've got bigger things to worry about," I said, looking at the float. At this point, the chances of us finishing it before the harvest parade were slim to none, especially since my priorities lay with proving Archie's innocence. "Listen, about Ginger—"

"I don't want to talk about Ginger. Let me bring Bruiser upstairs and get my step stool. We'll take a quick look in the dumpsters and see if we can find your missing float pieces," Baz offered.

"Thanks."

I awaited his return while considering what he said about me and Roman. I admit, I was keeping Roman at arm's length because of his reputation as a serial dater. Did that mean that I was afraid or that I was smart? I couldn't help but wonder if the chemistry we had would fizzle once we gave into it. Was fear preventing me from moving beyond our friendship?

Baz returned with a folding three-step stool. I stood

behind him in the alley as he used it to peek over the top of the dumpster to see what was inside.

"Nothing here." He climbed down and checked the recycle dumpster. "Nope. Let's check the ones in Carl's alley."

We walked the length of the building to the opposite alley where the dumpsters shared by Carl's Hardware and Lou's Market were kept. Baz stepped on the upper step of the stool and opened the top of the dumpster. He leaned over it and seemed to be fumbling with something.

"Did you find it?"

"No cheddar wheel, but look what I did find." With a grunt, he heaved a box out of the dumpster and turned around with it in his arms.

I recognized the publisher's logo immediately. It was a box of Phoebe's new books. Baz plunked it on the ground. The flaps of the box were tucked under each other, indicating it had been opened and reclosed. I peeled off a wilted leaf of lettuce and pulled open the top to look inside. Sure enough, a dozen brand-new books were inside. I opened one. It was signed by Phoebe.

"These are the books that were in Phoebe's car that day she came by. She brought a bunch she'd signed already."

"I know. I helped you carry the boxes from behind the counter to your office Friday night, remember? Did someone take them from there?"

"They were still there last night. This box was probably taken from the trunk of her car when Archie was carrying them in."

"They could be from the bookstore. After what happened with Phoebe, maybe they decided to dump their supply."

"Would they even carry them at Sharice's? Read More's a used bookstore."

"Phoebe was in town, so maybe they made an exception."

"But this is Carl and Lou's dumpster, not the bookstore's."

We had no other theories, so Baz took his step stool and I picked up the box of books.

"What are you gonna do with 'em?" he asked.

"I'll tell Heath about them. He might want to have a look." An odor remained even as we left the dumpster.

"Wanna trade?" He held out the step stool.

"Thanks, but I can manage." Heaving pallets of cheese on a regular basis kept my muscles in good form. The box wasn't a problem. "Has Ginger mentioned anything about Phoebe since you've been working on the float together? That she knew she was coming to town? Anything?"

"No. I think I would've remembered if she'd talked about her. How did they know each other?"

I filled Baz in on what I'd learned about Ginger and Phoebe's past relationship so far and about the stinging nettles recipes. "If Phoebe stole her recipes, that would give Ginger a motive for murder."

"That's a stretch. Didn't you say that first cookbook came out like five years ago?"

"Yes, but Phoebe had a lot of success. Maybe Ginger was angry and jealous. Why didn't she want to see Phoebe when she came to town?"

"I don't know. Even if you're right about Phoebe stealing her recipes, it doesn't mean Ginger killed her over some stinging nettles." Baz put a hand to his throat and looked somewhat alarmed. "Is that what I ate? What are stinging nettles, anyways?"

I ignored his question. "There's got to be somebody who knows the truth about their falling out."

He shrugged. "Ask Chet." Suddenly becoming wide-eyed, he snapped his fingers. "Hey, maybe *he* murdered Phoebe to avenge his girlfriend's stinging nettles."

"That's one theory." I refused to acknowledge the cheekiness of his remark. It was obvious he wasn't going to take my stolen-recipe theory seriously.

We reached the stairs to his apartment. "I gotta put this stool back and get Bruiser for my morning appointment. See ya later." He started up the steps.

I nodded goodbye and carried the books around to the alley door of my shop. They were too stinky to bring inside. I set them down and pushed them inside the door frame. The only cars allowed in the alley were delivery trucks and the sanitation truck, so it wasn't likely anyone would take them. I reclosed the top of the box again just in case.

"Whatcha got there?"

I turned, startled. It was A. J., who seemed to have a knack for sneaking up on me. They must've taught that in journalism school. I wasn't about to tell him about the books.

"Just something for the shop," I lied.

"People have been taking things from the floats. You probably shouldn't leave anything out."

"I don't have my keys right now, but thanks for the tip. What's up?"

"I hear you're asking around about Phoebe Winston's murder."

"Did Chet tell you that?"

"Chet's a friend, but no. I've got my sources."

"What if I am?"

"Then that makes two of us. Do you want to pool our resources?"

This was an interesting offer, but I had to think about it. After all, A. J. was on my list of suspects. He seemed to read my mind.

"I also heard you think I have something to do with those photos I printed in the paper." He brushed his wayward curls from his eyes and stuck his hands in the pockets of his green Salvation Army jacket.

"It only makes sense."

"You may have helped solve the last murder in this town, but you're way off base on this one."

"I have a hard time believing someone dropped off those photos without any note or compensation," I said.

"Ask Deandra. She found the flash drive on her desk."

"I already spoke with Deandra. Thomas didn't tell you where Phoebe was staying when you were having drinks with him Friday night?"

"I was hoping he would, but you took care of that." He glared at me.

I was guilty as charged. Even if he didn't take the photos, my gut told me he knew something more about them, but I'd have to change my tactics if I was going to find out anything new. "What do you mean by pool our resources?"

"Work together. I'm interested in the story, and you're interested in being the Veronica Mars of Yarrow Glen— the movie version. When she's older."

I sneered at him. If he was trying to get me on his side, he was doing a poor job of it. "And who are you trying to be? What's *your* experience investigating?"

"I did my time in L.A."

"So you went from working for the *L.A. Times* to the *Glen Gazette*?"

"I worked in Los Angeles. I never said I worked for the *Times*," he mumbled. "I freelanced."

"Oh. No shame in that. But what made you move to Yarrow Glen? The *Gazette* doesn't usually investigate more than which vegetables will be sold at the next farmer's market."

"To be honest, I got tired of trying to climb over everybody else to get noticed for a story. The editor position was open at the *Gazette* and I thought I might as well . . ." He shrugged.

". . . be a big fish in a small pond?" I finished his thought.

"Kinda. I only expected to stay for a little while, just long enough to have *editor* on my résumé, but . . . I don't know, I like it. People are cool here and I don't need roommates to afford my apartment. Did you know readership has gone up twelve percent since I took over?"

"The community would be lost without the *Gazette*. You've obviously done a great job with it, so why do you want to turn it into *True Crime*?

"It's the community's newspaper. You said so yourself. And you're right—murder doesn't usually happen in our town, which makes it more important than ever to let our neighbors know what's going on."

He had a point.

"Come on," he said. "You made things pretty interesting last year investigating Guy Lippinger's murder. Let's work together this time. We both want to solve this. I'm good at getting information from people, and Roman told Chet you were scrappy."

"Scrappy?" My face scrunched in disapproval.

"I think he meant it as a compliment."

There were a lot of ways I'd want Roman to describe me. "Scrappy" wasn't one of them. My thoughts about that would have to be put aside for the time being. It wasn't a bad idea to collaborate since I wasn't getting anywhere with my suspect list.

"Okay. We can try it," I agreed.

"Great."

"So what do you know?"

"Hold up. What's my end of the bargain?"

I thought about it. The biggest strike against Archie was that surveillance footage. If we could discover how the murderer entered the house, we could get Archie off the hook.

"I know where the house is," I told A. J. The police hadn't released the address so celebrity journalists and fans wouldn't converge on it for photos or try getting into the house. "It's completely fenced in with surveillance cameras—two of them in front, none in the back. The killer must've gotten in through the back door somehow." I wasn't about to tell him anything about Archie being on those cameras. I didn't want Archie's name plastered across the *Gazette* as a suspect. "Baz and I already tried finding a way in last night, but we were stopped by some thorny barberry bushes. It was too dark to see anything and there were forensics people inside, so we didn't want to stick around."

"You think they're still there today?" A. J. asked.

"I have no idea. We didn't even think they'd be there last night."

"We could check it out again. We might have more luck in the daylight. If we do find a way in, I'd have something worth printing."

"Wait a minute. What do you have for *me*?"

A. J. thought for a few moments and then replied, "The Uber driver who dropped off Thomas Doolittle at the house the day Phoebe was murdered didn't wait for him."

"He left?"

"Thomas had twenty-five minutes until another Uber picked him up."

I wondered if he was away from the surveillance cameras all that time. "How did you find this out? You talked to the driver?"

"I told you I have my sources, but the driver's not one of them. In fact, no one can find him, not even the police."

"Why not?"

"It looks like he got spooked when he found out the police were asking for him and bolted. Maybe he's got a record."

"That's just great." I knew Heath was all about the evidence and now there'd be less of it to gather on Thomas.

"You've got your info, now I want mine. Come to the *Gazette* about three o'clock. I'll be done with my meetings by then and I can drive us to the house."

I hesitated. Heath would kill me for bringing A. J. in on this and possibly having crime scene information leaked to the press. I considered reneging on our newly made deal. On the other hand, if word got out that there was a way the murderer was able to get into the house without being seen, then the surveillance footage of Archie may not hold as much weight. Letting A. J. do my dirty work might be a brilliant move on my part.

"Agreed?" He held out his hand.

"Agreed." I shook it, hoping I hadn't just made a deal with the devil.

CHAPTER 16

Since Curds & Whey was closed on Mondays, I had time for more than my quick breakfast of too many espressos and a chunk of good cheese. That didn't mean my morning meal would be cheese-less, however. The aged Gouda I had treated myself to last week was calling out to be finished off. I also still had some fresh orchard apples Mrs. Schultz had given me from a recent apple-picking excursion. Cheddar was the classic pairing, but it was time to give the more robust flavor of Gouda a chance to shine with the autumn fruit. I took out some puff pastry from my freezer to thaw.

It was time for Loretta's breakfast too. The tall metal stool the fishbowl sat on in the living room was one of the vintage pieces of furniture I inherited from my grandmother's house. I called it Loretta's island, and kept it near the TV, but away from direct sunlight. I sprinkled some food in the bowl and said good morning. She waved her red crown tail in return. She looked perky this morning, apparently recovered from her big day at the shop yesterday.

By the time I finished showering and made myself presentable, the pastry had thawed and I was able to put together my cheesy breakfast snack. I cut the pastry sheet into triangles, then chopped a large Granny Smith.

I mixed it with a little sugar to take off the sour edge and sprinkled in some chives. I scooped some of the mixture onto each triangle and accompanied it with a cube of the deep-flavored Gouda. I folded them like little envelopes, then stuck them in the oven.

While I waited for them to cook, I thought about Phoebe's books Baz found in the dumpster. If they were taken from the trunk of her car Friday afternoon, that meant they were thrown out by someone who hated her well before her carnivorous habits were discovered. Was it Ginger?

That question would have to wait. I had to tell the others that our float was pilfered again. I started to text Roman, but Baz's words stayed with me. Maybe Baz was right, and I shouldn't keep Roman at arm's length anymore . . . even if he did think of me as 'scrappy'. I had plenty of pastries to share, and maybe he could advise me of the best way to approach Chet about Ginger.

My nose told me the savory autumn pockets were baked before the timer did. I gave them several minutes to cool, then walked a container of them over to Roman's apartment above his shop. The businesses on our block of Pleasant Avenue, except for Lou's Market, were all closed on Mondays. This included the meadery, which was directly across the street from my shop.

As I knocked on Roman's apartment door and waited, I rehearsed a casual greeting and explanation for dropping by with breakfast.

Hi. I was in the neighborhood . . . No, we lived in the same neighborhood.

These cheesy pastries made me think of you . . . No. No one wants to be compared to a cheesy pastry.

Well, he wasn't answering my knock anyway. I checked my phone for the time before rapping on the door again. It was almost ten, not too early to call on someone even on their day off. Unless . . . someone stayed over last night. *Oh, gosh, maybe that's why he's not answering. Maybe he's got a woman in his apartment. Why didn't I think of that sooner? Why am I standing at his front door holding cheesy pockets?*

I turned and bolted down the steps, rounding the corner of the building and almost bulldozing Chet, who was coming from the opposite direction.

"Sorry," we both apologized, separating ourselves from each other. Luckily, the pastries didn't look worse for wear.

"You looking for Roman?" Chet asked.

"Well, um . . . I was just, um . . ." The last thing I wanted was for Roman to find out I was the one interrupting his romantic morning.

"He's checking on the new mead." Chet tipped his head for me to follow him to the back door of the meadery.

I rolled my eyes at myself for jumping to jealous conclusions and followed Chet through the back door of the meadery, which led directly into the tasting room. I'd been here plenty of times to deliver cheese platters to pair with Roman's mead for scheduled customer tastings.

Unlike the cool industrial feel of his shop, this part of the meadery was masculine in a cozy way. The transom windows along the outer wall added natural light to the room, which was separated from the retail part of the shop by a sliding barn door. A horseshoe of round, high-top cocktail tables hugged the walls, partially framing a grouping of comfortable-looking worn leather chairs and a sofa in the center. The focal point of the room was the striking handcrafted black walnut bar lined with stools for eight. On the olive wall behind the bar hung a large painting of Roman's Golden Glen label. His mead was simply showcased on a single glass shelf beneath it.

Roman emerged from a door near the corner behind

the bar. I'd been in that windowless basement-like room before. It was where he kept the large tanks of mead until it was ready to be bottled, along with his bottled inventory. His surprise at seeing me brought that slow smile of his, ending in a dimple that threatened to melt my restraint.

"Fancy meeting you here," he said to me.

"I made cheesy apple pockets." *Cringe.* Forget about what Baz said. It was easier to go back to just talking to my friend. "There's enough for you too, Chet." I set them on the bar and opened the container's lid.

"Thanks." Chet immediately took one.

"I came to give you some bad news about the float," I said to them.

"Ah." Chet held a corner of the pastry in his mouth and disappeared behind the bar. He popped back up, holding my cardboard cheddar wheel and their fake mead bottle.

"I-I thought they were stolen!"

He returned them behind the bar and used his free hands to catch the pastry as he bit into it. "Sorry, we should've told you," he said through a full mouth. "This is good."

"Everything ended so crazy last night, we made the executive decision to bring the float decorations back here instead of leaving them on the trailer since we hadn't fastened them well," Roman finished explaining.

"No, it's great. I'm happy we still have them," I said, relieved.

"We didn't have enough arms to take your cow scarecrow."

"That's all right. Guernsey's still there."

"We figured no one would take it," he said.

"Hey!" I couldn't help but be slightly offended, regardless of whether it was the truth.

"Sorry, I didn't mean anything by it."

"Uh-huh. I'm reconsidering my breakfast offering."

He quickly took a cheesy autumn pocket before I could change my mind, while Chet went in for his second. I tried one myself. The slight crunch of the cooked apples contrasted with the silkiness of the rich cheese encased in the flaky pastry, which made for a satisfying bite. I took another.

"How's Archie doing?" Roman asked.

"I texted him last night and again this morning. He's keeping up a brave front, but he's got to be scared. The only way I know how to help is to try to find out who killed Phoebe."

"I wish I could be of more help," Chet said.

"Maybe you can be. Ginger's really the only one around here who knew Phoebe well, besides Phoebe's assistant. What has she told you about her?"

"Nothing, really. She's never talked about her."

"Didn't you relay the message that Phoebe wanted to see her?"

"I did. She said she got her text but didn't want to see her."

"Did she tell you why?"

"I asked, but she said she didn't want to talk about it. I tried again later, but she shut me down, so I didn't bring it up again."

Roman mumbled, "Smart man." He and Chet fist-bumped.

That sounded like something more serious had happened than merely losing touch over the years the way Ginger claimed they had. She was even leaving her boyfriend in the dark about it. This meant Chet wouldn't be able to confirm whether Phoebe stole her recipes.

A cell phone on the bar rang. Roman reached for it. "I've been expecting this call. I've got to take it," he said. He stepped away to answer it.

Perfect timing. I wanted to talk to Chet about A. J. without Roman's nervous Nellie input.

"Chet, would you be able to meet me and A. J. at the *Gazette* at three o'clock?"

"Sure. I'll be done here in an hour or two. Why?"

Roman seemed entrenched in his phone call, but I still made sure we were out of earshot. "A. J. and I are going to Phoebe's rental house together," I told Chet.

His eyebrows shot up in surprise. "Really? You guys are working together on this now?"

"Well, I'm still not a hundred percent sure of his innocence, but if he didn't do it, he could be helpful to the cause. But that's where you come in. I'd feel a whole lot better if you could come with us."

"I've known A. J. for a couple years now. He rubs people the wrong way sometimes, but he's no killer."

"He's not at the top of my suspect list, but if Roman or Detective Heath or even Baz for that matter found out I went to the house alone with A. J., I'd never hear the end of it. Please?"

"Sure, no problem."

"Great. I'll meet you guys at the *Gazette*. Oh, and if you could keep this to yourself?" I looked back at Roman, who was still on the phone.

"I get it," Chet said with a wink. "My girlfriend's always on my case too. She's worth it, though."

"Roman's not my boyfriend," I sputtered.

"Oh sorry. I thought I sensed something. You and Baz then?"

"No. We're just friends."

"Oh. Ginger thought for sure you guys were together."

"He's just a loyal friend."

"Nothing *just* about it. Loyalty is everything."

"You're right. There's a lot to be said for someone who has your back no matter what. I was lucky to have that in my brother too."

"Was?"

"He died in a car accident eight years ago."

"That's rough, I'm sorry. I lost mine too. Not in the same way, but I can relate."

"I'm sorry for you too. It's not a feeling I'd want anyone else to know."

Roman, now finished with his call, returned to my side.

"Sorry about that, but it was important business. I had to take the call."

"Is everything okay?" I asked him.

"I'm thinking about getting some warehouse space to expand my mead making. That was the guy who's got a space that might work. We're meeting tomorrow night to have a look. It's farther away than I'd like, but the price is right. You can close up shop for me tomorrow night, Chet?"

"I got ya covered," Chet said.

"Expanding already! I'm really proud of you, Roman," I said.

"Thanks. It's all due to Chet. He might be coming into business with me." Roman patted him on the back.

"I thought you were just dabbling in it for the fun of it," I said to Chet. "So this is what's keeping you in Yarrow Glen. That's great."

"I know a good thing when I see it. Roman won't let me buy in until I know everything mead making entails. That's why I'm working on a new flavor with him."

Chet and Roman now wore matching grins.

"I'll let you guys get to it then."

Roman walked me to the back door. "I'll try to come by later to work on the float," he said.

"Sounds good. Text me first to make sure I'm around. I have some people I need to chat with today."

"I know you want to help Archie, but you know how dangerous it can be going around asking questions."

"You sound like Detective Heath. How do you even know I'll be asking about Phoebe's murder?"

He stared at me, not bothering to answer. I wasn't getting anything by him.

"I'll be careful," I said.

Standing in the doorway together dictated that we were only inches from each other.

"If you need back up, I'm here. Just in case you don't know, I'm happy to partner with you," he said.

"You'll be the Stabler to my Benson?" I referred to the *Law & Order* duo with a ton of chemistry. *Did I say that out loud?*

"Any time," he answered.

I only nodded, afraid to open my mouth for fear that another embarrassingly flirty comment might escape. I walked away and didn't breathe again until I heard the door close behind me.

CHAPTER 17

I hardly thought the crepe myrtle trees that umbrellaed Pleasant Avenue's sidewalks could be showier than their spring and summer blooms, but their blazing autumn leaves were just as flamboyant. This was my first fall season in Yarrow Glen, and it did not disappoint. I felt lucky to have Curds & Whey located on such a quaint street of shops and cafés. Some storefronts had flower boxes, some had awnings, and each had its own unique charm renovated from the hodgepodge of repurposed flat-roofed buildings that made up the eight blocks of the town center.

I still got a little thrill every time I saw my shop from the street. I was even happier at the sight this time, as Baz and Archie were in front playing with Buttercup. I crossed the street and joined them.

"It's good to see you, Archie." It was especially good to see him smiling.

"Hey, Willa. Baz called me with some questions about Buttercup. Uh, Bruiser. It was a good excuse to get out of the house," Archie replied from his crouched position, gently pulling on a toy in Buttercup's mouth. He picked up the dog and straightened.

"Back from your appointment already?" I said to Baz.

"It ended up being an easy fix, so it left me with the rest of the morning free."

"I just saw Chet and forgot to ask him if his landlord said he could take the dog. I'm sorry."

"That's all right," Baz responded. "You can ask him tomorrow or, ya know, whenever."

"I'm going to see him at the *Gazette* later, so I'll ask him then."

"Baz told me about the books in the dumpster," Archie said.

"We think whoever did it took them from Phoebe's car when you were bringing them into the shop. Did you see anybody around?"

He looked over to where the car had been that day in front of Lou's Market, likely playing the scene over in his mind. "There were people on the sidewalk, but I didn't notice anything suspicious."

"It looks like someone threw out her books *before* the photos were published. That means someone was already holding some kind of grudge against her."

"Do you have any ideas?" Archie asked.

"There is someone who's known Phoebe for a long time and may have had plenty of reason to dislike her."

"Are you talking about Ginger?" Baz asked.

"Ginger received Phoebe's text letting her know she'd be in town. She says she didn't see her, but I wonder . . ."

"I don't know, Wil." Baz shook his head in skepticism. "Stealing recipes?"

"Olive Berns said that when Phoebe was a student, she was accused of stealing the recipe for her final-exam dish, so it's not so far-fetched she would steal Ginger's."

"Then there must be other people who had grudges against her too."

"True. I promised Olive Berns a gift basket for her Sadler Culinary School raffle. If we bring it to campus, we can ask her what else she remembers about Phoebe's time at Sadler. Maybe she can tell us about some other people who had problems with Phoebe."

"I'm in," Archie said.

Baz's silence and focus on Buttercup told me he was still sulking about Ginger.

"Baz? Do you have time to come with us?"

He finally looked at me. "Yeah, I do. I'll come just so I can be there when you're proven wrong about Ginger."

"I'm not trying to pin this on Ginger. We just need to add to Heath's suspect list."

"All right, all right." Baz softened. "I'll drive. Bruiser likes the truck."

"Okay, let's go." I started for the parking lot but turned when I realized the guys weren't following. "What's the matter?"

"Aren't you forgetting something?" Archie asked.

"Right. I should call her to make sure she's in." I pulled out my phone.

"And maybe bring the gift basket?" Archie said.

"The gift basket! Archie, what would I do without you?"

We took Sonoma Highway north out of the valley almost thirty minutes to Santa Rosa where Sadler Culinary School was. I'd read a little bit about the school when I was doing my research before Phoebe's visit. It was undoubtedly overshadowed by *the* Culinary Institute in Napa, which probably explained the school's enthusiasm at having a celebrity alumna.

We followed the GPS to the campus, which seemed to consist of three older expansive buildings clumped together with a lawn, some trees, and several parking lots. Signs directed guests to the far lot behind student and staff parking, so Baz dropped Archie and me off at the front of the buildings and went to park the car.

"Archie? Is that you, Willa? What are you two doing here?" a female voice called.

I peeked around the large cellophane-wrapped gift basket I was holding and was surprised to see Archie's friend Hope approaching. I knew her from the bakery down the street from our shop, but her big smile was for Archie. They'd had a crush on each other for quite some time, but remained friends for now, as far as I knew. Although I got my daily sampling breads from her bakery, I hadn't seen her around much in recent months. I'd figured running the bakery on her own for the first time was keeping her busy behind the scenes. As usual, she had streaks of color in her pixie-style blond hair that matched her nail polish, this time a neon pink.

I told her about the gift basket for Olive. "What are *you* doing here?" I asked in return.

"Didn't I tell you? She's taking classes here now," Archie answered for her.

"That's great."

"You know how I always wanted to turn Rise and Shine from a bread bakery into a cake bakery? Well, I decided instead of hiring bakers to do it for me, I should learn to make fancy cakes myself. I started taking pastry classes in September," she said with pride in her voice.

"Congratulations. I think that's wonderful." That explained her frequent absence at the bakery. When I'd first met her, I underestimated how she would handle the demands of owning a bakery inherited from her mom at only twenty-one years old, so I was happily surprised at this news.

"Thanks. It's been therapeutic for me, too, with my aunt Vivian gone." Her eyes lost their brightness at the mention of her aunt.

"You went through a lot of changes all at once. I should've said this before, but if you ever need anything, I'm here for you. I know Archie's been a support, but I want you to know I am too."

"Thanks, Willa. Taking these classes has really helped me. I didn't know I'd love making cakes so much. It must be in my blood." Her smile was back at the thought of her mother, who died when Hope was only thirteen.

"I know you'll do your mother's bakery proud," I told her, meaning it.

"She's got mad decorating skills too. You should see some of her cakes," Archie gushed.

"I do enjoy it, but it leaves me even less time for fun. Sorry I haven't been around lately," she said to Archie.

"That's okay. Things have been crazy for us, too, with Phoebe Winston's death. Did you know she was supposed to give a talk at Curds and Whey the day she died?"

"That's right, I forgot! She's all anybody here talked about on Saturday after those pictures came out. Classes were almost impossible that day."

I recalled how devastated Olive was about Phoebe's death—mostly because of how it would negatively impact the school.

"You have classes on Saturday?" I asked.

"Sadler is geared toward the nontraditional student, so they offer weekend and evening classes too."

I'd been focused on whether Olive would have information about Phoebe, but maybe Hope would also be able to tell me something about her background. "Did you ever hear anything about what Phoebe was like when she went to school here? I know it was before your time here, but . . ."

"I didn't hear anything negative about her until after all this went down. Now everyone's saying they never bought into the 'new and improved' Phoebe and that she was always a phony. But before this, the instructors only said good things about her and made excuses for the bad stories we'd read about her. Ms. Berns practically has a shrine at the school for her."

"Olive!" I shouted in greeting, as the very woman we were gossiping about came up behind Hope, unnoticed.

Hope turned around, red-faced. "Hello, Ms. Berns."

"Hello." She joined our circle.

"Uh . . . I've got a class to get to. I'll call you, Archie." Hope scooted up the stairs and into the building, leaving me and Archie standing uncomfortably with Olive.

Olive brushed it off. "I don't blame her—Phoebe's name is on everybody's lips, especially after the Yarrow Glen police came by yesterday. I was working overtime trying to do damage control about the photos. I had no idea she was murdered! You want to bring that to my office?" The non sequitur threw me until I realized she was referring to the gift basket that was getting heavy in my arms.

"Yes." We started up the steps toward the building's entrance. "This is Archie, by the way. He works with me. And Baz," I added, seeing him and Buttercup walking toward us.

"Sorry, the dog can't come in," she stated. She looked at them again. "That looks like Phoebe Winston's dog."

"It is. We're taking care of him temporarily," I explained. I was beginning to realize how famous Phoebe's dog was.

Olive's shoulders dropped as she sighed. She looked a little worse for wear compared to the last time I'd seen her. She was once again dressed in all black, slightly disheveled this time, as if she'd been in a hurry and taken her blouse from the to-be-washed pile. I'd been known to do it in a pinch. Mrs. Schultz maintained that scarves were the best way to hide a crease or two.

"Poor dog. Phoebe's left *everybody* in the lurch, hasn't she?" She continued up the stairs to the front door.

Phoebe's predicament and death were hitting Olive hard, but not out of sympathy for the murdered woman. I shrugged at Baz, as Archie and I left him and Buttercup outside to follow Olive into the building.

She led us briskly through the lobby.

"Thanks for helping us out of this raffle debacle by providing the gift basket," she said.

"I'm happy to help," I fibbed. If it weren't for Archie's involvement, I'd want nothing more to do with Phoebe Winston.

Archie and I followed her up two flights of stairs and down a hallway, her low chunky heels clacking on the tile floors in short, rapid steps. Archie reached out his arms to take the basket from me, but I refused the offer.

Pretty historic buildings on the outside meant older cramped spaces on the inside, and Olive Berns's office was no exception. It was made worse by a desk crowded with stacks of picture frames. I stood looking for a place to set the gift basket.

Olive, appearing winded from the walk, looked at the stacks with exasperation written all over her reddened face. "I think we managed to take down all the pictures off the walls that had Phoebe in them. Now I just need a place to put them."

"I could set them in the corner for you," Archie offered.

"Thank you. I'd appreciate that. I don't need the constant reminder on my desk."

Archie carefully began to transfer the framed pictures, two at a time, to the corner of her office. When a small section of her desk was free, I gratefully set the cheese basket down, which felt like it had sprouted a few bricks since I first began carrying it.

"It's costing us to remove her name and photos from our brochures and we've had to revamp our website." She plopped down in her desk chair. Her face was becoming more pinched as she spoke. "I've spent my career pushing Sadler to the top. It's not easy competing with *the* Culinary, and in one evening with just a couple of paparazzi shots, she took us down."

"Were you able to give Detective Heath any useful information?" I sat in the chair opposite her without being offered it.

"Detective Heath?" She seemed confused, only half listening as she attempted to organize her desk.

"You said before that the police came by?"

"Oh. Yes, but he was too young to be a detective."

"Was it Officer Shepherd?"

"Shepherd. Yes, that's who it was. You know him?"

"I do." It was mostly because I was involved in the same murder investigations, but I left out that part.

"In that case, is it possible you could run these by the police station for me?" She thumbed through some manila folders piled on her desk and pulled one out, pushing it toward me. "He asked me to look for anything involving Phoebe Winston that might show someone had a grudge against her. I pulled up some emails that we've gotten over the years by people complaining of our affiliation with her. We got quite a few during that time when she wasn't so popular, about three years ago."

"Do you think there's a lead to her murderer in here?" I was chomping at the bit to look inside, but Olive squashed my hopes.

"The only thing they threatened was to withhold their donations if we kept using her name, but the notoriety the school got from her outweighed the few who refused to contribute because of her. There's nothing even remotely threatening in there, just complaints, but I thought I should give it to the police anyway. I don't want any more school visits. If you could save me the trip to Yarrow Glen, I'd appreciate it."

"Sure." Drats. I tried not to sound as disappointed

as I felt. "You told me yesterday that Phoebe and Ginger were close friends. Does that mean they were in the same classes and cooked side by side?"

"They were in the same program, so they'd have had most of their classes together."

"Do you think it's possible Phoebe might've seen some of Ginger's recipes and used a few of them as *inspiration* for her first cookbook?"

"Chefs usually take inspiration from each other, but there's always that fine line. In fact, I think that's what might've happened with Phoebe and Louis Pimbley."

"Who's Louis Pimbley?"

"He's the student I told you about? The one who accused Phoebe of stealing his recipes for his final dish."

"Oh, you remembered his name!"

"Thanks to those emails. There's a few of his in there and it jogged my memory. He seems to like to complain."

"You should let the police know he had a personal connection to her," I said as I made a mental note to look up Louis Pimbley.

"You think it's important? It was years ago."

"If he was sending the school emails still complaining about her, he's obviously not over it. What happened after he accused her?"

"She denied it and said he must've copied hers. So they were both asked to come up with another dish. It wasn't a big deal in the end, just petty jealousy."

"We'll mention it to the police when we give them the file."

"I hope that doesn't mean they're going to come back here asking more questions."

"Ms. Berns, do you know what this is a photo of?" Archie withdrew from the corner with one of the framed photos in his hand. He put it on the desk so we could look at it. It was a candid shot of Phoebe in what looked like a commercial kitchen surrounded by about a dozen enthusiastic-looking people. Her hair was different, and she wasn't quite as highly styled as when I'd seen her at my shop, but she was naturally stunning. She would've still stood out, even if she hadn't been in the center of the photo with all eyes on her.

Olive considered the photo. "That looks like it was taken here in one of our class kitchens, so it had to have been soon after *Fire It Up* . . . about five or six years ago? It was the only time Phoebe agreed to attend our open house for prospective students as an alumna. For a fee! Can you believe it? Most graduates come back to talk to new students as a favor. It's an informal thing. We invite many of our alumni to come."

"Do you know this guy?" Archie tapped the glass, indicating a man standing behind Phoebe.

I didn't know what Archie was getting at, but I looked more closely at the man, as did Olive. The guy looked like he was somewhere in his early twenties, brown hair and on the thin side. He stood out for having a sports coat on when everyone else was casually dressed. He looked at her the same way all the others did: with rapture.

Olive studied him but shook her head. "No, I'm sorry I don't. We had a stellar turn-out for our open house that year, but it seemed a lot of people just came to see her with no intention of attending Sadler."

"So he wasn't a student here?" Archie asked her.

"If he ended up being a student here, I don't remember him. But I don't get to know the part-time students as well as the ones who are here full-time."

"Could I have this picture?" Archie asked, ignoring my questioning stare.

"I'm sorry, that's Sadler's property. But if you want a picture of Phoebe, you can have a brochure in the box on the floor. In fact, you can have as many as you want. We'll be getting rid of all of them."

"That's okay. Thanks anyway."

"Look, I hate to rush you two out, but as you can imagine, I have a ton of things to do," Olive said. "This has been a nightmare for Sadler." She looked around her office at the chaos.

"Of course." I answered. I took the file from the desk and stood.

"Thanks again for the gift basket and for dropping those emails at the police station for me." Her smile returned.

"Happy to help."

This time I wasn't lying. I wanted a look at those emails, but as soon as Archie and I left the office, my attention turned to his inquiry of Olive Berns.

"What was that all about?" I asked him when we got to the stairs.

"That guy in the picture? That was the fan who sent his photo to Phoebe."

"What?"

Archie galloped down the stairs and I followed.

"I have to tell Detective Heath," he said.

"Wait. Wait." I finally caught up to him in the lobby. "Let's go back and get the picture."

"I've got it here on my phone." He brought it up to show me. "I took it when I first saw it, in case she didn't let me take the picture with me."

"Archie, you found the stalker!" Heath would have to believe him now.

CHAPTER 18

We caught Baz up on what had transpired in Olive Berns's office as he drove us back to Yarrow Glen. Archie sent the photo of Phoebe's possible stalker to my phone. He was excited to show it to Detective Heath, but I worried how Heath would take it. Would he believe Archie? I was determined to make sure this lead was followed whether the police looked into it or not.

"Did Olive say anything else?" Baz asked. Buttercup had one paw on the steering wheel, always needing to be in charge, apparently. "What's that on your lap?"

With Archie's discovery, I'd promptly forgotten about the folder of emails. I opened it. "These are emails from people who were disgruntled with the school for its affiliation with Phoebe. Olive wants us to give these to Detective Heath for her. There's one guy in here who had a beef with her when they went to school together, so that might be something. Let me find his. She said she wrote a few."

I flipped through the emails and read his aloud.

Ms. Berns,

I'm writing once again to tell you what a mistake it is to use Phoebe Winston as a notable alumna of Sadler Culinary School. Her character does not enhance the school's image and, in fact, degrades it. As long as you continue to sing her praises, I will not donate to this fundraiser or make any donations to the school in the future.

Sincerely,
Louis Pimbley

"That's from Lou?" Baz said, taking his eyes off the road for a moment to look at me and the paper in my hand.

"Lou?" I was confused for a second. "You mean Lou from the market? Is this *that* Lou?"

"Yeah. You said Pimbley, right?"

"Yes." I read the name again. "Louis Pimbley. I didn't know Lou's last name was Pimbley. You think that's him?"

"How many Lou Pimbleys do you think there are around here?"

"This means he went to Sadler with her." I looked through the other papers in my hands. There were two others from Lou from past years saying basically the same thing. "I wonder why Lou didn't tell me how he felt about her. The morning of her event, I told him why I was the first one in his store, but he still didn't say anything about her."

I took pictures of the emails before handing over the folder to Archie. He insisted he was confident going alone to the police with all this new information.

"I'm only a phone call away," I told him, as we pulled up to the security complex and he got out of Baz's truck and headed inside.

"Will you admit I was right about Ginger?" Baz said, driving away.

"That she's not a suspect?"

"Yeah. There's a stalker in the mix and we just found out about Lou. You still don't know about Thomas or A. J. It seems like you have enough suspects."

"It's not a game of Clue where there are a limited number of suspects. I'd like to find out what happened between her and Phoebe and why they didn't end up going into business together."

"There could be a hundred reasons." Baz pulled the truck into the lot next to the float but kept the car running. "Oh man, Wil, looks like someone messed with your float again."

I hurried out of his truck and ran over to the float. My immediate flash of anger dissipated when I looked it over. "No, nothing's different. I told you Roman and Chet have the other pieces."

He stuck his arm out the driver's-side window to point at the float. "It's not that. Someone messed up your scarecrow."

I smacked him on his arm. "There's nothing wrong with Guernsey!"

Baz cackled. He knew I was feeling sensitive about my homemade cow. His laughter finally trailed off. "You want me to ask Sharice or Ginger later to teach you how to make a scarecrow?"

"No. Guernsey's perfect the way she is. But I would like you to ask Ginger about Phoebe."

"I'm not interrogating Ginger."

"I didn't say to interrogate her. I just said to ask."

"I gotta get to my afternoon appointment. Catch you later, Wil."

As I watched him drive down the lot and out of the alley, I wondered how all the information Archie had for the police would go over with Detective Heath. I hoped the photo would convince Heath that Phoebe might've had a stalker. Lou's emails were another matter. How strong was his contempt for Phoebe? Heath or Shep were bound to talk to Lou once they read the emails. Before they did, I wanted to get some of my own questions answered.

CHAPTER 19

Lou could almost always be found at his market and today was no exception. He was restocking the pomegranates he kept in crates just outside the front door. He turned when he heard me approach and hitched up his sagging pants beneath his apron.

"Afternoon, Willa. Nice day, huh?"

"Perfect weather."

We saw each other practically every day—while he was outside sweeping the sidewalk or I was inside buying groceries—but by all accounts, we were merely acquaintances. Anything I knew of him was from others who'd lived in Yarrow Glen much longer than I. Pleasantries were the extent of our daily exchanges.

"Produce is fresh," he said, always the salesman. His salt-and-pepper hair made me guess him to be near Mrs. Schultz's age.

"It looks great. Pears, pomegranates, pumpkins . . . Look at that. It's like Sesame Street—brought to you by the letter P." I laughed. He didn't seem to get the joke. How was I going to ease my way into bringing up Phoebe? *Hey, here's another P word—Phoebe!* No, that wasn't going to do it. I noticed his cute scarecrow, tall with green overalls. "Your scarecrow looks great. I could use a lesson or two on how to make one. Mine's getting some flack."

"It doesn't take much to make a scarecrow look like a zucchini," he replied, unmoved by the compliment.

"Some people might say that about a cow." I was once again left chuckling by myself. The lull in conversation stretched and crossed into awkwardness. "We've been working on our harvest fair float, but we've had some things stolen from it. I heard that kids have been taking items from the floats and leaving them in dumpsters as a prank. I was wondering if the same has happened to you."

"I let my crew take the reins of that project. I don't have time for it. We're partnered with the bakery, so the float's over at Rise and Shine. Nobody's said anything to me about stuff being taken."

"What about books? Have you seen anybody dumping books?"

Lou went back to concentrating on the pomegranates. "I haven't seen anything."

"The reason I ask is that we found a box of Phoebe Winston's latest book in your dumpster this morning."

There was a pause before he spoke. "Have you asked Carl? It's his dumpster too." He said it without turning around.

"No, I haven't," I replied. I'd gone this far, I might as well go all in. "I thought you might know something about it since you went to Sadler with her."

He'd transferred all the produce. He had to face me. Oh, boy. This exchange was far from our usual pleasantries. In fact, it wasn't pleasant at all.

"I sometimes forget how small Yarrow Glen is," he said, turning toward me. There was no getting around the fact that gossip didn't have far to travel in a small town. "Yup, I went to Sadler. Call it a midlife crisis. My father was still running the market and he wasn't planning on retiring anytime soon, so I thought I'd dabble in something else and see if it stuck. It wasn't meant to be. My father opened this market when I was nine and named it after me. Where did I think I was going? Anyway, he had his heart attack and I took over the store."

"I'm sorry to hear that. He seems well now whenever I see him in the store."

"He's slowed down and grouses about living at the assisted-living complex, but he's still well enough to make me bring him to the market every day to tell me how to run it."

"Some parents have a hard time letting go."

My own parents would prefer I still be working on their dairy farm in Oregon, but I never loved it the way my brother did. After he died, I couldn't bear to stay. Almost ten years later, I have no doubt it was the right decision to leave, even though at the time it felt selfish.

"It's the market he's having a hard time letting go of, not me," Lou grumbled. "Anyway, that's the extent of my Sadler Culinary story."

It was clear he wasn't going to discuss the issues he had with Phoebe.

"Why didn't you ever mention knowing her when I told you she was having an event at my shop?"

"I never liked her and you were excited about it. I didn't want to rain on your parade."

"That's kind of you." *If it was the truth.* "So you must've known Ginger, too, when you were at Sadler?"

"Ginger was the one with the talent. She had something special and Phoebe could smell it like a hound senses a fox. Phoebe didn't walk all over her like she tried to do with the rest of us because she knew Ginger would come in handy someday."

"What do you mean?"

"Phoebe was competitive with everyone. She didn't need to be. We were all there to learn, but she was there to win."

"To win what?"

"Who knows? She had to be head of the class, teacher's pet, best in the school . . . But she *wasn't* the best and she knew it. She got to the top by climbing over people. It was no wonder she ended up on that reality show. It was made for people like her. It makes me feel old to say it, but this younger generation celebrates winners no matter how they win. She showed her true colors on that show, but she still walked away famous instead of infamous."

"I heard she and Ginger were good friends at school, though," I said.

"Phoebe played to her natural kindness. Ginger was always helping her out. Did you know Ginger was the one who was vegan? That was one of the reasons she stood out at school. When I heard that nonsense about Phoebe going vegan, I knew it was bull. Phoebe kept her close because she needed her skills. I tried to warn Ginger, but she was too nice for her own good."

"Do you know what happened between them to break up the friendship?"

"Ginger must've finally seen the light. It was only a matter of time."

I wondered if it was really only a matter of time or if something more serious had caused the falling out.

"You're sure you don't know anything about those books being in your dumpster?" I asked again.

"Can't say that I do. I have to get back inside."

"Okay. Have a nice day."

"You too."

And just like that, we were back to pleasantries.

I walked next door to Read More Bookstore where Ginger worked at the café. It was closed today, so it wasn't surprising that I didn't see any lights on or activity inside. I thought about what Lou had said about Phoebe and Ginger. It only confirmed there was more to their story I had yet to learn. But it also didn't stop me from questioning whether Lou was telling the truth about the books in his dumpster. Maybe Heath would get the truth out of him or maybe Phoebe's stalker would be identified, and this would have nothing to do with Lou or Ginger.

While suspects danced in my head like sugarplums, I heard the trill of a bell. It was Mrs. Schultz crossing the street from the meadery on her retro Huffy with the flower-appliquéd basket between her handlebars. We met at the bike stand in front of Curds & Whey where she wrapped the cable through the wheel's spokes and locked the bike. She was more casually dressed than I was used to seeing her, in jeans and an untucked blouse with flowy sleeves, but she still wore a signature scarf.

"You got your bike back from Roman," I noted after our greeting.

"It was nice of him to keep it safe for me. I also came by to see if we were doing float making today."

"We can. The others said they'd be by later." We walked to the rear of the building together, but I wasn't much in the mood for crafting cardboard cheddar wheels. I sat on one of the lower steps of my staircase and filled her in on the new information.

"You've had a productive morning—two new suspects," she said.

I made room on the step for her, but she declined. "How well do you know Lou? You're similar in age, aren't you?"

"Oh no. He's about ten years younger. His gray hair and grumpy attitude just make him seem older. I've mostly gotten to know him since working at Curds and Whey. I have another market closer to my house I've always shopped at," she added.

"How about Ginger from the bookshop café?" I asked. "Do you know her?"

"As a friendly acquaintance," Mrs. Schultz replied.

"She wasn't one of my high school students, so I don't know much about her."

"She moved here after going to Sadler. I tried to get her to talk about Phoebe, but she didn't seem to want to. Olive and Lou filled in some blanks about her friendship with Phoebe, but I still think there's some missing pieces to it."

"Does this mean you think Ginger's a suspect too?"

"We have to consider everybody until Archie's cleared. The only way to possibly narrow it down is to figure out what happened the night before she was murdered. Who took those pictures? Thomas refused to admit they were real, but we all saw the Mac's Big Mouth Barbeque bags and containers at her house."

"We did, didn't we?" Mrs. Schultz had a faraway look.

"What is it, Mrs. Schultz?"

"I was thinking of the plays I used to direct at the high school. When the curtain opened, we liked to have all the props in place to set the scene. Thinking back, that's what the house reminded me of."

"Are you saying you think someone staged it so we'd be sure to see the barbeque bags?"

"Why else would they have been all over?"

"I think you're right, which means the food, the photos, and the murder must be all connected."

"Now the question is, who's the connection?" Mrs. Schultz asked.

"There's one way to find out. Let's take a drive."

CHAPTER 20

The road to Mac's Big Mouth BBQ ribboned through groves of oak trees and bay laurels the colors of blood oranges and golden sunny squash. Mac's was a little out of the way, but the food was worth it. I pulled into the gravel parking lot, just starting to fill with the lunch crowd.

I was still satiated from this morning's cheesy apple pockets, but the vapors of slow-smoked brisket and short ribs curled its way through the late-autumn air and pushed my appetite out of first gear.

"It's divine," Mrs. Schultz said without preamble as we walked up to the counter of the open-air restaurant.

There was already a line. I wished I had a photo of Thomas to show them, but I'd looked through every social media and couldn't find an account for him anywhere. When it was our turn at the counter, I described him to the woman ready to take our order.

"The police were here yesterday with a picture of him," she told us. "We're nonstop on Friday nights. Unless he's a regular, none of us would remember a random customer. He didn't stand out to anybody. Sorry."

"Okay. Thanks, anyway."

"You going to order something?" she asked.

Mrs. Schultz and I looked at each other.

About ten minutes later, we were seated at one of the patio picnic tables, munching on sweet, smoky short ribs slathered with sticky barbeque sauce. We shared buttery cornbread and creamy mac 'n cheese. I detected Gruyère mixed in the pasta with cheddar, and an occasional kick of cayenne. Mac's was the only place in the area that paid proper respect to the side dish.

When my eyes weren't focused on the smorgasbord of delectable barbeque before me, I remembered to take in the sweeping vineyard views, their grapevines ablaze with color. All my senses were quenched.

Mrs. Schultz tucked a napkin over her scarf as a bib and rolled up her loose-fitting sleeves to enjoy her lunch unreservedly.

"At least the trip wasn't a total bust," I said. The meat fell off the bone with barely a tug.

"We don't have proof Thomas was here, but he doesn't know that. Should we try to talk to him about it?" she suggested.

"I think I've thoroughly gotten on his bad side. He wasn't a big fan of Baz either." I told her about our visit with Thomas the previous evening.

"Let me come with you this time and we can try doing good cop/bad cop. You're already the bad cop, so if I empathize with him and defend Phoebe, he might open up some more."

"It's worth a shot."

When we'd thoroughly had our fill, we used multiple packets of the handwipes they provided that seemed to be made for Barbie-sized hands and assessed each other to make sure any barbeque sauce hadn't been left behind on our faces, clothes, or teeth. I made a mental note never to come here on a first date.

We drove to the inn to speak with Thomas, but the reception clerk said he saw him head out about fifteen minutes earlier. We decided to give up on Thomas and make some progress on the float instead since the harvest fair was only five days away. I had been looking forward to it in the weeks before Phoebe's murder, but now it was hard to think about anything but finding out who killed her.

Mrs. Schultz tapped my arm with the back of her hand as we came upon our block of Pleasant Avenue. "Isn't that Thomas?"

I looked where she was pointing. A dark-haired man who looked a lot like Thomas, with jeans and a long-sleeved shirt buttoned at his wrists, was leaning over our flower boxes, crushing the russet chrysanthemums to peer through our window.

"It's him." I steered the car into a diagonal spot in front of the shop.

"Take my lead," Mrs. Schultz directed me. "Thomas?" she called as we got out of the car.

He turned. "Is the whole town closed today?" His voice bubbled with exasperation. "I'm tired of being imprisoned at the inn and even more tired of the food at The Cellar. Being stuck here is like a bad Twilight Zone episode."

I balked. "For one thing, there are no bad Twilight Zone episodes, and for another, Yarrow Glen is one of the most beautiful towns in the country." I was feeling defensive about my chosen town. I'd been here less than a year, but it was already home.

"Now, Willa, Thomas has a point. I'm sure if you're here on your own accord, it's a much different experience than being told you have to stay here," Mrs. Schultz countered. "Especially after what you've been through." She patted him on the shoulder. "We were just getting ready to make one of Phoebe's recipes for lunch in her memory. Would you like to join us?"

It was a little disconcerting how well Mrs. Schultz lied with ease, but it must've been her acting skills coming into play. Although I couldn't even think about eating another bite, I hurried to unlock the door before Thomas could protest. This was our chance to get more answers from him.

I shuffled him in ahead of us. Behind his back, Mrs. Schultz gave me the thumbs-up. We went to the kitchenette and offered him a seat at the farm table. He remained standing, and I thought for a moment he would change his mind and leave. Then I noticed his eyes looked teary.

"Things were very different the last time I was here." His voice dripped with melancholy.

"We're sorry. Would you rather go somewhere else?" Mrs. Schultz asked.

"No. I think it's a nice idea you had. Which recipe were you going to make?"

I decided to stick with one of the recipes Phoebe had chosen for the Book and Cook since I had all the ingredients. I'd taken down all her books from the shelves, but I recalled enough of her jalapeño popper grilled cheese recipe to make it on my own.

I stuck jalapeños that I'd cut and seeded in the oven. It was fortuitous that I'd put aside extra herbed vegan cream cheese from the pecan balls a few evenings ago. I took it out of the fridge and let it come to room temperature before slathering it on two slices of yesterday's ciabatta loaf. Thomas had started telling Mrs. Schultz stories about Phoebe. I listened in while I added American Ve-Cheez slices to the sandwich. I checked on the jalapeños. They were starting to blacken and blister, so I removed them from the oven and let them cool. Thomas had run out of steam for reminiscing. None of the anecdotes seemed pertinent to who might've murdered her.

"The sandwich is almost done. It's the jalapeño popper sandwich recipe she was going to make," I told Thomas.

"She was proud of that book. She said it was going to launch her career to another level," he replied. He leaned on the island and watched me finish making it.

"Do you know anything about how her first cookbook came about? How she came up with the recipes?"

"That was before my time with her. Jeremy was with her for that one. Huh. I pictured myself with Phoebe forever."

"Maybe there'll be a job out there that's not quite so demanding," I said in a clumsy attempt to make him feel better.

"Now, Willa, I'm sure Phoebe was an excellent boss, wasn't she, Thomas?" Mrs. Schultz said, still fully in good-cop mode.

Thomas finally sat down at the table. "There was never a dull moment, that's for sure."

"It must've been glamorous, traveling all around the country," she prompted.

"I wouldn't say glamorous exactly. There was a ton to manage."

"Not just anybody could do what you do. You helped carry her to the top." It was interesting that Mrs. Schultz was using Phoebe's technique of over-complimenting him. Maybe she hadn't been so charmed by her after all.

"It was a tough job; I'm not saying it wasn't. But I bet there were thousands of guys who would've loved to have been Phoebe Winston's confidante."

The sandwich only needed a few more seconds on the pan for the natural crunch of ciabatta to turn golden. I served it to Thomas and joined them at the table.

"You two aren't going to eat lunch?" he asked.

My hand went to my very full stomach. "We had a late breakfast." I decided to get as intensely into my role as Mrs. Schultz was. "Thomas, what did Phoebe confide in you, her confidante? Maybe she told you that she wasn't really vegan?"

"How can you say that? Especially right now when you just made one of her recipes." Thomas sulked.

"I admire your loyalty, Thomas. It's no wonder she allowed you to know her deepest, darkest secrets," I said, hoping he'd share some.

"My loyalty to her won't change just because she's gone."

"Loyalty is great, but truth is also pretty awesome. You were recognized as the person picking up Mac's Big Mouth Barbeque," I bluffed. I'd made him lunch, now it was time to get right to the point. "The police showed them your picture. They remembered you from that night."

Thomas swallowed hard and stared intently at the sandwich he didn't touch. "They couldn't have." His denial came out squeaky.

"Thomas, we understand. You were just doing your job," Mrs. Schultz said in a soothing tone.

"It would help the police do theirs if you confirm that you gave her the food," I said, taking it down a notch. "Isn't that what you want? For Phoebe to get justice?"

"Of course I do."

He took a bite of the sandwich and requested some water. I suspected it was to buy himself time to think. He drank from the bottle I gave him while I waited for him to say more.

"I didn't like it," he finally said.

"Sorry. It was my first try at making it," I replied.

"Not the sandwich, the deception. I didn't like being involved in it."

Mrs. Schultz and I looked at each other, surprised we'd softened him.

I approached carefully. "Was it always a lie?"

"She didn't mean for it to be. It was my fault."

"How is that?"

"She'd impulsively announced she was going vegan after she got so many positive comments about the Buttercup video. It was something she said she planned to do. Then Ve-Cheez called her because they wanted a celebrity's face on their cheese and she had some great vegan recipes in her first cookbook. They said they could get her another cookbook deal, as long as it was a vegan cookbook featuring their cheese. So she pretended to be vegan to get the contract. She was desperate for any good exposure at that point."

"And that's when she found you working at Ve-Cheez and hired you?" I recalled Thomas telling me as much.

"Yeah. And that's why it's my fault. She hired me because she thought I could help her out with the whole vegan thing, but I didn't know that. I only ate vegan during work hours. She tried going vegan, she really did, but she couldn't stick with it. Jeremy and I tried to help her, but it didn't last."

"You mentioned Jeremy last time. You sure you don't remember his last name? Where he's from?" Maybe it was time to take a harder look at Jeremy.

"I never knew it. We only worked together for a couple of months. We'd talk when Phoebe wasn't around, so we got to know each other some, but that was about it. I think he said he was from Alameda."

"You still think he wasn't fired? You said he left abruptly. Maybe something happened between him and Phoebe? Did they have an argument any time before then?"

Thomas slowly shook his head. "Not that I know of. She snapped at us whenever she felt like it, but there was nothing different about that. I don't think Phoebe would've lied to me about why he left."

Luckily his eyes were back on his sandwich as he took another bite, because I couldn't contain my eye roll. Trying to get information out of Thomas was like squeezing an unripe lemon. Mrs. Schultz must've sensed my frustration.

She put a gentle hand on his forearm. "Can you remember when you found out Jeremy left? What did you think at the time the reason was?"

Thomas considered this for a moment. "I thought he might've quit to see his family more often. He'd been estranged from them—he hated his stepdad, but he'd started to reconnect with his brother and sister again. So when Phoebe said he left, I thought maybe it had to do with that. He never had the time to visit them when he was working for her. Phoebe made sure we were her constant companions. We didn't have much of a life outside of her."

"Maybe he resented that," I said.

"I don't think so. He was as committed to Phoebe as I was. We knew she was destined for more than being a cookbook author and we wanted to help her make it happen. When we talked about her, we used to call her Phoenix instead of Phoebe, because she was rising from the ashes." He smiled at the recollection.

"How did she do it? How did this cookbook go from a vegan cheese cookbook to what it ended up being?"

"Ve-Cheez paid the bills, but Phoebe had bigger dreams. Her star was rising fast again and this time, she didn't want to let it fall. She was trying to get another deal for a book about her life, but the publisher wasn't convinced, so they let her combine the ideas into one book. She planned to leave all the vegan stuff behind once the book tour was done to move onto something bigger."

"Her authenticity brand?"

He nodded.

"She didn't see the irony in that?"

"You know, 'fake it till you make it.' She thought if she promoted the idea of authenticity as being above all else, then when she stepped away from being vegan, it could be seen as going back to her authentic self and people would be okay with it. The vegan chef thing was just a stepping-stone. She wanted to brand herself to have her own empire someday." Thomas slouched on the bench. "She would've. She had what it takes."

"Someone wanted to make sure that didn't happen. Who knew you were going to Mac's Big Mouth Barbeque? Did you tell anyone?"

"Are you kidding? No way. That was just between me and Phoebe. I paid cash and we didn't even text about it. It used to be her favorite place when she attended Sadler."

"Someone had to have known. Unless it was a very big and happy coincidence for whoever took those photos. You sure you didn't tell A. J. anything about it or where she was staying?"

"I'm positive. That's not something I'd let slip, especially not over one beer. He did follow me out to the lobby after you outed him, but I told him I wouldn't talk to him and pretended to go to my room."

"Do you think he followed you to Mac's and then to Phoebe's?"

"I saw him go back to The Cellar, but maybe he was also pretending. I should've known something was up with him. Before you came along, he tried to talk to me about Phoebe as if he didn't know who I was."

"Did you tell him anything?"

"I didn't want to talk about her. I signed an NDA when she hired me, so there was nothing I could say even if I'd wanted to, whether he was a reporter or not."

"An NDA?" Mrs. Schultz inquired.

"Non-disclosure agreement. It basically said she could sue me if I ever talked about her private life. I don't blame the guy for trying to get something out of me. Phoebe would've never given him an interview. She had *People* magazine running stories on her. She wouldn't have bothered with your little free newspaper."

This ruffled Mrs. Schultz's feathers, forcing her good-cop persona to slip. "If Phoebe was such a big shot, why did she agree to do an event here in Yarrow Glen at all? Wouldn't Curds and Whey be small potatoes for her too?"

"The culinary school got in touch with her about their annual fundraiser. They do one every year, but this year she figured it could help her sell some books. And then there was Ginger."

"Ginger was one of the reasons she came here?" I asked. Finally, we might be getting somewhere.

"She wanted to see her again. Phoebe said they were best friends at culinary school. She knew Ginger had moved out here when they graduated. Ve-Cheez would help sponsor the trip if it was in your shop because you carried their cheese, so it was enough for her to come."

Now I knew for certain Ginger hadn't been completely truthful with me. Phoebe had still been under the impression they were friendly. She and Chet were still at The Cellar when I left with my half of a Reuben sandwich, so she couldn't have followed Thomas to the house. She may not have taken the photos, but that didn't clear her for the murder the following day. It was possible she was invited by Phoebe herself. But how did the photos fit in?

Thomas rose from the bench. "I don't want to talk anymore. You're not going to tell that newspaper editor about any of this, are you?"

"You don't have to worry. We won't say a thing to him." Even though I had a pact with A. J., I didn't feel any compulsion to share Thomas's information with him. I was already showing him Phoebe's rental house, so it was his turn to reciprocate. "But you should tell the police the truth about bringing Phoebe the food."

"The police?" he groaned.

"They're wasting manpower that could be directed elsewhere trying to figure it out," I said.

"I thought you said they knew it was me."

Oops. "It was just a hunch. They will find out eventually."

"You know it's the right thing to do, Thomas. Do you want me to go with you to the station?" Mrs. Schultz offered.

Thomas hesitated.

"You don't have to be nervous about Detective Heath. His bark is worse than his bite," she said. I knew Mrs. Schultz's offer to Thomas was completely her own doing, not any good-cop role she was playing. With some reluctance, he left with Mrs. Schultz for the police station, but not before snatching half his sandwich.

I brought his plate to the sink. Out of curiosity, I bit into the half he hadn't touched. The kick of the jalapeño was only slightly tempered by the blanket of creamy cheeses. Even though it was no longer warm, I could see how the sandwich could easily be addictive. It was only because I was still so full from lunch that I didn't finish it.

I cleaned up the kitchenette and thought about what Thomas had told us. Should I believe he brought the barbeque to Phoebe, yet didn't take the incriminating pictures of her eating it? Did Phoebe being distraught over the photos give Ginger an opportunity to kill her? I recalled seeing A. J. return to The Cellar to grab his forgotten coat. Maybe he followed Thomas. Maybe they were working together. Or was it possible neither Thomas nor A. J. took the photos? A glance at the clock told me it was time to go to the *Gazette*. The only way I was going to get some answers was to trust A. J., but that was a scary prospect.

CHAPTER 21

On the seven-minute walk to the *Glen Gazette*, I changed my mind three times about meeting A. J. I'd much rather walk across the street and get a few Let's Talk Tacos. I stood at the door to the old stucco building on the west end of Main Street, still uncertain. I should've put my old Magic 8 Ball to use and asked "Should I trust A. J.?" After all, it was still in the box of childhood bedroom stuff I'd lugged through every move across the country since leaving Oregon. In lieu of its helpful advice of *Signs point to yes* or *Very doubtful*, I went with my instincts and entered the building.

I stepped into an open ground-floor partitioned into cubicles like a Dilbert comic strip, except for the desk by the door where I entered. The older woman behind it, dressed casually in jeans and a long-sleeved shirt, was gathering her things. She stood and slipped the straps of her handbag over her shoulder before pausing to take notice of me.

"Can I help you?" she asked politely enough.

"I'm here to see A. J. He's expecting me." There was no turning back now.

"Take the stairs in the back alcove."

"Thanks."

She nodded and blew past me out the front door, probably wanting to be sure there were no more delays to her afternoon break. On my way to the stairs, I peeked into the closest cubicle. No one was in it, but a framed family photo on the cluttered desk indicated it was Deandra's workspace. It was only several steps to the front door, as she'd said.

The room was surprisingly quiet except for the soft sounds of taps on a keyboard and the rustling of what sounded like a bag of chips. In my imagination, newsrooms bustled with activity and noise—phones ringing over the sharp clicks of multiple typewriters. I must've watched too many old movies. The *Glen Gazette* wasn't the *Washington Post*. It was a free paper that came out three times a week and covered the happenings in Yarrow Glen. It wasn't likely there'd be any pressing harvest fair report that needed immediate attention. The only big story was Phoebe's murder, and as Deandra had told me, A. J. was covering that one. Was there a more nefarious reason than ego for assigning the story to himself?

I found the mentioned alcove in the rear of the building with an emergency exit and staircase, which I climbed to a propped-open door. Through the doorway was a loftlike space with only one window on either side looking out to the stucco exteriors of neighboring buildings.

My gaze hardly knew where to land, as if I'd just come upon too many trinkets at a flea market. A large oak table was a disorder of piled folders, newspapers, and a rogue keyboard without a monitor. I spotted several mismatched mugs, some used as pencil holders and some with leftover coffee I noted as I walked farther into the room. Two wheeled office chairs flanked either side of a desk where a computer monitor with pink sticky notes covering it like chicken pox parted the clutter. I recognized A. J.'s canvas satchel on one of the chairs.

A second workstation shared the cluttered space. Chet sat facing an oversized monitor, his back to me. Hearing me enter, he swiveled his chair to face me. "Hi, Willa."

"Hi. Good to see you." I walked over to him, relieved he was here.

His work space was in stark contrast to A. J.'s. The computer monitor was on a simple table he used as his desk. Next to it sat a lone succulent in a clay pot and his cell phone. I wondered how he and A. J. were friends, considering their apparent differences.

His phone chirped announcing a text and I couldn't help but furtively look. Ginger's name appeared on the screen. He ignored it.

"Is A. J. around?" I asked.

"Yup." His phone chirped again, indicating another text message from Ginger. He grabbed his phone. "Sorry, let me just . . ." He rolled a few feet away and texted.

A. J. suddenly appeared behind me as if out of nowhere. I wondered if his habit of slinking around people might prove to be more palatable once we were working together.

"You have secret passages in here?" I asked.

"Bathroom." He pointed to a door I hadn't noticed. "Are we good to go?" He always had a nervous energy about him, like he was ready to bolt at any moment, and often did.

"I suppose so," I replied. "Chet, you want to come along?" I made the request sound casual so A. J. wouldn't suspect I'd already asked him.

Chet looked up from his phone. "Sure, why not?" he replied, not giving anything away.

"I gotta get my bag," A. J. said. He nipped to his desk.

I mouthed a silent *thank you* to Chet and we met A. J. at the doorway to the stairs. I suspiciously eyed the camera he was placing in his bag, as we followed him downstairs and out of the office.

I had to power walk to keep up with him as we hoofed it to the public parking lot across the street at the end of the block. My nerves sputtered to life again as soon as I hopped into the passenger seat of his older-model Jeep Cherokee with a dent in the back fender.

Chet got in the back. I still wasn't one hundred percent sure I was doing the right thing letting A. J. look around the house. But I had to risk partnering with him to get Archie off the suspect list, even if it meant breaking some of Heath's rules. Besides, A. J. had no motive I was aware of for killing Phoebe.

"Take Valley Road west," I said when he started the car. He did as I directed, and we drove in awkward silence. "So who do *you* think murdered Phoebe?" I asked. Since I was leading him to the house, I wanted my fair share of our deal.

"That may depend on what we find out at the house," he answered vaguely. "My money's on her assistant, Thomas. I bet he had some kind of weird obsession with her."

"Thomas mentioned Phoebe's other assistant, Jeremy, but I don't know what to make of it. He left a few months after Thomas started working for Phoebe, which sounded a little sketchy."

"What's sketchy about that?"

"They were together all the time at work—both totally committed to Phoebe, according to Thomas—but Jeremy left unexpectedly, without a word. Thomas said Phoebe told him Jeremy got another job, but then why wouldn't he tell Thomas? And if Jeremy was so committed to her, why would he leave in the first place?"

"What's your theory?"

"He was either fired, in which case he could be a suspect, although it was almost three years ago. Or Thomas lied to me about it, and he did away with him to be Phoebe's number one."

"I'd go with theory number two," A. J. said. "What else do you know about the guy? His name's Jeremy what?"

"That's another thing. Thomas claims he doesn't know his last name. He said he thinks he's from Alameda." I raised my voice so it would carry to the back seat: "What do you think, Chet?" I looked over my shoulder. Chet's head was lowered and he was texting on his phone. "Chet?"

He looked up. "Oh, sorry. Ginger's giving me grief. I was supposed to see her this afternoon. Did you say something?"

"Never mind." Ginger had given me the impression that Chet was the one always checking in, but it seemed the other way around. I was starting to think maybe Baz was unknowingly lucky that she was already taken. I changed the subject. "Did you talk to your landlord about Buttercup?"

"Oh yeah, I forgot to tell you. He said no problem. And Roman said Buttercup's welcome at the meadery as long as he stays out of the tasting room. You're good with the dog being at the office, right, A. J.?"

"I guess," A. J. responded, unenthused.

"Oh good," I said. "That really helps us out."

A glance out the window told me we were almost at the poorly marked road Baz and I had missed last night. If my memory served, it was just after the gas station coming up. I was about to say so when A. J. slowed down and made a right turn. I was going to correct him, but I realized he'd turned onto the correct road. This was the way to Phoebe's rental house.

"How did you know . . . ?" My confusion gave way to a certainty I didn't want to admit. There was no way A. J. could know the way to her house unless he'd been there before. My stomach sank. I stared at him, but he didn't answer me. I knew he heard me start to ask the first time, but I asked again so there'd be no mistake. "How did you know where to turn?"

"That detective gave out the address," he explained lamely.

"No, he didn't." I knew Heath too well for that. "You know your way to this house."

A. J. made a point of staring straight ahead at the road. I didn't need to consult my Magic 8 Ball for this one. *Outlook not so good.*

CHAPTER 22

The road was a windy one that followed a creek. I remembered it well. There were no traffic lights, no people. We hadn't even passed another car the last two times I'd been en route to the house. I knew there would be no opportunity for the car to come to a stop so I could make an escape. Still, I had to somehow find a way out.

It was like A. J. was reading my thoughts. The car seemed to be speeding up. It began hugging the nonexistent shoulder as it rounded each bend.

I didn't know what to say to make him let us go. He appeared nervous now. His hands gripped the steering wheel tighter.

"A. J.," I began.

"My brakes aren't working," he uttered.

"What?" I watched him pump the pedal, but the car didn't slow down.

We were swinging from side to side now. It would only take one missed curve and we'd end up down in the creek or wrapped around a tree. The next curve slammed me into the passenger door.

Chet's attention was finally ripped from his phone. "What's going on?"

"I don't know what's wrong!" A. J.'s focus went from the road to the pedal and back to the road.

"Downshift!" Chet yelled from the back seat.

A. J.'s hands seemed glued to the wheel. I looked at the shift panel between us. The emergency-parking brake caught my eye and before a complete thought went through my mind, I pulled on it. The car went into a skid. I sensed A. J. trying to keep control, hand over hand on the steering wheel, but all I saw was everything spinning, like when I was eight years old on the playground carousel. I grasped for something to hold onto.

The sound of tires eating gravel resounded in my ears just before we came to a dead stop. My body was thrust forward until my seat belt caught and bit into my collarbone.

We all froze, as if any movement might push the car into motion again. Breathing hard, A. J. carefully pried his hands off the steering wheel, shifted the car into park, and turned off the ignition.

The three of us assessed one another, ourselves, then our surroundings. Somehow A. J. had managed to steer the car toward some high grass.

"Way to go, bro. That was Nascar-level driving." Chet gave A. J. two firm pats on the shoulder. Although he was trying to lighten the mood, sweat had broken out on his brow.

A. J. let out a long breath, and a shaky laugh followed.

"What happened?" I asked.

"I don't know. I haven't had any trouble with it since I had the transmission fixed a few months ago. The brakes should be fine. Are you guys okay?"

We nodded. Just as my adrenaline was subsiding and allowing relief to seep in, I remembered what I'd realized before the brakes went. A. J. had lied to me. I still had to get away from him.

I fumbled with my seat belt and the door lock like a teenager in a bad horror movie. Realizing it was already unlocked, I pushed my way out of the car. A. J. and Chet followed. A. J. took his jacket off and threw it on the passenger seat. Sweat stained his T-shirt.

"I'm calling an Uber," I said, keeping plenty of distance between me and the two of them. I held up my phone like a weapon for them to see. "Or Baz. He knows I'm with you guys if anything happens to me," I fibbed.

"What do you mean, if anything happens to you?" Chet said. "A. J. just saved us."

"He already knew how to get to the house. That means you were the photographer that night," I said to A. J. "Or the both of you were in on it for all I know."

"You're talking crazy now," Chet said, wearily plopping down on the grass. He obviously held no credence to what I just said. "Let's just get back."

A. J. bent over and put his hands on his thighs. I thought maybe he was going to be sick.

"You okay, A. J.?" Chet asked.

A. J. straightened, but his shoulders drooped. He pushed his curly hair, damp with sweat, away from his forehead. He looked spent.

"It was me. I took the pictures," he said. Then hastily added, "But I didn't kill her."

Chet looked stunned.

I wasn't going to be so gullible this time. "If you only took the pictures, why didn't you give yourself credit for them?"

"Her fans are so rabid. I thought I'd get too much backlash. Besides, I didn't know if she was the type to try to sue me. I just wanted some recognition for the paper."

I wanted to hear the whole story. "How did you know where she was staying?"

"Someone put a note in my jacket pocket with her address."

"Bro . . ." Chet shook his head.

Even his friend apparently didn't believe him.

"A note in your pocket? Along with the deed to the Brooklyn Bridge?" I asked.

"I swear! There was a note. I think Thomas knew who I was all along and put it in my pocket because he wasn't allowed to tell me. Plausible deniability."

"How did you know she'd be eating barbeque?"

"I didn't. That's why I think it was Thomas who tipped me off. He *wanted* me to come to the house that night to see that."

I paced in front of the car to absorb what A. J. was telling me. A minute ago, I'd thought for sure it was him, but I had to admit, his story made sense.

Chet left his seat in the grass to get some space from A. J. too.

"I'm sorry I lied to you," A. J. said to him. "It was just journalism, nothing personal."

Chet stopped walking just a couple of yards from him, but didn't turn around. I sensed this betrayal was hitting him hard.

A. J. looked defeated, but I still had more questions. "Why did you let me take you here if you already knew where the house was?"

"I wouldn't have been able to come again to get more information for the story without implicating myself. I needed to be able to say that you showed me where the house was."

"So you were using me for your story?"

"We were using each other. That was our agreement, wasn't it? You think I don't know about Archie?"

I felt my face burn hot at the mention of Archie.

"I'm not a monster, I'm just a journalist. Unless the police tell me otherwise, I want to get the whole story before I accuse anyone," he said.

"I appreciate that," I said. Had I pegged A. J. all wrong?

"And I'd appreciate the same consideration from you," he said.

"You should give the police the note, then."

"I can't," he replied.

"You have to."

"I got rid of it."

"What?"

"At the time, I didn't want any evidence linking me to the photos, so I ditched the note that night. I didn't want any clues to reveal my source—I thought Thomas was doing me a favor. I mean, until Phoebe was murdered. Now I think he was just setting me up."

I was still skeptical.

"Look, when I followed Thomas out of The Cellar to the lobby, he told me how Phoebe would never do an interview with me. So later on that night when I found the note and went to her house, I knew I was going to have to settle for getting some candid shots of her. I got so lucky with the house and all those windows, but unlucky with that fence. I was still able to get some great shots with my telephoto lens. And then I saw it—she was eating the ribs. Thomas had to be the one who set it all up."

"Why didn't you tell this to the police?" I demanded.

Chet finally turned around to face us. He likely wanted to know the answer to that too.

"Because it makes me look pretty guilty, don't you think?" A. J. said testily. "Besides, by the time we knew she was dead, I'd already made up the whole thing about the anonymous photos. I'd copied the pictures onto a flash drive and left it on Deandra's desk, then acted like I didn't know about them. How was I supposed to tell Chet and Deandra that I lied about it?"

With eyes lowered, he hesitantly looked at Chet, who still said nothing. I had a feeling this lie between them was going to test their friendship.

"You're going to have to tell the police. If Detective

Heath finds out before you tell him, you'll really look guilty," I warned.

"I didn't kill her. I swear."

Now that my heart was pumping at a normal pace, I saw A. J. and Chet once again as the guys I knew. I believed A. J. about the pictures and about the murder. For now.

"We still need to get back home," I said.

"You guys can catch an Uber back if you want. I gotta wait for a tow. I'm going to have to pay for a loaner car." He grumbled to himself, "Does my insurance cover this?"

"You really ought to read your own newspaper. You guys just did an article on Triple A's services," I said.

A. J. snapped his fingers. "I do have Triple A."

He leaned in the passenger side and rifled around inside the glove box. He emerged staring wide-eyed at a piece of paper in his hands.

"What's going on?" Chet stepped to his side to see what it was. "What the . . . ? Where'd you find this?"

"It was in the glove compartment."

Curious, I moved next to them to see it too: *STOP ASKING QUESTIONS OR YOU TWO WILL BE NEXT.*

We looked from the note to one another. I searched their faces for answers.

"You think someone messed with my brakes on purpose?" he asked.

I had a past experience with a threatening note. I knew exactly what this meant. "A. J., someone was trying to kill you."

A. J. went pale. This time I think he really was going to throw up.

CHAPTER 23

We nixed the tow truck and Uber, and called Detective Heath instead. He arrived with Shep trailing him in a patrol car. Heath's presence had a disconcerting way of making me feel both safe and anxious.

He glanced at me without a word before reading the note. With latex gloves, he slipped it into an evidence bag. A. J. explained to them what had happened.

"When was the last time you looked in your glove compartment?" Detective Heath asked A. J.

A. J. ran a hand over his mop of curly hair. "Who knows? Could be months. I don't remember."

"Where do you keep your car?"

"It's usually either parked in front of my rental house or at the business lot on West Main."

"Do you keep it locked?"

"Overnight, but not when I'm working. The food trucks are there—people are always around, and I take my bag wherever I go."

"So anyone could've put that note in your glovebox," I said, following along.

Shep lifted the hood of A. J.'s Jeep and scanned the car's innards.

"You know what you're looking for?" Heath asked him.

"No idea," Shep answered.

A tow truck pulled in front of A. J.'s car. It belonged to Richie—Richie Muscles, as I'd privately nicknamed him when I met him through Baz. Almost as well-known around town as Shep, he seemed to like everyone he met. He was especially fond of himself.

He stepped down from the truck and approached us, his ballooned biceps keeping his arms slightly aloft at his sides. Richie silently said hello to me in his usual manner, with raised eyebrows and a quick once-over followed by an approving nod. I shot him a wave. He exchanged bro handshakes and half hugs with A. J. and Chet.

"Transmission again, A. J.?" he said, nodding to the car.

"No, man, the brakes went," A. J. answered.

"Whoa. Glad you're all okay. The detective's here, too? You must be a VIP," he kidded A. J. He'd done this enough to know not to ask any probing questions, at least in front of Detective Heath. He was close friends with Shep and was the police's go-to guy for towing vehicles related to car collisions or criminal cases. "Where am I towing her?" He directed his question to Heath.

"Bring it to the station impound. We're going to have to take a closer look," Heath answered.

"Will do." He went about putting the car on the bed of his tow truck.

"When will I be able to get my car back?" A. J. asked Heath.

"When we're done with it." Heath turned to Chet. "Do you have anything to add about what happened?"

"Not really. I was texting with Ginger and wasn't paying attention until I got knocked into the door. That's when I realized we were going too fast and A. J. said his brakes weren't working."

"Where were the three of you going?"

I was afraid he'd ask that question. We looked at one

another, at our shoes, at the sky . . . everywhere but at Heath.

"I can't help but notice this is on the way to Phoebe Winston's rental house," Heath said. It was the only time he looked at me.

"I think A. J. has something to tell you about that," I said, throwing A. J. directly under the bus. He had lied to me, though, so every man for himself.

A. J. glared at me then sighed, resigned. "I was the one who took the photos of Phoebe Winston eating barbeque at the house that night."

Heath didn't look too surprised. Then again, his poker face was always on point.

"You'll need to come to the station for further questioning. Who else knew?" Heath asked A. J., but his gaze darted to me and Chet too.

"They didn't know. Nobody else knew."

"Chet, do you mind accompanying A. J. to the station to go over the statement you gave on Sunday about the photos?" Heath asked.

"No problem," Chet said.

"You can go with Officer Shepherd," Heath directed.

"Let's go, guys," Shep said.

"Let me get my bag from the back of my car first." A. J. started toward the Jeep.

"Nope. It's evidence now," Heath said.

"It's got my camera and my notebook in there. You're going to put me out of a job?"

"You might've done that all by yourself." Heath nodded at Shep, and Officer Shepherd led both guys to the cruiser.

That left Heath and me alone on the side of the road. I put on my most innocent face, as if we just happened to run into each other waiting for a bus.

"I'll take you home," he said. His tone was gruff. My innocent act had no effect on him.

We drove in silence for several long minutes. As uncomfortable as the silence was, I knew having to confess what I was really doing with A. J. and Chet would be even worse. Maybe I'd just keep it to myself.

Another five minutes passed in silence. *Ugh.* The vow I'd just made to myself went out the window at his reverse psychology interrogation technique of not interrogating me. Or maybe it was just my own guilt that made me spill everything. Heath listened but didn't stay silent for long.

"You weren't sure if A. J. was a suspect, but you got in a car with him?" he reiterated needlessly.

Why did it sound so much worse when he said it?

"I made sure Chet came with us," I replied weakly.

"And your plan was to cross the police tape and try to get on the property?"

"No. We just wanted to see how to get in. We wouldn't have actually gone in."

"Semantics. When did you plan this?"

"*Plan* makes it sound so . . . planned."

"Willa." He took his eyes off the road momentarily to look at me. He wasn't letting me get away with anything.

"We talked about it this morning," I confessed.

"Did anyone overhear you?"

"Not that I know of. I suppose it's possible—we were in the alley by my shop. You think this happened because we were going to the house? If A. J.'s been asking questions about the murder, it could just be coincidence that I was in the car with him."

"Did you read the note?"

"Of course I did."

"It said, 'Stop asking questions or you two will be next.' You *two*."

"You think I was one of the two? I assumed it was Chet."

"If someone overheard you, or if A. J. or Chet told

someone your plans, you might've been directly targeted. We'll ask them who they talked to about it. When did Chet know?"

"I asked him to come along this morning when I saw him at the meadery." I thought back. "He was saying how Ginger always wants to know his every move. Maybe he told her." All roads seemed to lead to Ginger. "Do you know that Ginger went to culinary school with Phoebe?"

"Yes, we do."

"Oh, and the books in the dumpster!" I remembered.

"What are you talking about?"

I went on to give the details of that morning when Baz found the box of Phoebe's signed books in the dumpster between Carl's Hardware and Lou's Market.

"They could've been taken out of Phoebe's trunk when Archie was bringing the boxes into Curds and Whey. He made two trips and left the trunk open. The car was parked right in front of Lou's," I told him.

I stared at him from the passenger seat, waiting for him to show any signs of excitement at this new development. Of course, I was disappointed.

"We've been getting reports of float decorations found in the dumpsters. The books could've been thrown in as another prank," Heath said, unwilling to hop on my theory train.

I wasn't giving up. "Or they could've been thrown in by someone who hated Phoebe Winston. I think it was Ginger or Lou. You saw the emails from Olive Berns, right?"

"We'll be talking to Lou."

I peered at his profile as he stared at the road. Nothing. Not one ounce of enthusiasm.

"Okay, what about the stalker angle? Is there a way to find out who that guy in the picture is?" I asked.

I detected a pause before Heath said, "We'll look into it."

"You paused. Why did you pause?"

"I didn't pause."

"There was a definite pause. You're not still question-ing whether there really was a picture, are you? I mean, Archie found the guy in another photograph *with* Phoebe Winston! He was in classic stalker mode, dressed up for her and lurking behind her at a public event. Maybe she gave him some attention once and he exaggerated it in his mind, and then when he didn't hear from her, he got upset. That's why he sent the picture. It said 'Remem-ber me?' He was obviously mad that she'd been ignoring him." I splayed my hands in front of me to show him I'd just given him a credible theory on a silver platter.

He glanced at me. "I said we'll look into it."

"We'll, meaning we *will*?" I said.

"Yes. We will."

"Why not 'we *are*'? Why are you putting this off? This guy could be the answer."

"We *will* look into it. We only have so much manpower. This mystery guy is a long shot and not our only suspect."

"Right, there's Thomas. Did you talk to him this after-noon? He confessed to bringing the food to Phoebe that night, so Mrs. Schultz went to the station with him so he could tell you about it."

"We talked to him."

Silence.

"You're welcome," I said.

An intensity crept into his voice. "I'm not going to thank you for putting yourself in harm's way to get con-fessions out of people."

"That wasn't my intention," I said, feeling duly scolded. "But the fact is, we now know what happened on Friday night. Thomas had been to the house multiple times before the murder, so he could've scoped out the house's perimeter. The two surveillance cameras are in the front, so all he had to do was find a way in from the back of the house the next day."

"Do you think we're not working on this? Really, Willa? Is that what you think?"

This time when he turned to face me, his irritation with me was fully apparent. I was the one who looked away first.

"Of course you are, but—"

"We've checked for breaches in the fence. There is no way in. The back door was locked and deadbolted from the inside. We asked about the house keys too. The home's owners only left one set of keys and they were still in her purse. And before you ask, we've checked into the owners. They're not suspects at this time."

That put a crimp in my theories. "Maybe Thomas made an extra set?"

Heath's voice relaxed, his annoyance with me dissipated. "It's possible. There are only two people who had that kind of access to her, and Thomas is one of them."

"Who's the other?"

Heath glanced over at me, then went back to staring at the road ahead of him. I understood what the look meant. The other one was Archie.

"We know it's not Archie, so we need to focus on your other suspects," I insisted. "We know the surveillance footage isn't definitive because there was none of Thomas when he delivered the food that night. The question is, why not?"

There was a hint of approval on Heath's face this time. "Good question."

"When I was looking into getting a surveillance system, they said access to it would've been through a passcode on my phone. It would alert me if there was movement within sight of the camera and it would record for a certain amount of time I select. They said only the person with the passcode has the ability to delete the recording." Now saying it out loud I had my answer. "Thomas said they only talked about the barbeque when they were alone together—she didn't want any trace of it in writing. Do you think she deleted Thomas's visit herself Friday night as a precaution?"

"Good deduction."

"If someone only needed access to her phone, that means whoever came to the house after Archie could've also deleted their surveillance."

"They could've deleted coming to the house, but not going. We have her phone."

"What if he knew her passcode and deleted it remotely? Thomas probably even set up the app on her phone for her, so he would know the passcode. Archie said she didn't do anything for herself."

"Merely downloading the app and knowing her passcode isn't enough to get you into the system. During the setup, the homeowner activated it on Phoebe's phone with his personal passcode, which is different than the passcode he gives to her to use the system."

"Well, *somebody* found a way to access it." There were still too many possibilities. "Her murderer knew where she was. That puts Thomas and A. J. at the top of the suspect list. And don't forget about Ginger. Phoebe could've called her that afternoon. Maybe she wanted her old friend to help her through all of this."

"It would explain how she was killed in the short window of time she was alone, but there's no record of a phone call to Ginger's number. It could've been merely luck that Archie wasn't there when the murderer showed up."

My breath hitched. "Oh Heath, I never thought of that. If the killer didn't know he was with her that day, Archie could've been in the house and been killed along with Phoebe!" A heavy blanket of self-reproach covered the guilt that had been eating away at me because of Archie's involvement. I looked out the side window and held back my tears.

"Hey." Heath rested his hand on my thigh. "That didn't happen. Archie's fine."

"He's a nineteen-year-old kid suspected in a murder investigation. He's not fine."

His hand returned to the steering wheel. He slowed the car as he turned onto Main Street.

I collected myself as we neared my shop and told Heath the box of Phoebe's books was by the side door. He pulled into the alley where A. J. and I had planned our disastrous excursion and cut the engine.

"That's the box," I told him as we got out of the car. "A little smelly, but otherwise they look untouched, except for being signed by Phoebe."

"I don't think anything will come of it, but I'll bring them to the station to see if there are any clues as to who took them. What are you going to be doing now?" It wasn't a casual inquiry.

"We have a float to finish before the harvest fair this weekend."

This answer seemed to mollify him. "I know it's a little late to say this and maybe I shouldn't," he began, then hesitated. "But I have to be honest about how I feel." He stepped closer to me, his dark eyes never leaving mine.

I felt my heart pick up speed. I caught a hint of his rich cologne. I inhaled, trying to breathe in more of the intoxicating undertones of citrus and wood. "Go on." It came out in barely more than a whisper.

He hesitated a moment more, then finally spoke. "Don't do anything stupid."

Wait, what?

I took a step back, the pull I'd felt immediately broken like a snipped wire.

"I know it won't make a difference," he continued, "but I have to say it. I thought keeping you somewhat in the loop would make you stay out of dangerous situations, but that apparently hasn't happened."

I said nothing while I recovered from the whiplash of my foolish thoughts.

"Willa, what can I do to get through to you?"

I finally dared to look him in the eye. "Clear Archie's name."

He was the first to look away. He rubbed the back of his neck, perhaps trying to release some tension. His hands fell to his waist, fanning his suit jacket—his usual position of frustration. "I have to get back to the station. I've got interviews to do with A. J. and Chet."

"Let me know how it goes," I said.

I didn't appreciate his hearty sarcastic laughter as he stuffed his hands into a pair of latex gloves and took the box of books to his car.

CHAPTER 24

With Heath gone, I contemplated what to do next. I didn't want to admit it to myself, but I was still feeling shaken up from the car incident. My thoughts went to my brother, Grayson, who had died in an automobile accident. I never wanted to know the details of what had happened. I avoided reading or hearing anything about it except for the most general information—he was out with his friends the weekend before his college graduation, the car rolled over, and he was killed. I knew my mind would do what it was doing now, imagining what his final moments might've been like. I always wanted to think of it as instantaneous, but now I had to contemplate an alternate scenario. Had the car my brother was riding in gone out of control like A. J.'s? Had he experienced that same fear I had before the crash took his life?

I shook my head of the thoughts and wished I could also get rid of the unease now festering in my stomach. Time to occupy myself.

I let myself into the Curds & Whey stockroom where I could retrieve the toolbox and the materials to finish making the float. Roman still had some of the decorations we'd made from last night. I considered texting him, but I wasn't sure if being in my vulnerable state was the best way to see him. I decided against it and started hauling everything to the float. On my third and last trip, Baz's pickup truck came through the lot and parked in his assigned spot beside my car. My mood lightened. I could really use my best friend right now.

He parked and got out of his truck with the moppet dog in tow. "Baz!" I called, flagging him down with a wave.

"Hey, Wil."

He hung around his truck, so I met him there. I greeted Buttercup with some ear scratches.

"You won't believe what happened," I began.

Before I could recap my near miss and the note that might've been targeting me as well as A. J., the truck's passenger door opened and Ginger emerged.

"Oh!" I blurted. "Hi, Ginger."

"Hey," she answered half-heartedly. She was focused on the phone in her hand.

With my back to Ginger, I gave Baz an exaggerated O mouth.

"Her place was on the way back from my last job. We're going to the bookstore to work on the float." He returned my surprised face with a stern look that warned me to *act normal or else.*

I complied. "I need to gather my team too. We only have a few more days to finish."

Ginger looked up from her phone. "If Chet comes to work on it, tell him to come by the bookstore. He's ignoring my texts."

"I don't think he's ignoring you. He's um . . . he's with the police."

"What?" She finally stopped giving an annoyed look at her phone and instead directed it at me. "Why?"

"It's a long story, but A. J. admitted to taking the pictures of Phoebe eating Mac's barbeque."

"Chet wasn't involved in that." She looked at her phone once again as if she'd find answers there. "Was he?"

"No, he wasn't. A. J. lied to him and Deandra, but Detective Heath still wanted to talk to both of them."

"I should go down to the station," she said.

Baz looked disappointed.

"Don't bother," I quickly told her. "They won't let you into the interview room."

"I need to get in touch with him at least. I'll meet you inside the bookstore, okay Baz? I need to call him."

"Sure," Baz said to Ginger's retreating back. She was already scurrying away with the phone to her ear.

"Thanks a lot, Wil," Baz complained.

"Sorry. Don't get too upset. She hasn't been ruled out as a suspect. In fact, I left out some important parts to the story just now, because it's possible she was involved."

"She's not a viable suspect. You really need to let that go."

"Lou told me some stuff about her background with Phoebe."

"Maybe Lou's trying to deflect from those emails."

"Possibly. But Ginger's one of the few people Phoebe would've let into her house that day. I know you think stealing the recipes is a lame reason for murder and maybe it is. But they were family recipes handed down to her. Phoebe seemed to have taken on Ginger's whole vegan image after talking Ginger out of opening a vegan café together. At least I think that's what happened. You could ask her about it later."

"I told you before, I'm not interrogating Ginger."

"There's more." I still hadn't told him that Ginger might've known I was going to be in A. J.'s car this afternoon and messed with the brakes.

"I don't care. I don't want to hear it." Baz started to walk away.

"I thought we were partners in this," I called after him.

He stopped and turned on his heel. "You know what? You're right."

"Thank you!" *Finally! He admitted I'm right.*

"Here." He pushed Buttercup into my arms.

"What are you doing?"

"I'm out." He lifted his hands as if in surrender.

"You're out?" I was so confused.

He ticked off his argument on his fingers. "The police have A. J.'s confession about the photos. Archie gave them the stalker picture and Lou's angry emails. The police have enough information to figure out who did this. I'm washing my hands of the whole thing and I think you should too."

I half expected his clenched lips to break into a smile—I'd almost thought he was kidding. I'd never seen Baz like this, especially not toward me.

"Are you serious?"

"I'll leave his food on the deck."

Baz threw a peace sign up with his fingers and walked away toward the bookstore without another word, leaving Buttercup and me staring at each other.

CHAPTER 25

I didn't move for several minutes. Frankly, I was in shock. Baz and I had never had an argument. I couldn't believe he would abandon us like this.

Archie and Mrs. Schultz emerged from the alley, she on her bike and he on his skateboard.

"Hey, you starting without us?" Archie called.

It felt great to see their friendly faces, but it made me feel even more hurt about Baz—this investigation wasn't about me, it was about Archie. I decided to keep Baz's outburst to myself. I didn't want to create any bad blood between them.

Buttercup immediately began to wiggle in my arms at the sight of Archie, which I tried not to take personally.

"What's he doing with you?" Archie took the happy dog from me. "I thought Baz was starting to get the hang of taking care of him."

"Chet said he could take him." It was the truth, even if it wasn't exactly the reason the dog was with me. "Detective Heath told me he interviewed Thomas at the station," I told Mrs. Schultz.

"He was a little nervous about going, but he seemed okay when we got there," she replied, dismounting her bike.

"Did you two see each other at the station? Don't tell me you've been there this whole time," I said to Archie.

"No, I left hours ago. I texted Mrs. Schultz to see if she wanted to work on the float. We thought we might be able to finish it tonight."

"Are you really in the mood to do this?" I asked him.

"It keeps my mind off things."

"I think we could all use a happy distraction," Mrs. Schultz said.

I couldn't have agreed more.

We took the fresh materials I'd taken from my stockroom and decided what each of us would work on. While Mrs. Schultz was drilling a plywood Curds & Whey sign onto the back of our float, I was second-guessing the bleu cheese crumbles I was trying to make, which were looking more like giant pieces of popcorn.

"How did it go with Detective Heath?" I asked Archie after we'd gotten started on our projects.

"He wasn't too impressed by any of the stuff I showed him." Archie seemed disheartened.

"That's just his way. He doesn't let on what he's thinking."

"Then we should get this stalker ourselves," Mrs. Schultz proclaimed. She raised the drill and pointed it into the air, hitting the trigger so it whirred.

We laughed with her at her bravado.

"You do have a point, though," I said. "Maybe we should focus a little more on Phoebe's stalker. Phoebe said she was staying at her secluded location because of paparazzi, but that could've been a cover."

"But you asked Thomas, and he said he didn't know anything about a stalker. Don't you think she would've told him?" Mrs. Schultz pointed out.

"Possibly," I responded. "Maybe she was afraid of this guy and didn't want to admit it."

I didn't want to dismiss the stalker angle as easily as Heath seemed to be doing.

Mrs. Schultz and Archie raised their hands in a wave with sudden smiles on their faces. I turned to see Roman approaching with my cardboard cheddar wheel and a laden tote bag. He raised the cheddar wheel in a return greeting, but the slow grin I'd come to look forward to was absent. Buttercup circled his legs once, then ran back beside Archie.

"Chet texted me about what happened with A. J.'s car. Are you okay?" Roman said.

"What's he talking about?" Mrs. Schultz asked. Their previous smiles had vanished.

"I'm okay, thanks," I replied.

"What happened?" Archie asked.

I proceeded to recount the car incident and how A. J. confessed to being the one who took the compromising photos of Phoebe and those barbeque ribs.

"You're lucky the car didn't flip or end up in the creek," Archie said.

"That's a dangerous road even with proper brakes," Mrs. Schultz said.

The two of them spontaneously hugged me.

"I know, but I'm fine. Thanks for your concern, guys." I wasn't comfortable being doted upon, and gladly changed the subject. "What's in the bag?" I asked Roman.

Roman looked at the bag he seemed to forget he was holding. "This is the first time Chet and I have collaborated." He pulled out an ordinary-looking wine bottle, not one of the sleek ones he sold his mead in. "It's apple-pie cyser, freshly bottled. Who wants to try it?"

We all volunteered readily. We temporarily left our crafting and pulled chairs out from under the deck.

"What are you going to do now?" Roman asked me, opening the mead bottle as we sat in a circle next to the float.

"About what? A. J.?" I said.

"About continuing to investigate the murder. You could've been killed. The police can handle it from here, don't you think?"

"The note mentioned two people, so I don't know if Chet was the other target or me."

"Does it matter? You still could've gotten seriously hurt or killed. Don't you think it's time you stop investigating and leave it to the police?" Roman said, not for the first time.

"Roman's right. I know you're doing this for me, Willa, but I don't want you getting hurt," Archie said.

I didn't want me getting hurt either, but I wasn't ready to give up entirely. "There's nothing dangerous about discussing theories with each other, is there? We can still do that."

"And if we come up with something new, we'll tell Detective Heath," Archie said.

We all nodded in agreement.

"It's probably for the best," Mrs. Schultz said. "Now that Detective Heath knows Thomas delivered the food to Phoebe, and A. J. took the photos, he can get a clearer picture of what happened the night before she died. I'm sure he'll be able to figure it out soon."

"That's pretty lousy that A. J. lied about the photos." Roman poured the mead into plastic cups he'd brought.

"Did Chet know?" Archie asked.

"A. J. said he didn't," I told them. "Chet looked pretty hurt by it. A. J. left the flash drive on Deandra's desk for her to find from an 'anonymous source.' A. J. went through the whole ruse with both of them."

"I would've been very surprised had Chet gone in on something like that," Roman said.

"I'm surprised he and A. J. are such good friends. They seem so different from each other. A. J.'s like a rat in a maze always going after the next piece of cheese. Chet seems more laid back, like you."

"I think Chet used to be a lot like A. J. until he got burnt out. He told me about the brutal schedule that was expected working for one of those big Silicon Valley companies."

"I wondered how a guy working two part-time jobs could afford a boat," Archie said. "Here I am just trying to get out of my mom's house."

"You're doing just fine, Archie," Roman said, patting him on the shoulder.

"Roman's right. That's the problem when we compare ourselves to others. We don't know their backstory," Mrs. Schultz said.

"Wise words, Mrs. Schultz," I said.

"Maybe it's a good thing he and A. J. are friends. Chet could start to rub off on him," Mrs. Schultz, ever the optimist, said.

"I wish I knew more about our *Gazette* editor. He's told me a few things about himself, but he's still pretty mysterious. What do you know about him, Roman?" I asked.

"We haven't had much opportunity to cross paths. I remember when the *Gazette* was looking for a new editor and it was controversial that they got someone from out of town. That was the year after I moved here, so about three years ago now."

"Nothing about his family or hometown? You never chatted him up over drinks at The Cellar?"

Roman slowly shook his head. "Here and there, but he talked mostly about L.A. in general. Maybe it was a hazard of being a journalist, but if anything, he was usually the one asking questions."

"He told me he used to freelance there, but I don't know any more than that. Maybe you could ask Chet about him?"

"Sure," Roman agreed as he handed out the cups of mead.

"What did you say this was? Cyser?" Mrs. Schultz peered at the bottle in Roman's hand.

"There's no label—it's just a sample bottle. It's a variety of mead that's apple-based," Roman explained.

"Like a hard cider?" Archie asked.

"It's still fermented with honey like my other meads, so it's a little sweeter than hard cider." Roman apologized for the plastic cups, but none of us minded. "You only get a taste of it, Archie."

Archie inspected his cup with a frown. "This is less than the amount of mouthwash I use every night."

"Sorry, bud. I don't want to contribute to underage drinking."

"Here's to Roman expanding his mead making with a new partnership," I toasted before any of us drank.

He returned the toast. "And to you and Chet and A. J. all coming through unharmed."

"And to Detective Heath solving this case soon," Mrs. Schultz added.

"I'll rinse to that," Archie joked, making us all laugh.

We tapped our cups and drank.

"My poker-night girlfriends would love this," Mrs. Schultz said, smacking her lips.

"Come by the meadery. We're just starting to bottle it. I've got several in the back room I can give you."

"I'm happy to buy them from you, Roman."

"That won't be necessary. You'd be helping me spread the word about our new flavor."

Mrs. Schultz raised her glass again and took another sip. She declined a second cup, as she had to drive home, albeit on a bicycle. Roman and I, however, started a second bottle while we made good progress on the float. Was it just my mead goggles or was Guernsey starting to look good?

Before we knew it, the streetlights had blinked on and we were rubbing our arms from the sudden chill of the evening. Mrs. Schultz had to grocery shop for the aforementioned girls' poker night the following evening, so with a wave and the trill of her bicycle bell, she was off.

Archie had been texting with Hope about grabbing dinner together. "We're meeting on the corner in a few minutes," he told us.

"A date?" I asked, eyebrows raised.

"Nah, just dinner," he replied, but his eyes didn't meet mine.

Archie and Roman gathered the last of the materials, and I took charge of Guernsey, as the cow scarecrow had to return to her post outside Curds & Whey tomorrow. Arms full and Archie coasting on his skateboard, we headed down the alley with Buttercup trailing us. We came upon Hope at the alley door. She was dressed in ripped jeans, an off-the-shoulder sweater, and heels— definitely date attire.

"Hi, guys," she said. "I brought a couple of cranberry scones for you, Willa. I noticed you eyeing them in the bakery the other morning."

"Was I that obvious?" I laughed, taking the small paper bag from her. "That's really nice of you. Thanks."

"It's also kind of an apology for this morning—I hope I didn't make things awkward with you and Ms. Berns when she overheard us talking about her in front of the school."

"Don't worry, it was fine. In fact, she gave us some interesting information. We had no idea Lou from the market went to Sadler."

"I could've told you that," Hope said.

"You knew?"

"He was really nice to me when he found out I was going. He told me to finish and get my certificate no matter what. That was the thing he regretted—not finishing the program."

"I thought he was an alumnus. I know they've asked him for money to support the school."

"They send those flyers to anybody who goes to school there. I even started getting them already and it's only my first semester. Everybody says Olive Berns is a pit bull when it comes to fundraising."

"Did he say anything else to you about Sadler or Phoebe?"

She shook her head. "Not really. Lou's not much of a talker. I was surprised when he said what he did."

My arms were starting to itch from the scarecrow. "Thanks, Hope. You two go on. Roman and I can take this stuff inside."

"Are you sure?" Archie said.

"Go. We got it."

"Thanks." He handed off his armload to Roman and me, tucked his skateboard under his arm, and off they went.

Roman and I clumsily made our way into the stockroom with Buttercup at our feet.

"They're cute together. I'm glad they made dinner plans," I said, peeking around my armload of craft supplies to find my office.

"Speaking of dinner, do you want to grab some food before I spend the rest of the evening bottling mead?" Roman asked.

It sounded like a nice offer, but the mead was working its way through my system, and I was afraid I'd fall asleep in my soup. "Thanks for asking, but it's been such a crazy few days. I'm going to give myself a spa evening at home, watch *Rebecca*, and call it an early night."

"Who's Rebecca?"

"The movie *Rebecca*. Alfred Hitchcock?"

"I've never seen it."

"What? That's just a shame. I've seen it enough times for everybody."

"Well, you deserve to relax after what you've been through. You sure you're okay?"

I nodded. "Just tired. Rain check?"

"Of course."

I was relieved to drop everything I had on the old couch in my office. Floor space in the cramped, windowless room was at a premium. Roman had to reach around me to do the same. As he leaned across me, his chest briefly pressed into my back.

"Sorry," he mumbled. I could feel his breath on my ear.

The moment simultaneously paused time and passed in a flash. He stepped back and we moved out of the office into the roomier stockroom.

"There was something else I wanted to ask," he said. "Um . . ."

His eyes wouldn't meet mine at first. Was he still upset about the car incident? Was he going to be like Heath again and warn me one more time against investigating?

"Do you want to come with me to the harvest fair?" he finally asked.

It wasn't the question I'd expected. "Aren't we going together on the same float?" I answered without thought.

"Yes, but I mean, do you want to hang out together for the bonfire after we close our booths? Like a . . . you know, a date?"

A date? I tried to rearrange the surprised expression I knew would be apparent on my face before answering, "I'd love to."

"Great. Go enjoy your relaxing evening. I'll talk to you soon." He was back to his chill, confident self. He pushed open the door and left through the alley.

I suddenly felt lighter, like a hot air balloon lifting off, purely fueled by endorphins. Roman asked me out on a date. I hated to admit when Baz was right.

Baz. I sighed, disappointment dulling my previous elation. Would things continue to be awkward between us? Normally, I would've texted him right away with this new development. This time, I left my phone in my jeans pocket. He would've just berated me for declining dinner with Roman anyway. Maybe he'd be right again. Why didn't I say yes to dinner with Roman?

I situated my grandmother's knit throw on the couch in my office and Buttercup immediately jumped on it, re-arranging it some more to make himself comfortable. "I'll bring you back some dinner," I promised him, impulsively changing my mind about tonight's plans.

I walked through the stockroom and pushed open the side door, only to be stopped short by a figure looming in the shadows of the alley, blocking my way. A clipped scream escaped my throat.

CHAPTER 26

The figure shuffled to the side where the spotlight caught his face.

"Lou." I put my hand over my rapidly beating heart, my shock subsided. A thread of apprehension remained, however.

"Sorry, I was just about to buzz. I wasn't sure where to find you." He looked serious. Then again, Lou was not a smiler. "We need to talk."

Before I knew it, he'd sidestepped past me and continued inside. I followed after him, the door clunking closed behind me, reminding me too late that everybody else was out of reach. It was only Lou and me.

"What can I do for you, Lou?" I called to him, not wanting to walk much farther into the bowels of my stockroom alone with him.

"Is this your office?" I saw him paused in its doorway. He sounded a little incredulous.

I gave in and walked all the way in. His surprise made me reassess the cramped, cluttered room. Two boxes of Phoebe's latest book were stacked on the floor. Guernsey sat on my office chair while the couch was overtaken with my fake cheddar wheel and the rest of our float designs, plus our leftover materials. It didn't help that

Buttercup was turning the tissue paper I'd carelessly put within his reach into confetti.

"Let's go into the shop," I told Lou. I took the decorations I didn't want destroyed and transferred them to a shelf in the stockroom, not that Buttercup could've done much to make the recycled Styrofoam bleu cheese crumbles look any worse.

I led Lou out of the stockroom through the swinging door and switched on the lights to the kitchenette. I turned the dimmers up to high. This normally cozy space at the rear of my shop felt eerily isolated since I was alone with Lou. I kept ahold of my phone as we sat across from each other at the farm table. His short-sleeved buttoned white shirt was clean and crisp. I realized it was the first time I'd seen him without his market apron on.

"What's up?" I asked, my nerves simmering just beneath the surface. This wasn't a neighborly call.

He leaned forward and crossed his arms on the table. "I threw out the books," he said matter-of-factly.

Hearing him confess was still jarring, even though I had an inkling he'd done it. "Why?"

Sitting across from him, waiting for the confession he was working up to, I saw a vulnerable man I hadn't seen before. I looked past his perpetual scowl at his powder blue eyes, his broad nose, and skin still undamaged from the California sun. Mrs. Schultz was right—it was his demeanor that made him appear older.

"I despise people like Phoebe Winston," he began. "You know the ones—they don't work for anything. Success just falls into their lap. They draw people in and then feel entitled to take from them." He paused and looked toward the large windows at the front of my shop. "I was sweeping the sidewalk and saw her massive SUV pull behind the cars parked in front of our shops. I went over to tell her she can't block the customers in like that.

She had the nerve to tell her minion to 'keep her fans away.' A fan? She didn't even remember me! When they parked the car right in front of my place a little later, I went out to remind her I was no fan of hers. It was Archie who got out of the car, though. He carried a box of books to your shop and he left the trunk open. It was petty, I know, but taking those books and tossing them in the trash made me feel better. I don't regret doing it."

"What happened with Phoebe at school?"

His surprise was only apparent for a split second. "I suppose you've already heard or you wouldn't be asking."

"I'd like to hear it from you."

"We were in a class together my last semester there. She always acted real interested in what I was making. She'd compliment me, tell me she wished she could think of such clever dishes. When I told her what I'd be making for my final-exam meal, she said it sounded so good, she wished she could eat it. So I invited her over. I thought she looked up to me, like a father figure. I've never had that before. What she really wanted was to see how I made it. She was a quick study, I'll give her that. I don't think she wrote any of it down, but when it came time for class, she made the same thing. It was then I realized she'd been playing me all along."

"Is that why you left the program without finishing?"

"No. I told you my father had a heart attack." I noticed his fingers digging into his thin arms.

"Oh. Sorry," I mumbled. "Why did you decide to tell me the truth after all about taking the books?"

"It was bothering me that I lied to you. If she hadn't gotten herself killed, I would've proudly confessed to it. You can see how it looks bad under the circumstances."

"You should tell Detective Heath."

"Why? It doesn't have anything to do with her murder."

"He knows about the books. It ties up a loose end."

"You told him?" Lou growled.

I leaned away from him and gripped my phone tighter. "Yes. I wasn't trying to get anybody in trouble, but I thought he should know. It'll look better for you if you voluntarily go to him before he comes to you." I wanted Lou to feel we were on the same side.

"Why would he think it was me? Did you put that in his head?"

I swallowed hard. "No. They were in your dumpster, that's all. He's bound to question you and Carl about it." I didn't want to give him a heads-up about the emails Heath had from Olive Berns.

"Oh." He sat just as ramrod straight and his mouth was still in a grim line, but somehow I sensed he had eased ever so slightly. "I guess I'll go see him tomorrow."

He swung his legs over the bench and rose to leave. I followed him through the stockroom once more.

"Lou, since you sort of knew Phoebe from school, do you have an opinion on who killed her?"

"I have no idea. It's too bad, though. I would've enjoyed seeing her squirm after those photos were published. Kudos to A. J."

"How did you know A. J. took the pictures?"

"They're in the paper he runs, weren't they? He's the only one there who'd do such a thing. She was due for some karma, but not the kind she got. I hated her but I didn't wish her dead."

I was glad to hear him say it, but I still felt much better after he left and I heard the satisfying clunk of the door as it closed behind him.

Lou had no problem admitting his distaste for Phoebe, which coincided with the emails he sent to Olive at Sadler Culinary. But why confess to me? Was it because he felt bad, like he said, or did he want to make sure I didn't suspect him? Did he want me to stop asking questions the way the threatening note said?

I felt Buttercup scamper under my feet. The sound of

the door must've startled him. He could've really used a bell on that fancy collar of his so as not to get stepped on or tripped over.

"I promised you dinner. Let's go home."

Roman was probably already nose deep in mead by now, so I went back to my original plan of pampering myself. It would come as no surprise to anyone who knew me that a spa evening didn't come in the form of a bubble bath. For me, cheese was the direct route to relaxation. I popped back into the shop for a tea-rubbed variety I'd recently acquired from a creamery in Utah. Made from Jersey cows' milk, creamy Teahive was perfect for a little nosh. I'd slice the citrusy fragrant cheese onto one of the cranberry scones Hope had brought me from Rise and Shine bakery. Dollops of marmalade would complete the delicious snack.

The autumn chill left me yearning for a steaming cup of Earl Grey tea to go along with my cheese-topped scone, as Buttercup and I made the quick walk to my apartment. The anticipation of sitting with my satisfying treat while watching *Rebecca* for the umpteenth time was just what this cheesemonger ordered.

The spotlight clicked on as soon as we climbed the stairs, allowing me a good look at the float. The few items we'd secured on there were still intact. As I crested the stairs, I noted Buttercup's bag of food and toys in the corner of the deck next to the door of my apartment. My internal happy dance halted. It looked like Baz hadn't softened his stance. Buttercup sniffed the bag as I unlocked my door.

"Willa!"

Startled, I turned to see Thomas at the bottom of the stairs. He marched up, uninvited.

"Buttercup." He picked him up. Buttercup seemed much more amenable to being held by a sober Thomas. "You still have him."

"What did you expect me to do with him? Are you here to take him?"

"Well, no."

"So what *are* you doing here?" I quickly recalled he wasn't aware that I still considered him a possible suspect. We'd parted on good terms. Keeping myself in his good graces might be for the best, so I changed my tone. "Did things go okay at the police station?"

"That's what I wanted to talk to you about," he said.

We stood awkwardly at the door. Buttercup barked to get inside.

"Come on in, I guess. Can you grab that bag?"

I allowed Thomas into my apartment, which I supposed was only fair since Baz and I had barged into his hotel room. Then again, there wasn't a possibility that I was a murderer.

CHAPTER 27

Thomas followed me and Buttercup inside my apartment.

"I have company coming," I told him just in case he was planning something nefarious that the protection of a five-pound fluffball and a flashy betta fish couldn't handle. "What did you want to talk about?" I opened a can of dog food for Buttercup and looked longingly at my Teahive cheese. I'd really be earning my relaxing evening.

He put Buttercup down and said, "I told Detective Heath everything I told you about that night, but he's not letting me go back home. He says I'm still a person of interest."

"Think of it this way. You're helping him put the pieces of the puzzle together. The sooner he figures it out, the sooner you'll get to go home." *Or to prison, whichever fits.*

Thomas made himself comfortable on the love seat. I fed Loretta and sat not so comfortably on the chair beside him. Thomas didn't look satisfied with my answer.

"What do you want me to do about it?" I was trying to be nice, but I could feel my relaxing evening watching *Rebecca* slipping away. I needed to practice the Mrs. Danvers staredown.

"I wanted to know if you figured something out. You're the one asking questions, right?"

The note from A. J.'s car flashed in my mind. *STOP ASKING QUESTIONS.* All thoughts of my cheese-and-movie night disappeared.

"I came up empty," I said. It was only a half lie. I had a lot of information, but none of it led anywhere definitive.

"Maybe I can help."

"I'm leaving it up to Detective Heath." I wasn't about to share information with Thomas. He might've given A. J. the address to Phoebe's house so he'd take those pictures. He was still one of my top suspects regardless of his willingness to go to the police.

"You think it's me, don't you?" he said.

"Noooo," I replied, exaggerating the point too much. Gosh, I was a bad liar.

"Listen, I didn't kill her. I know how that sounds. What else would I say, right? But I didn't. I was probably one of the only people who lov—," he coughed, ". . . liked her. I'm going stir-crazy at the inn. I need to do *something* to help resolve this," he pleaded.

I could never be sure how much of what Thomas told me was the truth, but I did believe that he loved Phoebe. Whether it contributed to her demise, I was still uncertain. There was something I could use his help with, however.

"Maybe you could help me with this. You said you didn't know anything about a stalker, but Archie recognized this guy." I grabbed my phone and brought up my photos. "This man sent a picture to Phoebe. Maybe you've seen him before." I showed Thomas the photo Archie had sent me. "Do you recognize him at all?"

Thomas took my phone to get a better look at the photo. "Sure. That's Jeremy, her old assistant I told you about."

"That's Jeremy?"

He studied the photo again. "Where was this taken? We weren't allowed to have our own social media."

"Really?" That explained why I couldn't find Thomas's picture on the internet.

"She didn't want us posting something that could look bad for her by association, so it was radio silence for us," he explained.

"This one's from Sadler at one of their open houses. Olive Berns said it was after Phoebe finished *Fire It Up* when she was first becoming famous."

"That makes sense. That's when he started working for her."

I had to forget about the stalker angle and pivot my thoughts to Jeremy as a strong suspect. "Jeremy couldn't have left under good circumstances like Phoebe told you. Archie said she seemed freaked out by his picture and wanted Archie to throw it out."

"I don't know why she'd act that way. She wasn't upset when he left. She seemed happy for him that he found a better job. She said it was probably for the best now that she had me."

"I know you don't want to believe it, Thomas, but I think she lied to you about why he left."

Thomas, looking confused, wiped his glasses with the hem of his shirt before replacing them and answering, "I don't know. Everything's starting to look a little different now that she's been gone. I guess it's possible. I've been thinking about it since we talked this afternoon. She might've not wanted to be associated with him because of his past."

"What about his past?"

"He told me once that he used to have a substance abuse problem. It started when he was a teenager. His mom remarried a few times, so he didn't have a stable childhood. His latest stepdad wanted to ship him off to a military school, so he ran away and never went back. He got into drugs, but when I met him, he'd been clean for years."

"Did he keep it a secret from Phoebe?"

"No, it wasn't a secret. She knew about it."

"Hadn't he been working for her for a while, though? Why would it suddenly bother her?"

"This was her second chance. Things were finally starting to happen for her again and I remember she was very particular about nothing tainting her new image. You'd think I was applying for the CIA by the way she looked into my past before she hired me."

I thought about the possible scenario. "Jeremy was with her through her first success and stayed by her side during her downfall. Then he helped her rebuild her image and right as she's peaking again, he's replaced by you."

"I never saw myself as replacing him."

"I'm not blaming you, Thomas. I'm just saying if that's what happened, he could've been very angry about it."

"Jeremy didn't have a temper. He was a nice guy. I don't think he'd come back three years later to kill her."

"So then tell me this. Why did he send her his picture with 'Remember me' written on it?"

"That's a good question."

It was one I needed answered.

I finally got Thomas to leave, but I was no longer hungry for my fun snack. That didn't keep me from making and eating my Teahive and marmalade scone, however. Eating cheese was a tonic—it had little to do with hunger. I let the creamy cheese and crumbly scone soothe me as I searched for information about Phoebe's first assistant on the internet but came up with nothing. With Buttercup on the love seat at my feet, I sipped hot, fragrant Earl Grey tea as I worked out in my head the possibility of Jeremy being involved in Phoebe's murder.

Something must've happened between Phoebe and him, something she didn't even tell Thomas. Perhaps he'd been stewing these last three years about it and finally decided to take his revenge. The only thing I couldn't work out was that he didn't seem to be involved in her take-down before her murder. Thomas was the one who brought Phoebe the barbeque ribs, and A. J. was the one who took the pictures. Was it all just coincidence that those things happened before she was to be murdered?

I studied the photo on my phone again. This was Phoebe's former assistant, possible stalker, and now my number one suspect. I texted Heath.

Rebecca was still in my DVD player from the last time I watched it, so I turned it on and waited for Heath's return text. Buttercup was now nestled in the crook of my bent knees. The two of us were the perfect size for my love seat. I felt a little guilty leaving Loretta on her island stool. I usually brought her over to the wide bench I used as my coffee table so we could watch TV together, but I didn't know how Buttercup would react to her being within his reach. I'd bring Buttercup to Chet tomorrow, and Loretta and I would go back to movie snuggling, such as it was with a fish. I had to admit, having a cute ball of fur resting on me was nice, too, but I wasn't up for the responsibility of a dog. It served as a reminder that I wasn't ready for marriage or children. Friends and cheese were all I needed, at least for now. And maybe a date with a cute meadery owner. It also wouldn't hurt to have a detective who took my suspicions seriously, but Heath never returned my text.

CHAPTER 28

Mrs. Schultz and Archie usually came to work a few minutes before we opened, but this morning they were both in early. I think we were all eager to get back to our routine to feel the comfort of normalcy. I'd wanted Archie to take as much time off as he needed, but it was sure good to have him back.

Since we had some extra time, I decided today's samples would include some more autumn comfort food. We tried our hand at another beer cheese, this time in soup form.

By the time I placed Guernsey outside to greet customers, the aroma of cooked onions, carrots, and celery had begun permeating the air until the Yuengling was added, and the beer's malty aroma overrode the root vegetables. We boiled out the alcohol before cooking it with chicken stock, Worcestershire sauce, and Dijon mustard. After blending in the milk, Archie added the most important ingredient—the cheese. He was excited to use the immersion blender to mix in the extra sharp cheddar so it would be nice and smooth. Mrs. Schultz typed up the recipe and cut the printouts into cards as Archie and I finished making the beer-cheese soup before customers arrived.

"I have some promising news. It's about the guy in Archie's photo," I said, as I grated smoked Gouda to add an extra depth of flavor to the cheddar base.

"The stalker?" Archie replied expectantly, looking up from the pot of soup.

"He's Phoebe's former assistant, Jeremy."

Archie and Mrs. Schultz took a minute to digest the news.

"We have to tell Detective Heath," Archie said. With his free hand, he reached into the pocket of his cargo shorts for his phone.

"I already texted him about it last night."

"What's Jeremy's last name? We can look him up on the internet," he suggested.

"I tried already and couldn't find him anywhere. Thomas doesn't know his last name. He said she didn't allow them to have their own social media pages, but it occurred to me this morning that maybe Jeremy was on hers."

"I already tried looking for him on her Instagram before I found his picture in Olive Berns's office. There was nothing."

I peeked into the soup pot. The cheese was melted and fully integrated with the rest of the ingredients. I carefully carried it to the front sample counter where I poured the warm soup into the waiting crockpot.

Even as Mrs. Schultz gathered the recipe cards and rounded up paper cups for customers to sample the soup, her mind was still on the investigation. "She might've deleted any photos of him if there was bad blood between them," she said. "Do you want me to clean that?" She offered, referring to the pot.

"Sure, but first . . ." I took three plastic spoons from under the sample counter. There was beer-cheese soup that hadn't made it out of the pot.

The velvety soup hit my tongue and cascaded down

my throat, packing all of its rich, smoky goodness into one spoonful. We all went in for a second round before Mrs. Schultz took the pot to the sink.

I remained at the counter and took out my laptop. "Maybe now that we know who we're looking for, we'll spot him. It won't hurt to look again. We have to go back a few years, at least."

I opened my laptop and found Phoebe's Instagram page. It took Archie quite a bit of time to scroll back that far, but once he did, we skimmed the pages.

"I don't see any of him," Archie confirmed. "None of Thomas, either."

"I shouldn't be surprised that her ego wouldn't allow her to share the spotlight with her personal assistants."

"Do you think Detective Heath will go after Jeremy as a suspect?" Archie's eyes were scared and hopeful all at once.

As if saying his name aloud summoned him, the well-dressed detective walked through our front door.

"What are you doing here?" I closed my laptop and stowed it under the counter. I wasn't in the mood to be polite if he was here for Archie again, who'd suddenly gone a shade paler than he already was, which made him almost translucent.

"I got your text," Heath said to me.

I heard Archie release a breath. Mrs. Schultz joined us at the front counter, still holding the kitchen towel she used to dry the soup pot.

"Let's talk in the back," he said to me, as if I wasn't going to tell Archie and Mrs. Schultz everything verbatim.

I led Heath to the kitchenette, and we sat side by side on the farm table bench, our knees accidentally touching as we shifted to face each other.

The last time I'd been this close to him, we were dancing together at The Cellar. The memory of that night last spring accelerated my heartbeat. I put a little more space between us.

I wondered how he always looked this put together no matter what time of day I saw him. A five-o'clock shadow made an appearance on his strong chin eventually, but he always started out clean-shaven, as he was this morning. No matter how many hours he put in on the job, his thick, jet-black hair was always in place and his suit was never rumpled. He laid his hands on his thighs—even his nails looked better manicured than mine. I also noticed he was no longer wearing his wedding band. Was he finally healing from his wife's death?

He leaned in, jolting me out of my thoughts. He kept his voice low. "Thanks for telling me about the books. We interviewed Lou and he admitted to throwing them out."

I nodded. No sense in telling Heath that I'd had a visit from him too. "You think he's involved any further than that?"

"We're still keeping him on our radar. Ginger too."

"So they don't have alibis," I deduced.

That poker face was back, but I didn't need confirmation. If he was still considering them suspects, then I must be right. I moved on.

"What did you find out about the information I gave you last night?" I asked.

"We've looked into it and there's nothing to pursue any further."

"What do you mean? You think it's a coincidence Jeremy used to work for her, left under suspicious circumstances, sends her his photo which freaks her out, and then she's killed? You're just going to ignore that?"

Heath hesitated. "He's got an alibi." Before I could react, he finished, "And I'm only sharing this information with you so you understand that a lot of our police work is behind the scenes. Just because you don't think you see us investigating, doesn't mean we're not. Understand what I'm saying?"

"Yes, I understand."

"Good." He nodded, satisfied.

I echoed the nod in agreement. Now that we understood each other, I waited, but nothing else was forthcoming.

"So that's it? That's all you're going to tell me?" I asked.

"Yeah. Jeremy's not a suspect at this time."

"You once told me not to rely too heavily on alibis."

"This one's airtight."

"But you're not going to say what it is? I was the one who handed him to you."

"I appreciate that and, as I said, we looked into it. Can you trust me for once?"

That was a good question. I'd leave this one in his hands, but I wasn't ready to give up entirely. "Have you found out anything about A. J.'s car?"

"We had the brakes looked at. They're in excellent condition and work perfectly fine."

"How is that possible? I know he was trying to stop the car."

"Are you positive he was hitting the brake?"

I thought back on the incident and realized I couldn't be sure. "It all happened so fast."

"It's possible your adrenaline filled in the blanks to what he was telling you was happening."

"Do you think he was faking it to take the heat off himself? That's pretty risky."

"It might not have been too risky until you hit the emergency brake."

"I didn't realize it would go into a skid. But you're right. He might've been pretending to be out of control until I did that. That would mean he planted the note himself too. We could've been killed! What an awful thing to do."

"There is one other possibility. It could've been re-motely tampered with."

"What do you mean?"

"Someone could've been anywhere and controlled the car through a computer. All they needed was to know your GPS coordinates. If someone knew where you were going, they could find the car and hack the brakes."

"But how?"

"That type of car has digital features—it enables phone calls, Wi-Fi hotspots, navigation features . . . all of it leaves the car vulnerable to possibly being hacked. It's a long shot—someone's really got to know what they're doing—but it is a possibility."

"How will you know for sure?"

"We can't. There's no black box to tell us what was happening in the car's computer system. So it's only a guess."

"Unbelievable. So we'll never know if A. J. was fak-ing it or if someone really targeted us?"

"We're still having the car checked out to see how likely it is. It's an older model, so we're looking into whether the software was updated to match the newer models that have stronger security."

The thought that the car was hacked was even more frightening than A. J. being behind it. For once I was glad to own an old car with none of the digital bells and whistles.

"If hacking a car is possible, then couldn't someone do that with the surveillance camera at Phoebe's rental house? That's used through her phone," I said.

"After speaking with the owners, there's another more likely scenario. They never bothered to change the ac-count password, which they gave to every person they've rented to."

"You're kidding."

"Since the password was only for the camera, and didn't

control opening the gate or the doors, they didn't think it was a big deal. They figured renters would delete the app with the owner's access code when they left, so there was no point in changing the password every time."

"So that means . . ."

"Everyone who rented from them could've had access to the recordings and deleted the last one."

"Great."

"We're working through the list they gave us to see if any names have a connection to Phoebe. The good news is, they used to live in the house full time and have only been renting it for a year."

"There's nobody obvious on that list, then? None of our suspects?"

"Nobody we have our eye on. It's going to take some time."

"That means there's still nothing definitive."

"Not yet, but we're getting there."

My mind spun like a slot machine with all the suspects names landing in a row: Lou, Ginger, A. J., Thomas. I still didn't know what they found out about Jeremy. I couldn't seem to get enough evidence against even one of them.

"What do we do now?" I asked Heath.

"*We* don't do anything. You didn't get that information about Jeremy by staying out of things like we talked about, did you?"

"I didn't seek out Thomas. He came to my apartment last night uninvited."

"You think that makes me feel better?"

I had no retort. I walked him to the door and we stood outside my shop. At least my window-box chrysanthemums bounced back after the crushing they got from Thomas yesterday—the only good news of the morning. Not only was my best suspect Jeremy a bust, but Heath was annoyed with me again.

"You'll be happy to know I'm out of leads, anyway," I told him.

"Good. I'm sure you can keep yourself busy with the harvest fair coming up. Looks like you've got a scarecrow to finish."

He walked away before I even had time to defend Guernsey.

CHAPTER 29

I returned inside and filled Archie and Mrs. Schultz in on what Heath had just told me, or rather, anything they missed while they were eavesdropping. Apparently, someone else wanted in on the conversation too—Buttercup nosed his way through the stockroom door. I picked him up and he got pets from all of us.

"I don't blame you, little guy. It's time to take you to the meadery so you can have more fun," I told the amiable furball.

"Baz is okay with Chet watching Buttercup?" Archie asked, letting Buttercup lick his cheek.

"I haven't told him yet. We had a little tiff yesterday."

"You and Basil? About what?" Mrs. Schultz sounded surprised.

"I wanted him to talk to Ginger about her relationship with Phoebe, but he's got a crush on her, so he refuses to consider her a suspect."

"Having love goggles on can be dangerous," Mrs. Schultz observed.

"I know. I don't want him getting hurt or be in danger if she ends up being the murderer. Last time I talked to Chet about Ginger, he told me she didn't want to talk about Phoebe, but I wonder if that changed last night after Chet got back from the police station."

"Are you going to ask him about it?" Mrs. Schultz asked skeptically.

"Since I'm bringing Buttercup over anyway, I'll try to bring it up. I may have to butter him up first."

"You mean cheese him up?" Archie lifted the lid of the crockpot.

"Good idea. Get me a container of that for Chet and I'll get Buttercup's food and toys from the back."

I thought poor Buttercup ought to have a doggie suitcase for all the resettling he was having to do. I hoped he was appreciated in whatever home he ended up in. He never complained as long as he was in the middle of the action.

Once I gathered the dog's things and the soup, I crossed the street with Buttercup. A man was lurking by the front door with an Oakland A's cap pulled low over his eyes. He hissed my name as soon as I neared, startling me.

It was A. J. He wasn't wearing his usual jacket and I'd never seen him with a hat on. His dark locks curled around it.

"Oh, jeez, A. J. You scared me."

He glanced quickly up and down the sidewalk, pausing to stare suspiciously at a couple who emerged from the consignment shop and a woman wheeling a stroller up the block. "I saw that detective at your shop. Did he say anything about my car?" he said under his breath.

"Like what?"

"Like they found evidence of who tried to kill us." He whispered the word *kill* and pushed the stiff bill of his baseball cap even farther down.

"He said they're still looking into it."

"That's it?"

I couldn't tell if he was paranoid about the thought that someone tried to kill him or that he might get caught lying about someone trying to kill him. He was making a good show of trying to be incognito, however.

"Come on, give me something," he pleaded. "Quid pro quo."

"Last time we did this, you lied to me."

"That was about information you gave me about the house. The information I shared with you was the truth."

"Semantics."

I tried to push past him, but he blocked my path and said rapidly, "I'll go first then. Remember Phoebe's first assistant you told me about? The one who left and wasn't heard from again?"

I halted. "Jeremy? What did you find out?" I had to know what Heath wouldn't tell me.

"Quid pro quo?"

I growled at him under my breath. "Fine, yes. What do you know about Jeremy?"

"His full name is Jeremy Jillcott. He's in rehab in Austin, Texas. It's one of those intensive in-patient treatment facilities where they're not allowed to come and go or have visitors for the first ninety days. He's been there for the last two months."

"How did you find out all this? I couldn't find anything on him."

"As a journalist, I pride myself on having more research skills than a cheesemonger. Anyway, he's a dead end as a suspect."

Disappointment shot through me. Heath was right—airtight alibi. This explained why he was no longer Phoebe's assistant and why Thomas couldn't find him. He must've relapsed.

"So?" A. J. said.

"So what?"

"Where's my quid pro quo? What did the detective say about my car?"

"I told you. He said they're still looking into it."

"Come on. I see how you two are together. He must've shared some information with you."

"What do you mean 'how we are together'?" Now I was the one eyeing the sidewalk, hoping no one was listening in.

"I'm a journalist. I observe people. You two stand very close to each other. I've seen you talking low with your heads together. There's some kind of relationship going on there."

I sputtered in protest, "Th-There's no relationship."

"Hey, that's your business, I just want to know about mine."

"You want a tip?" I said, getting his full attention. He leaned in as I whispered, "You might want to take the price tag off your hat." I flicked the white tag dangling on the side of his cap.

He grabbed it from his head and pulled on the tag until it snapped off, then adjusted the cap again, pulling it even farther over his brow if that was possible. Huffy, he walked off without another word to me and not even a pat for Buttercup. I shrugged it off, half hoping he'd run into a lamppost with that silly cap covering his eyes.

I paused at the door to the meadery. I needed to get Chet to talk to me, but I was already feeling bad that he'd gotten sucked into being questioned by the police because I'd ratted out A. J. Now I was going to ask for another favor. Was my beer-cheese soup delicious enough to get him to confide in me after all that?

The tinkling of a small bell on the door announced my arrival with Buttercup and soup in hand, hoping one of them would soften Chet. The Golden Glen Meadery had an industrial feel with its poured-concrete floors, painted gray beams, and exposed brick. The starkness of it was sure to draw a customer's focus to the hardwood shelves of translucent sleek mead bottles in a spectrum of golden hues and flavors from crisp pear nectar to a deeper blackcurrant.

The meadery was quiet, just Roman and Chet in the

shop. I was glad to see Chet smile alongside Roman when I entered, although it might've been at the sight of Buttercup. It was hard not to smile at the dog.

"He's here. I hope it's a good time," I announced.

Chet came over and took him from my arms. Buttercup's back end wagged excitedly, so that he almost fell out of Chet's arms. I told myself he must have a preference for men, so as not to feel slighted. I set down his bag of food and toys.

"You must've been reading my mind," Roman said. "I was about to come and see you. We're having a tasting tomorrow and I need to order a cheese platter for it." Then he leaned in and said more quietly, "And I wanted an excuse to see you."

"You never need one," I replied.

It looked like I'd surprised him as much as myself with that answer. Eyebrows raised, he nodded. "Noted."

"I hope it's still okay that Chet watches Buttercup until we can figure out a more permanent situation."

"He'll be great for business as long as he stays out of the tasting room," Roman said.

"I even bought a doggie bed for him," Chet said pointing to a cushy one next to the register.

Roman noticed the bowl of soup in my hand. "You came bearing food too?"

"Don't get too excited. This is actually for Chet."

"For me?" Chet put Buttercup down and let him explore the shop.

"It's beer-cheese soup. I hope you like it," I said.

"I'm sure I will. But why?"

"I'm sorry I dragged you into the nonsense with A. J. yesterday. I feel bad that I accused you of being in on the lie with A. J. and that you were questioned by the police."

Chet scoffed and accepted the soup. "It wasn't your fault. A. J.'s the one who took the pictures and lied about it."

"I hope I didn't make it worse by mentioning it to Ginger. I happened to run into her when I got back and I thought she would've known since you'd been texting her in the car before it happened."

"Yeah, I kinda didn't tell her because I didn't want to worry her."

"Oops. Sorry."

"It's not your fault. I'm learning she can be a little high-strung."

A bell jangled, but I paid it no attention. "What did Ginger say about it?"

"About what?" a voice behind me asked.

I turned to see Ginger had entered the meadery.

Awkward.

"Hi, Ginger. I didn't know you were there," I said, plastering a smile on my face.

"Obviously. You know, Willa, if you have something to ask me, you can do it directly. You don't need to go through Chet." Her high ponytail bounced as she approached us in a denim miniskirt and a Read More Bookstore & Café T-shirt, carrying a small paper sack. She handed it to Chet. "I brought you lunch." She noticed the container in his hand. "What's that?"

"It's soup. Willa brought it for me."

I was *definitely* not getting in her good graces now.

"You're right," I said to her. "I should've talked to you directly. Do you think we can do that now?"

"You can talk in my tasting room," Roman offered, striding to the back of his shop and sliding the barn door open for us. I loved having him on my side.

I could sense Ginger's reluctance, but she allowed herself to be shuffled into the room. He turned on the lights and shut the door behind us. She finally took a seat in one of the leather chairs.

"Why are you asking Chet and Baz about me?" she

said before I even fully sat down on the sofa across from her.

"Baz?" Did Baz tell her I suspected her?

"He was asking me questions about Phoebe last night. Now that you're here asking Chet about me, I figured you must've also told Baz to get what he could on me."

I couldn't help but be happy that Baz asked her even after our argument, but I didn't want it to get in the way of his budding friendship with her—if she wasn't a murderer, that is.

"No, I didn't. I'm sure Baz was just making conversation," I lied. It was for a good cause. "You've known Phoebe the longest out of anybody around here, so I just had more questions about her."

"I told you, I haven't talked to her in years. We went to school together and then went our separate ways. People do that, you know. I'm not friends with everybody I knew at UCLA, either, and I was there for just as long."

"But when you heard Phoebe wanted to see you, Chet said—" I stopped myself, but not in time. Ginger's deep-set eyes narrowed. Uh-oh. I was going to owe Chet a lot more than beer-cheese soup. "Believe me, Chet didn't know why I was asking when he said you seemed angry with her and didn't want to see her."

Ginger sighed and looked away.

Had I been too direct? I seemed to play bad cop even when I didn't intend to.

She looked back to me. "Fine. We didn't go in on a café together after culinary school because she kept telling me there was no money in going vegan. She'd changed her plans without letting me know and tried out for that reality show. Now here she is, a few years later, branding herself as the vegan queen. So you're right, I didn't jump at the chance to see her when she came to town."

"I don't blame you for not wanting to reunite with her, especially if she stole some of your recipes?"

"How—? What makes you say that?"

"I saw the stinging nettles recipes in her first cookbook, and Lou said you taught her a lot about vegan cooking."

"Lou said?" She forced a laugh. "He's probably trying to cover for himself. He was the one who dropped out of Sadler because of her."

"It wasn't because of his dad's heart attack?"

"No. That happened months later."

"Are you sure?"

"Positive. I remember because I heard about it at the market after I was already living here. Personally, I think he was too embarrassed to go back because he'd allowed her to charm him like that. He felt like a fool, but almost every guy reacted to Phoebe that way. I mean, you saw her. Phoebe got all the attention from students and teachers."

"Even more than you?" I'd noticed how Chet and Roman both seemed to appreciate her lithe figure when she walked into the meadery.

"I don't have what Phoebe had. It wasn't just about her looks. She made everyone feel they wanted to please her to be a part of her inner circle. But once you were in it, it was more like you were in her web." She looked off past me and I could tell her thoughts were far from the tasting room.

"Why didn't you stand up for Lou?"

"I didn't know who stole from who. It was only later—" She cut herself off.

"When she stole some of your grandmother's recipes?"

"I have to get back to the café." Ginger left the chair, then turned when she got to the door. "And to answer the question I know you want to ask, no, I didn't murder

Phoebe Winston." She used both hands to slide open the barn door and walked out.

I guess I shouldn't have expected her to be any less defensive about herself than she was. She never admitted Phoebe stole those recipes from her grandmother, but I had a good indication. It was a shame Phoebe seemed to use all her good qualities to take advantage of others.

That was quite a revelation about Lou. He and Ginger didn't mind pointing the finger at each other. As far as I was concerned, it meant I couldn't trust either of them.

CHAPTER 30

I sat for another minute to make sure I wouldn't run into Ginger on my way out of the meadery. Roman came into the tasting room.

"How'd it go?" he asked.

"Is she gone?"

"Yup. She wasn't too happy with Chet."

"I didn't mean to get him into trouble with her. I'm not her favorite person."

He sat on the sofa next to me. "Do you really think it's her?"

"I don't know. It could be her or Thomas or Lou . . ."

"Lou? From the market?"

"It's a long story. Then there's A. J."

"Wait a minute. Didn't someone clip his brakes and threaten you two?"

"It's complicated. For a minute there it looked like it was going to be Phoebe's old assistant, but he's got an ironclad alibi."

"What made you think it was him?"

"There was a picture." My mind zeroed in on Archie's story about the picture.

"Willa?"

"There was a picture and now there's not."

"You've lost me."

"His name is Jeremy Jillcott. He has an alibi but maybe . . ."

"I know that look, Willa. The wheels in your mind are spinning."

"I thought his alibi cleared him, but maybe he got someone else to kill her or someone killed her on his behalf. There was a photo he sent to Phoebe, but it disappeared and was never collected into evidence. I'd be willing to write Jeremy off, except where did the picture go?"

I took out my phone and retrieved the picture I had of Jeremy Jillcott. "Do you remember seeing this guy around any time last week before Phoebe's event? Or anybody who looks like him? Thomas says he has a brother and sister."

Roman studied it. "I can't say that I have, but I might not remember him if I did. Sorry I'm not more helpful."

We leaned back on the couch together shoulder to shoulder. It was the first time I was this close to him without a zing going through me. It felt comfortable, which was a nice feeling too.

"You're helpful just by being here," I said. A slow smile crept over his face and before I knew it, the zing was back. It was the only explanation for my ensuing outburst. "Do you want to go for dinner later?"

"I'd love to, but I'm going to the new warehouse tonight to check it out. The one I told you about in Penngrove?"

"Oh right. That's exciting. I hope it works out for you."

"Rain check?"

"We're piling up the rain checks."

"That's okay. Winter's just around the corner and it's our rainy season," he said with a wink.

"We've got the fair this weekend."

"Yes, we do," he said, his eyes never leaving mine.

A series of yips popped our romantic bubble and

alerted us to Buttercup just before he ran down the stairs to see what he was missing. Chet charged in after him.

"I'm sorry. He seems to know this is the only place he's not allowed." Chet scooped him up.

"We'll keep the door closed when we can," Roman said, unfazed.

Feeling much better, I said goodbye to Roman and Chet, and walked back to Curds & Whey. I recognized Baz's stocky frame in his Carl's Hardware T-shirt and loose-fitting jeans as he leaned over the sampling counter. He was talking beer-cheese soup with a customer while Archie and Mrs. Schultz rang up the older woman's purchase.

"I can't wait to make it when I get home. Earl's going to love it," the woman said. She waved to them and passed me with a smile on her way out the door.

"Basil, you're an excellent salesman, if you're ever thinking of changing professions," Mrs. Schultz said to Baz. As his former high school teacher, she was the only one allowed to call him by his full name, if you didn't count his mother.

"I'd get too stir-crazy having to stay in one place, but I do like the perks." He ladled himself another sample of soup.

"You do realize there's another cheese besides cheddar in there," I warned him. Slowly but surely, I'd been introducing his provincial palate to a wider array of cheeses, determined to broaden his cheese horizons.

"The beer compensates," he answered. "I was waiting for you."

"What's up?" I hoped Ginger hadn't just told him about our conversation. We weren't on the best of terms as it was.

"Can we talk?" he asked me.

"We got it covered," Archie said, referring to the shop. There were a few customers milling about.

"Thanks," I replied. I led Baz through the stockroom door and into my office.

I sat on the arm of my old leather sofa that took up any extra space the cramped office might've had. He plopped himself in my desk chair and swiveled it to face me.

"I'm sorry," we said in unison.

I couldn't help but smile. Hard feelings with Baz were impossible to harbor.

"I shouldn't have put you in that spot by insisting you question Ginger," I said. "I hope I didn't ruin anything between you two."

"Don't worry about that. Why didn't you tell me about A. J.'s brakes going out and the threat? I heard it from one of my clients. It's all over town already. You could've been killed."

"Maybe. Maybe not."

"What do you mean?"

"Heath thinks A. J. could've been faking it to move suspicion off himself."

"Wow. What do *you* think?"

"I don't know. It looked like he was pumping the brakes and he did seem really freaked out, but we know he's capable of lying since he made up all that stuff about how he got the photos. Heath says it's possible the brakes could've been tampered with remotely."

"Like a hacker?"

"Yeah. He says it's a long shot, but possible."

"Someone would have to be a computer engineer or something to do that."

A computer engineer. Didn't Ginger say she was an engineering major at UCLA before she went to culinary school? I wondered what kind of engineering she majored in, but I wasn't about to ask Baz if he knew anything about it after we'd just made up.

"Our suspect list doesn't seem to be getting shorter," he said, as my suspicions about Ginger ignited again.

"Nope." It was good to have Baz back as my partner in crime solving. "Oh, and I solved the mystery of the books that were dumped. It was Lou." I went on to explain to a surprised Baz about Lou's former relationship with Phoebe and what he had to say about Ginger. "So that's why I suspected Ginger, but guess what Ginger just told me." I proceeded to fill him in on Lou dropping out of school because of Phoebe, which he had lied to me about.

"No wonder this place is a mess. You got a lot going on." Baz scanned the disarray my office was in.

"I do, but this office is Buttercup's fault."

"Where is Bruiser, anyway?"

"Mrs. Schultz and Archie didn't tell you? I brought him to the meadery. Chet said he would take care of him."

"Oh." Baz crossed his arms over his chest.

"I told you about Chet, remember? And then you gave him to me, so I thought you'd be fine with it."

"Yeah, of course it's fine. I couldn't take him to all my appointments anyway, so it's better this way." His drooping bottom lip told me he felt otherwise.

"You can always go visit him, you know."

Baz guffawed. "I don't need to visit a dog."

"Suit yourself, but he *is* right across the street."

"Does Chet know how he likes his dry food mixed in with the wet? Did you give him the squeaky blue toy? That's his favorite. Maybe I'll stop by just to be sure."

"Good idea."

We left the office and stockroom and walked into the shop together.

"Are you two best buds again?" Mrs. Schultz asked from the checkout counter she was tidying.

"Never stopped," Baz said, hooking my neck in his arm for a hug that was more like a wrestling move.

"I appreciate the love, but less is more." I wriggled out of his friendly embrace.

"Now that the team's back together, we can solve this thing," Archie said. It was the first time in days I'd seen him back to his optimistic self.

I didn't want to bring him down again, but I had to be realistic. "I'd like to think so, but our suspect list is longer than ever."

"Did Heath find out anything about the stalker?" Baz asked.

I told him about Jeremy, and we mulled over the possibilities of the vanishing photo to no conclusion.

"Thomas talked a little about Jeremy when we walked to the police station yesterday, but nothing that we didn't already know," Mrs. Schultz said.

"There's another angle the police are following." I let Baz in on what Heath told me about how the owners never changed the password to the surveillance camera access, so anyone who'd rented that house could've erased the footage.

"Can we get a list of who rented the house?" he asked.

"Heath says they're working through it. There were no obvious suspects on the list, so they're checking everyone for any kind of connection to Phoebe. But it's a long list."

"Great." Archie's excitement dissipated.

"It sounds like we have to be patient and let Detective Heath do the legwork on this," Mrs. Schultz said.

We all agreed, but my mind was still ticking off possibilities. Patience was not my strong suit.

CHAPTER 31

Baz went back to work, and we stayed busy with customers as the day wore on. We ran out of beer-cheese soup and made a late second batch so the three of us could each steal a bowl of it at closing time.

"I hope you remembered I can't stay tonight to do the float," Mrs. Schultz said afterward as she began to count the stock of refrigerated cheeses. "It's poker night."

"I did. No worries. Roman has to meet with someone out of town, so I already decided to cancel it for tonight. You're hosting, aren't you? Why don't you leave now? Archie and I can handle the closing ourselves, right Archie?"

"No problem. You filled in for me this weekend, Mrs. Schultz." Archie held out his hand for her to relinquish the inventory sheet.

"Go on, Mrs. Schultz. Have fun," I urged.

"Okay. I appreciate it. There's always so much to do before they come," Mrs. Schultz said.

She gave the clipboard to Archie then swapped her apron for her windbreaker before scooting out the front door. I relocked it behind her.

"Could we work on the float tonight anyway?" Archie asked.

"You want to?"

"My mom's been too much lately. She won't leave me alone since the murder. I've said it before, but I really gotta move out."

I chuckled. Archie's mother was a mama bear, but we were all a little protective of him. "We do need to get it done by the weekend, so let's do it. It's you and me tonight."

After cashing out the register, I pushed a dry sweeper across the polished floor, lamenting how great the burgundy Aubusson rugs I'd picked out would've looked on these floors. Phoebe's event didn't pan out, to say the least, so I'd have to stop pouting and wait a little longer to afford them. I couldn't even think of doing another event until Phoebe's murder was solved.

After a few more tasks, the shop was readied for tomorrow.

"Are we all set?" We'd shed our aprons and I was about to dim the lights.

"Yup. Oh, don't forget Guernsey."

"Good call." I unlocked the front door and Archie walked out ahead of me to retrieve the scarecrow. "It's breezy tonight. Lucky you remembered."

Archie picked her up, then halted. "Why is Mrs. Schultz's bike still here?"

He was right. The unmistakable cherry red bike with the flowered basket was still locked in the rack under the streetlight where she'd left it this morning. She only lived eight blocks away and always rode it home unless Baz offered to give her a ride. Even then, unless it was raining or very late, she would decline.

We looked up and down the street with no sign of her. The sidewalks were empty, as pedestrian and car traffic dwindled quickly on our block as soon as six o'clock struck and all the businesses closed.

I patted my pockets. "My phone's inside."

We returned inside with the scarecrow. I looked around for my phone, but Archie had already taken his out of his shorts pocket and dialed her number. He put it on speaker. It rang once and then silence. He tried again. One ring, then silence again.

The concern on Archie's face mirrored my own feelings. I pushed away the nagging twinge in my stomach that something wasn't right. There could be a logical explanation for why Mrs. Schultz's bike was still on the sidewalk and her phone was off.

"Let me try her with my phone. I'll check my office." I didn't have any reason to believe my phone would produce different results, but I hurried to my office in search of it anyway. I found it on the desk and returned quickly to the shop, tapping the phone to life.

"There's a message from her." I let my anxiety ease as I hit play on my voicemail. Archie and I both smiled in relief.

Mrs. Schultz's voice said, "Willa, I think I know who killed Phoebe. Arthur—." The phone cut out.

"Is that it?" Archie said, his smile vanished. "What did she say? Arthur?"

My anxiety climbed again like an elevator and this time it hit the top floor. I played the message again. It sounded like she'd been cut off.

"I'm calling Heath." I tapped his name on my phone contacts and waited an interminable few seconds for the ringing to end. Only his voicemail picked up. "Heath, it's Willa. Call me as soon as you get this. We think Mrs. Schultz has been taken by somebody named Arthur. We have to find out who Arthur is." I ended the call. "Let's get the car and go to the police station," I told Archie. "Maybe Heath's there."

We left out the front door and I hastily locked it behind me. We ran around the building and down the alley, where we almost blew past Baz at the foot of my stairs.

"I just got back and was coming up to see you," he said. He saw our panicked faces. "What's the matter?"

With heavy breaths, I managed to say, "Get in the car with us. I'll explain on the way."

Archie played Mrs. Schultz's message for Baz while I drove above the speed limit to the security complex.

I pulled beside the curb in front of the police station and threw the car into park. We exited and made a run for the doors. They didn't budge with our tugging. The complex was locked for the night.

Archie spotted an emergency phone off to the side. I picked it up. A dispatcher came on the other end.

"Yarrow Glen police. What's your emergency?"

"Our friend is missing. Is Detective Heath in?"

"Name?"

"What?"

"What's your name?"

"Willa Bauer. Please, we don't have time for this. Can you please let us in so we can see Detective Heath?"

"Is the missing person a minor?"

"No, but—"

"How long has the person been missing?"

"Thirty minutes maybe? She's not answering her phone and we know something's happened to her."

"Would you like to file a missing person report?"

"No. I need to speak with Detective Heath."

"I can patch you through to his phone. Hold just a moment."

"No, wai—"

Detective Heath's voicemail played in my ear again. I hung up the phone. "Where is he when I need him?"

"How can we figure out who Arthur is?" Archie said.

I racked my brain. "Have you guys heard of the name Arthur? There hasn't been any suspect named Arthur, has there?"

Archie and Baz shook their heads. "Did Detective

Heath ever mention an Arthur to either of you?" Baz asked. "Someone associated with the case?"

"Not to me," Archie said.

"Heath said they were going through a list of renters who all had the surveillance camera's access pass and password. Maybe there's an Arthur on the list," I suggested.

"How do we get that list from the police?" Baz asked.

"They're not going to give us the list. We have to get in touch with the owners ourselves," I said.

"We could find them online. Remember when we were at the float and Roman said their names would be on the rental listing?" Archie already had his phone out, typing in the search bar "vacation rentals in Yarrow Glen."

"I should have looked online for the listing that night. Why didn't I?" I paced impatiently and silently berated myself.

Archie looked up from his phone. "The theory that the owners were involved didn't pan out, that's why."

I went back to that conversation in my mind. "That's right! *Thomas* rented the house. It's in his name. He would have their phone number."

We raced back to the car and hightailed it to the inn. We ran into the lobby, startling Constance.

"Have you seen Thomas?" I barked at the poor woman.

"In The Cellar," she said, obviously sensing my urgency.

We sprinted down the hallway, sprung open the red door, and skittered down the stairs. An unsuspecting Thomas was having a beer by himself at a table. We quickly surrounded him.

"Thomas, you have to help us. Mrs. Schultz found out who killed Phoebe," I sputtered.

"What?" He looked from one to the other of us trying to make sense of our panic.

"We think Phoebe's murderer has kidnapped Mrs. Schultz," Baz said more clearly.

Thomas's eyes widened in comprehension. "How can I help?"

"We need you to call the owners of the house you rented for Phoebe and ask if the list they gave the police of renters included anybody named Arthur. That's all we have to go by."

Thomas took out his phone and found their contact information. He called and put them on speaker. He quickly explained what was happening.

The man on the phone said, "I don't recall off the top of my head. Let me look at the list again. Honey, where's that list of renters we gave to the police?" We all hovered over Thomas impatiently while the guy and his wife found the list. "Here it is." We held our breath. "No. No Arthur. Sorry."

"All right. Thanks anyway." Thomas ended the call.

I dropped into a chair at the table, dejected. Archie and Baz did the same.

"I thought for sure he'd be on the list." I tried to pick out another possibility from the heap of information we knew about the case, but everything was whirling in my head. I couldn't think clearly. "Who could Arthur be?"

"Jeremy's brother is named Arthur," Thomas said almost casually.

"What?" I grasped Thomas by the arm wanting to squeeze more information out of him. "Why didn't you say that in the first place?"

"It's just a guess that it's the Arthur you're talking about," he replied.

"It would be a heck of a coincidence if it wasn't." Baz snatched Thomas's mug of beer and took a healthy swig.

"But how would Mrs. Schultz know about Arthur?" I said. "You told us Jeremy had a brother and sister, but you never told us the names."

"I'm pretty sure I mentioned it to her when we were walking to the police station together yesterday," Thomas said.

"Now you tell us," Baz groused.

"Sorry, it just came up in conversation."

"Okay, so she knows his name. How did she find him?" I said.

"How are *we* going to find him?" Archie tapped the table with nervous fingers.

"He's probably been right under our noses, but all this time I've been looking at Ginger and Lou and A. J. . . ." I chastised myself.

"To be honest, I wanted it to be A. J. Stringer, myself," Thomas said. "I don't like the guy."

"A. J. Stringer," I repeated. "He told me he used to be a freelance journalist. Isn't that what a stringer is?"

"Beats me," Baz said.

Thomas and Archie shrugged, confused.

"Does that sound like a real name to you guys?" I asked. Suddenly the puzzle pieces clicked into place. "A. J. Those are the same initials as Arthur Jillcott, Jeremy Jillcott's brother."

We all stared at one another, absorbing the revelation. Archie, Baz, and I bolted from our seats without a word and headed for the stairs, with Thomas following suit.

CHAPTER 32

We piled into the car and spilled out three blocks later at the *Glen Gazette* building. As Deandra had told me, the *Gazette* was open at odd hours and tonight was no exception. We burst through the door and startled Deandra at her desk.

"What's going on?" she said.

"Where's A. J.?" I demanded.

"I-I don't know. He left a while ago. Is something wrong?"

"Do you know what his initials stand for? Is his real name Arthur Jillcott?"

"Gosh, I don't know. What's this all about?"

"I'm sorry I don't have time to explain right now, Deandra. Is there any way to find out? Trust me, this could be life or death."

"I suppose you could check his employment file."

"Great. Can you get it for us?" I looked around the room for file cabinets.

"They're stored in the home office."

"Okay, where's the home office?"

"In Santa Rosa. Nobody will be there this time of night."

"There aren't any files on the computer?"

"The only people with access to them would be the people who work at the home office."

We were going in circles.

"What now? How are we going to find out if A. J. is Arthur Jillcott?" Archie pleaded.

"Who is Arthur Jillcott?" Deandra asked.

I ignored her question. "We have to find A. J., Deandra. Do you know where he lives?"

"Sorry, I don't know that either. I do have his number, though. Do you want me to call him?"

"You can try. If he answers, don't tell him we're looking for him. Just try to find out where he is."

Deandra called and we all waited. My heart beat faster with each faint ring I heard through her phone. His voicemail picked up.

"Should I leave a message?" she said.

"If he's got Mrs. Schultz, he's not going to be answering his messages," Baz said.

"You can hang up. Thanks anyway," I said.

"Does anybody want to tell me what's going on?" she asked.

"When all this is over, I'll be sure to give you the story," I told her.

We plodded back to the car.

"How are we supposed to find A. J. now?" Archie said. His eyes pleaded with me to do something, but I was out of ideas.

"Chet might know," I suggested. "But I don't know how to find him either."

Baz retrieved his phone from his baggy jeans pocket. "Ginger," he said in explanation.

While he called Ginger, I checked my own phone. No missed texts or calls from Heath.

"Don't you think we should go to the police?" Thomas said.

"I left a message with Detective Heath, but maybe we

should fill out a missing person report." I felt the minutes ticking away and wondered if each one was putting Mrs. Schultz in more danger.

Baz was done with his call. "She hasn't heard from Chet, but she said he lives in the Old Mill neighborhood on River Street. Apartment 207. She gave me his phone number too." Baz was already punching in the numbers as we got back in the car. Chet's voicemail picked up after two rings. I started the car and Baz left a message.

In less than ten minutes, we arrived at the Old Mill neighborhood where a cluster of early twentieth-century warehouses were repurposed into studio and one-bedroom lofts. I parked in the first free space about ten spaces from the door of Building 200, even though there were signs everywhere warning Residents Only.

"I sure hope he's home," Archie said.

"I'm leaving my key in the drink holder. Archie, you and Thomas stay here in case you need to move my car. The last thing I need to do is get towed or blocked in. We'll be right back."

As Baz and I walked briskly toward the entrance, we caught sight of Chet about to go inside.

"There he is. Chet!" I called.

He stopped, one hand on the opened door. Baz and I trotted over to him.

"Thank goodness we found you," I said. I didn't give him a chance to ask questions, as his furrowed brow suggested he wanted to. "We need to find A. J. Have you heard from him?"

"Not recently. Why?" He allowed the door to close without going in.

"First, do you know his real name? Does A. J. stand for Arthur Jillcott?"

"What's going on?"

I didn't blame him for looking alarmed at our obvious panic. I told him our theories as succinctly as possible.

"Oh wow."

"I know he's your friend, but it's a strong possibility he murdered Phoebe and kidnapped Mrs. Schultz," I said. Even saying that out loud ran an icy chill down my spine.

Chet rubbed his forehead and shook his head in disbelief.

"Do you know where he lives?" I asked.

"Uh, yeah." He shook himself out of his bewilderment to answer. "He rents half of a duplex on Quarry Ridge."

"Great. Why don't you come with us? We could use your help."

We turned and started back toward the car.

"Wait. I can't," Chet called, remaining in place.

We turned around to face him again. "You can't help us find A. J. and Mrs. Schultz? Why?"

"I uh—I didn't want to have to tell you, but I lost Buttercup."

"Oh no," Baz said.

"We were taking a walk and he slipped the leash and took off. I'm just running in for a flashlight to check under the bushes."

First Mrs. Schultz went missing and now Buttercup. I couldn't handle much more. "All right, you'd better go find him then," I said.

Chet gave us A. J.'s address and we wished each other luck as we went our separate ways.

Baz took out his phone again.

"Who are you calling this time?"

"The police station. I'll see if Shep's in and ask him to meet us at A. J.'s house, just in case he's there," Baz said.

"That's a good idea. He can update Heath on what's going on."

Baz left a message with Shep and we returned to the car. Baz was familiar with the street where A. J.'s duplex was located, so he directed me to the neighborhood where the houses toed the sidewalk with only short driveways separating them. I slowed so my headlights could flash on the house numbers.

I detected A. J.'s number just as Archie said, "This is it!"

A harsh yellow light illuminated the narrow front porch with four steps leading up to it. A man was leaning over the railing smoking a cigarette. I couldn't make out who it was, but he didn't have A. J.'s signature bushy locks.

I parked at the curb in front of another car and we all approached the house. The man straightened. Light seeped through the curtains of the window behind him and the door was cracked open. The upstairs windows were completely dark.

"Is this where A. J. Stringer lives?" I asked from the first step.

The man pointed a finger to the sky. "Second floor. The stairs are through the door behind me."

We climbed the steps to the porch.

"He's not home, though," he continued.

"Are you sure?" Archie said.

"It's an old house. We can hear him when he's home. He doesn't usually get home until after nine. He's a good neighbor that way—mostly just sleeps here."

Struck out again.

An interior door creaked open. "Martin, dinner's ready," a woman called from the house, slamming the door shut immediately afterward.

Martin took a deep drag off his cigarette and stubbed it out in a small saucer balanced on the railing filled with cigarette stubs and ash. He nodded and went inside, closing the outer door behind him.

"What do we do now?" Archie asked.

"Wil, we could be completely off track. We don't even

know for sure if it's him," Baz said, frustration piercing his words.

"But it makes sense. He was able to tell me all about Jeremy Jillcott. He said suspecting him was a dead end. He obviously didn't want us looking any further into his brother." He must've been afraid we'd find out about him and took off. But where did that leave Mrs. Schultz?

My phone rang. In my haste to take it out of my pocket, I almost dropped it. Heath's name flashed upon the screen. I hurriedly tapped the answer call icon. "Heath! Did you get my messages?"

"Yes. We sent a car to Mrs. Schultz's house. Her poker group is gathering, but she's not there. We've got everybody on the case looking for her and we're looking into Arthur Jillcott."

"We're at A. J.'s now, but he's not here. We think it's him."

"Shep told me. Go home now. We're on it."

"Are you going to look into A. J.?"

"Willa."

"But—"

"Go home. We don't have the manpower to rescue you while we focus on tracking down Phoebe's murderer and Mrs. Schultz's possible abductor. Please, just stay out of trouble so I can do my job."

"All right, all right."

"I'll be in touch." He rang off.

"He wants us to go home," I told the others.

"Probably a good idea," Thomas agreed, looking relieved.

"Do they have any idea where Mrs. Schultz is? We can't stop looking for her," Archie said. "What about A. J.? Do they think he's Arthur Jillcott?"

The brass mailboxes, one above the other, glinted off the porch light. On a hunch, I lifted the lid to his and stuck my hand inside. My fingers found three pieces of mail and I pulled them out.

An advertisement flyer was addressed to A. J. Stringer, but the second envelope gave us the answers we were looking for.

CHAPTER 33

Baz read the envelope over my shoulder. "Alan Feckle Jr."

"Alan Junior. A. J." I connected the dots.

"So it's not even him?" Archie grabbed fists of his hair in frustration.

"I'm sorry, guys." I just wasted a ton of time.

"You had the right idea. A. J. Stringer wasn't his real name," Baz tried to console me.

"But it's not Arthur Jillcott either." I made another call to Heath about A. J. so they wouldn't waste time chasing down that lead. As usual, I left it on his voicemail.

We returned to the car. I was hoping that being behind the wheel would propel me to the right place, but I sat there, still as perplexed as ever.

"I'm going to try Mrs. Schultz's phone again." Archie pulled out his phone, but it was Thomas's that rang.

"It's the owners of Phoebe's rental house," he said. He answered it and tapped the speaker. "Hello? This is Thomas."

"Hi," the voice on the phone said. "We thought of something that might help. My wife just told me there was someone not on the list who had the access code and password. He wasn't a renter, which was why we forgot to put him on the list. We hired him twice a couple years ago. His name was Arthur."

"Was his last name Jillcott?" I yelled into the phone.

"It could be. Sorry, it was a few years ago."

I took the phone from Thomas. "What did you hire him to do? Maybe we can find him that way."

"He stayed at our house for a few days to take care of our dog."

Another detour.

"Okay, thanks. If you find his full name, can you call Thomas back?" I asked.

"Sure."

"Thank you."

The call ended.

"That doesn't narrow it down any," Baz complained. "Do you think dog sitters advertise and we can find Arthur Jillcott?"

"Who knows?" It was all I could do not to throw the phone in frustration. I gave it back to Thomas instead.

"What now?" Archie said. I looked at him through the rearview mirror. His eyes pleaded for answers, but I had none.

"Don't you think we should follow Detective Heath's orders?" Thomas said.

"I can't sit and do nothing," Archie said. "I'll keep looking for her on my own."

"You don't have to go on your own," I told Archie.

"We're not giving up," Baz agreed.

"I really think we should listen to the police," Thomas muttered.

"You don't have to come with us, Thomas. I didn't want to say anything, but you should know that Buttercup's missing. Chet's out looking for him now."

"Buttercup's missing?" Thomas cried accusatorily.

"You can help Chet find him. We'll drop you off at his apartment."

"I can help find him from here." He took out his phone.

"What do you mean?"

"The tracker," Archie supplied.

"Buttercup's collar has a tracker," Thomas explained.

Baz and I turned around in our seats to watch Thomas go into the app on his phone, which brought up a map.

"Where is he?" Baz said when we saw the blinking red dot.

Thomas tapped the pulsing dot. "Ninety-five Pleasant Avenue."

I was confused. "That's the meadery. Chet said he lost him outside his apartment. That's nowhere near the meadery, not for a little dog to walk."

"Maybe he already found him," Thomas said.

"We could use the extra help to look for Mrs. Schultz," Archie said.

"We sure can. Roman might even be back from the warehouse. Let's get to the meadery." I agreed.

We drove to town in silence, each in our own thoughts. I hoped Roman or Chet could come up with a new theory about where Mrs. Schultz might be.

"I hope Buttercup didn't get hurt while he was missing," Thomas complained. "You should've gotten somebody who knew how to take care of a dog."

"I'm sure he's fine, Thomas," I snapped. "Listen, you didn't offer up any suggestions for taking care of him. You left it up to me and I did the best I could." My worry about Mrs. Schultz was boiling over and I was happy to redirect my frustration at Thomas.

Archie leaned forward from the back seat. "Didn't Chet say he used to watch people's dogs sometimes? When he agreed to take Buttercup?"

"That's right. He did. So he was more than qualified. Any dog can get lost," I said to Thomas.

"That's not what I mean. He said he used to watch people's dogs. Maybe he was the dog sitter," Archie said.

"Chet?" I replied skeptically.

Baz weighed in. "He *was* acting kinda strange when we saw him."

"That's just because Buttercup was missing," I said.

"He said he slipped his leash, but he didn't have a leash—he never went far. And he said he was going inside to get a flashlight, but why wouldn't he just use the one on his phone?" Baz questioned.

"Maybe he didn't have it with him. I don't know. Besides, his name's not Arthur," I contended.

"It's probably not Chet. Mine's not Baz. Does anyone know his last name?"

I didn't. From the rearview mirror, I saw Archie and Thomas shake their heads.

I was having a hard time trying to wrap my mind around Chet killing Phoebe or kidnapping Mrs. Schultz, but I pressed the car's pedal a little harder.

"How would Mrs. Schultz find out Chet's name was Arthur?" I said, trying to work it out in my own mind.

"You know she likes to use people's proper names. She might've asked him," Baz said.

I could feel the pit in my stomach expanding as everything Baz was saying made sense. "But she was in a hurry to get home for her poker game."

"Didn't she want that new mead Roman had for her poker night?" Archie said.

"Oh no, Archie, you're right. I bet she went to the meadery as soon as she left the shop."

I gunned the accelerator.

CHAPTER 34

I'd barely swung the car into a diagonal spot directly in front of the meadery when everybody climbed out.

The streetlights glared outside onto a deserted sidewalk, but it was dark inside, as expected. We pressed our faces to the glass, but the few dim lights only cast shadows in the shop. I rapped on the door.

"Mrs. Schultz!" I called

"Mrs. Schultz!" the others echoed, as several of us banged on the door and front windows.

We ran to the back of the building. A bad feeling grew with each step. The light above the back door that led to the tasting room flickered and buzzed. I pressed the bell and heard it chime inside.

Baz pounded on the door. "Chet! Let us in."

"Do you think he's got her in there?" Archie asked, his voice rising with worry.

Headlights glared at us. Instinctively we gathered behind the pillars of Roman's small deck and tried to hide. I suddenly realized none of us had a weapon.

The lights went off and we heard the slam of a car door and footsteps approaching. I peeked out from behind the pillar. It was Roman.

"Roman!" I practically cried at the sight of him.

"What are you guys doing here?" he asked.

I gave him a shorthand account of what happened.

"Chet? I can't believe that," Roman said.

"Can you let us in just to make sure?" I asked.

"Sure, my keys are in my apartment. But why do you think it's Chet?"

We followed him upstairs.

"We think Chet's not his real name and that it's Arthur," Baz explained.

"Do you know what it is?" Archie asked.

"Sure, it's on his application and his tax forms. Arthur Stevens. His nickname comes from his middle name, Chester," Roman said.

"His last name's not Jillcott?" I said. Disappointment landed on my chest like a boulder.

"No. I told you I didn't know anybody named Jillcott. It's Stevens. If Mrs. Schultz is missing, we'd better call the police."

"I told you we should leave it to the police," Thomas said.

The rest of us glared at Thomas as Roman unlocked his door and we all tromped into his apartment. With a flick of the light switch, modern track lighting illuminated a lived-in apartment reminiscent of his shop, with a black-and-slate color scheme and brown leather sofas.

"We've talked to Detective Heath. He doesn't want us in on this, but we really thought it was Chet," I said. "It's gotta be."

"If Chet knew Mrs. Schultz was onto him, why would he stick around? It just doesn't make sense," Roman said.

"Maybe he hightailed it to his parent's house in Alameda after we saw him at his apartment and told him we were looking for Arthur Jillcott," I said, shaking my head at how I'd bungled things.

"I don't think he'd go home," Thomas said. "Jeremy told me he and his brother both hated their stepfather."

"Stepfather? Does that mean Arthur could be a half brother or stepbrother?" Baz said.

"Jeremy did say his mom got married a few times."

"So his brother could have a different last name!" I said.

"Let me check the meadery." Roman started for the door.

"Not on your own. He might still be in there. Let's all go," I insisted.

"Let's go in through the front door where we can see what we're getting into at least."

We hustled down the steps and around to the front of the building.

"Archie, you and Thomas stay out here." I gave Archie my phone. "If Detective Heath calls, let him know we're checking out the meadery. Don't do anything dangerous."

"Me? You're the one going in there," he said.

Archie and Thomas stood by the car while Roman unlocked the door and led the way in. I followed close behind with my finger hooked into his belt loop. Baz remained just as closely behind me. Someone looking through the window might've thought we were starting a conga line.

The overnight dimmers were on, which shone just enough light to see the austere store. We peeked behind the checkout counter and in one shadowy corner, where a dark shape made my heart stop for an instant, only to realize it was the outline of Buttercup's food bag. I pointed to the sliding barn door to the tasting room. It was closed.

"Is that usually closed?" I whispered in Roman's ear.

He nodded. "Let's check it out, though."

"What if he has a weapon?"

Roman grabbed a bottle of mead by its neck, ready to swing it like a bat. I grabbed one, too, and lifted it behind my shoulder ready to strike, but it accidentally connected with Baz's head.

"Ouch!" Baz rubbed his head where I'd conked him.

"Ooh, sorry," I said.

"That'll do as a weapon," he said, grabbing a bottle for himself.

Roman slowly slid open the door and hit the lights.

The room awoke in brightness, but nothing moved. Roman snuck up to the bar, but no one was behind it. No sign of Chet or Mrs. Schultz. We all lowered our mead bottles.

"They're not here. There doesn't look to be any sign of a struggle either," Roman said, glancing around the room some more.

He was right. Nothing looked out of place.

"Where could he have taken her? And why?" I could feel my exasperation about to spill over into tears.

"Maybe it's not what you think," Roman tried consoling me.

"It has to be him. It all fits," I said.

Footsteps sounded from the shop and we all raised our bottles again.

Archie and Thomas appeared at the barn door, each grasping a bottle by its neck.

"We thought you might need backup. Nothing?" Thomas said, as we all lowered our bottles.

"No," Roman answered.

Baz and Roman slumped on the couch. We placed the mead bottles on the center table, but I continued to pace.

"Where could they be?" Archie echoed my silent desperation.

Thomas held his phone in front of him at arm's length, Still staring at it, he took steady paces all the way into the tasting room. He turned one way, took a few steps, and then turned in the other direction.

"What are you doing?" I asked him.

"I'm trying to find Buttercup. It's like a game of Hot and Cold." He continued to walk robotically toward the bar.

"What's he talking about?" Roman asked.

"We tracked Buttercup here through his collar," I explained. "That's why we thought Chet might be here."

"There." Thomas pointed at the door behind the bar.

"The mead-making room!" Roman cried. He sprung off the couch.

The rest of us rushed the door with our bottle weapons while Roman fumbled with his keys. How stupid that none of us thought of it. A windowless basement-like room—a perfect place to hide. Roman unlocked the door and opened it. The motion-activated fluorescent lights had barely blinked on in the low-ceiling space when we raced down the five steps and advanced like King Arthur's knights, holding our bottles aloft like swords, not taking heed to what Chet might have in store for us.

We found Mrs. Schultz, propped against the far wall, seated on Buttercup's doggie bed with Buttercup lying on her lap. They both roused when we entered.

"You found me already," Mrs. Schultz said, a little sleepily.

Archie, Baz, and Roman hurried over to her to help her stand. I leaned on Thomas, feeling faint from the flood of relief.

"Thanks. A hard floor and old knees don't mix. Did Chet tell you where I was?" she said.

"Why would he? Isn't he the one who locked you in here?" I said.

"He did once he realized I figured out his brother worked for Phoebe. But he left some water for Buttercup and me. And a glass to drink any of the bottled mead stored in here. He knew Roman would find me in the morning. I did drink a glass or two. I hope you don't mind, Roman."

"Mrs. Schultz, you can have the lot," Roman said, as he helped her up.

We walked her out to the tasting room where she could sit on one of his comfortable leather couches. We sat around her. Buttercup went from lap to lap and finally settled again on Mrs. Schultz. Roman slipped behind the bar and returned momentarily with a glass of water for her.

"Unless you'd like another mead?" He handed her the water.

"I might need something stronger than mead even, but this will do for now." She took a long draft.

"Are you okay?" I asked her. Even though she was sitting right next to me, I couldn't shake my earlier dread.

"I'm fine," she insisted, her hand absently petting the dog. "I'm more worried about Chet."

"Isn't he the one who murdered Phoebe?" Thomas spoke up for the first time since finding Buttercup.

"Yes, but he seemed so distraught."

"No kidding. He's going to be caught now," Thomas muttered.

"What happened, Mrs. Schultz?" I asked gently.

"I was about to bike home when I saw the lights were still on at the meadery and I remembered about that apple-pie mead Roman had brought us. You'd mentioned I could get a few bottles for my poker night, so even though it was after closing, I came over. Chet let me in and said Roman had put some aside in the back for me. We both came in here and I waited by the bar while he went into the mead-making room to get them. There was a folder on the bar. Buttercup startled me and when I turned around, my purse knocked the folder off the bar and the papers went everywhere. They looked like some kind of legal papers."

"Chet and I were working up a partnership so he could buy into the meadery. I had an agreement drawn up for him to read and sign. I gave the papers to him today," Roman explained.

"That must've been what they were then. Anyway, I began to gather them and saw that Chet's legal name was on the document—Arthur Chester Stevens. I recognized the name Arthur right away—when Thomas and I were talking on the way to the police station yesterday, he'd mentioned the names of Jeremy's brother and sister. But the last name wasn't the same as Jeremy's. I wasn't sure what to think, so I called you, Willa."

"If only I had my phone with me and picked up!" I was furious with myself.

"Don't feel bad. How could you have known?" Mrs. Schultz patted my knee.

"What happened then?" Archie asked.

"He saw me crouched over the papers and heard me on the phone. I'm afraid my acting skills kicked in too late, and somehow he knew that I knew."

"He was in the car when I told A. J. about Jeremy, and he might've overheard me talking to Roman about him when I was here today," I said. "Chet must've known we'd started looking into his family."

"He didn't hurt you, did he?" Archie asked.

"No, no. I tried to play innocent, but he took my phone and shuffled me into the mead-making room. Buttercup followed me in. He locked the door behind us but then came back a minute later to leave the water and the glass, and the dog bed and bowl of food for Buttercup. I tried to get him talking, but he wouldn't say anything."

"Nothing?" Roman asked her again.

"He apologized to me and said you'd be back in the morning, then he locked me and Buttercup in."

I tapped Heath's name on my phone again. To my surprise, he picked up. "We found Mrs. Schultz," I told him. "Chet locked her in the mead-making room. She's all right, but you need to find Chet. He's the guy you're looking for."

"We know. We contacted Jeremy's mother and got Arthur's full name. She's on her third husband, so her last name didn't tip us off to Chet's. She'd been out of touch with him, so we ran it through the system to locate his place of employment—the meadery and the *Gazette*. We've got Alameda officers at their house now in case he shows up. Did Chet give Mrs. Schultz any clues as to where he was headed?" Heath said.

"No. Maybe he went back to his apartment?" I told him when we'd last seen Chet.

"We're at his apartment now. It looks like he was here briefly to get some things. He's not at Ginger's place either. He's on the run. Stay where you are. We'll be right over."

CHAPTER 35

In a matter of minutes, Detective Heath arrived with Shep, directing another officer to tape off the mead-making room. Paramedics followed them in.

"Are you all right?" Heath asked Mrs. Schultz. "Do you need to go to the hospital?"

"Of course not," she answered.

We had to leave Mrs. Schultz's side so the two paramedics could attend to her. Buttercup remained on her lap. They opened their medical kit and wrapped a blood pressure cuff on her arm.

"This really isn't necessary," she protested. "It was probably worse for Buttercup. He's the one who's used to being pampered."

"Chet didn't say anything about where he was going?" Heath repeated his earlier question, this time directly to Mrs. Schultz.

"No, I'm sorry, he didn't," she answered.

"Your blood pressure and oxygen levels are good," the female paramedic told Mrs. Schultz as she ripped the cuff off her arm and took the pulse oximeter off her finger.

"I told you I'm fine."

"We can still take you to the hospital if you'd like," the paramedic said.

"Why would I like that? Thank you, but you can go now."

They collected their equipment and left.

Detective Heath picked up where he left off. "You all know Chet. Do you know any place he might go?"

"If he's not at Ginger's . . ." I shook my head, fresh out of ideas.

"He's got a boat," Roman reminded us.

"Where does he keep it?" Heath asked.

"A marina near Alameda. Uh . . ." Roman snapped his fingers trying to jog his brain. "Safe Harbor. That's it."

"Mrs. Schultz, are you okay to go to the station with Officer Melman and give your statement?" Heath said.

"Of course," she answered.

He turned to Officer Shepherd. "Shep, you're with me."

"Don't hurt him, Detective," Mrs. Schultz implored.

"Mrs. Schultz, I'm grateful he didn't harm you, but there's a firearm registered to his name and an empty safe in his apartment. He's a fleeing felon who could be armed and dangerous." Heath turned to Shep. "Let's go."

"Be careful," I called after him.

He nodded, and he and Shep were out the door.

"I'll go with you to the station, Mrs. Schultz," I said.

"Me too," Archie said.

"Don't be silly. There's no sense in any of you sitting in the lobby all evening."

"You're not going on your own," I insisted.

"Let me take her," Roman said. "I feel terrible that I didn't suspect Chet, even when you thought he was the one."

"It's nobody's fault," Mrs. Schultz insisted. "He fooled all of us. Even A. J., the investigative reporter."

"Still, I'd like to go with you," Roman said gently.

Baz interjected, "You probably need to stay here while

the police are here. Let me go. I'll take her home afterward."

"I've never had so many men fighting over me," Mrs. Schultz said. "I could get used to this." Her grin allowed the rest of us to relax a bit.

Buttercup jumped off her lap as she stood. Despite her earlier protests, she suddenly appeared a bit frail—a word I never would've associated with the indominable Mrs. Schultz.

"I'm coming too," Archie insisted.

Buttercup yapped twice as Baz and Archie started to leave.

"What are we going to do with him?" Baz said about the dog.

I picked up Buttercup. "We'll figure it out. Just take care of Mrs. Schultz."

The three of them left with Officer Melman.

"I can't believe we finally know who killed Phoebe. I thought it would feel different," Thomas said as he watched them leave.

"Yeah. It's a little overwhelming," I said. Unfortunately, I had some experience with it.

"I'm not sure what to do now." Thomas stood in the middle of the room like a lost kid. "I guess I'll go back to the inn and get some dinner. I'm suddenly starving."

I handed the dog to Thomas. "How about you take *him* to dinner."

"Me? *I'm* going to take care of the dog?"

"Yes, Thomas, you're going to take *good* care of the dog."

They looked at each other. Buttercup's big black eyes could melt anyone's reserves.

"Fine. But Phoebe never let us feed him anything but dog food. Do you think he likes The Cellar's hamburgers?"

"If not, he's a big fan of the carnitas at Let's Talk Tacos."

As Thomas walked out with Buttercup, I faintly heard him approving of the dog's palate.

I turned to Roman now that it was just me and him . . . and two police officers. The ever-present twinkle in his eye wasn't to be found.

"It's not your fault," I assured him. "I was the one who let Chet in on practically every clue I found. I even wanted him around to protect me from A. J. and apologized to him for suspecting he had something to do with the photos."

"Let's hope Detective Heath catches him."

"Mr. Massey?" A female officer at the door to the mead-making room called to him.

"I'll let you go. We'll talk tomorrow." I squeezed his hand.

I walked out of the meadery with a heavy heart. I should've felt elated that we'd solved the murder, but there was no celebration in the culprit being Chet. Without Chet in custody, it felt incomplete.

The cool burst of air as I walked out the door felt good. I was too antsy to go back to my apartment. I needed to move. I left my car in front of the meadery and walked toward Main Street where the security complex and my three best friends were. My thoughts were clearer when I walked, and I wanted to put all the clues into place.

Chet insinuated himself into Phoebe's circle from the day she came to my shop. He must've known who she was already. Phoebe may have even recognized him. She had asked, "Do I know you?" but at the time I thought she was being snarky about why he was there. Maybe Jeremy had shown her a picture of his half brother at some point, and he looked familiar to her. Did Chet wait outside Curds & Whey after seeing Phoebe at my shop on Friday and follow the car to her rental house?

He must've, then realized it was the house where he had dog sat before. He'd be familiar with the house's layout with all the windows in the back. I wondered if he set up A. J. to take those photos of her. He could've been the one who put that anonymous note in A. J.'s coat pocket that night at The Cellar. How much did A. J. know about his good friend Chet?

I stood at the corner of Pleasant Avenue and Main Street. I could go left to the security complex to meet Baz and Archie or I could go right to the *Gazette* to see if A. J. was there. I wanted more answers. I went right.

CHAPTER 36

The door to the *Gazette* was unlocked. The receptionist was still absent from the front desk, which wasn't surprising given the time. Deandra's desk lamp was on, but there was no laptop or purse in her cubicle.

"Hello?" I called out.

Nobody answered. Was it the eerie quietness of the newspaper office that made the fine hairs on the back of my neck stand up? I went to the rear alcove and walked up the steps. The door to the second floor was closed this time, but I heard a muffled voice. I was determined to get some answers from A. J.

I threw open the door and charged into the room. A. J. started as if I'd given him an electric shock through the chair where he sat in the middle of the room. It was no wonder. Just a few feet across from him sat Arthur Chester Stevens.

Chet had been startled at my sudden appearance too. He stood from the chair. I noticed a duffle bag at his feet.

"You two are in this together," I said, looking from one to the other while my mind tried to make sense of it all.

"In what together?" Chet said to me. He made an effort to act casual, but he shifted his gaze back and forth between A. J. and me. A. J. was uncharacteristically quiet.

"We found Mrs. Schultz," I blurted out.

"Already?" Chet plopped back into the chair. "How did you know I was here?"

"I didn't. I came to see A. J."

"You don't want to leave your story unfinished," A. J. said to Chet.

"It's too late now. There's not enough time." Chet leaned over his lap and put his head in his hands.

"There's time," A. J. insisted. "Nobody's coming for you. Right, Willa?" A. J. widened his eyes and stared at me.

I had no idea what he was talking about, but I wasn't about to let them know I came on my own. "The police are after Chet," I said. "They know you killed Phoebe because of your brother Jeremy."

"Willa," A. J. chided.

A. J. was agitated. It suddenly dawned on me that being in the room with a murderer and his accomplice was a bad idea. I began to back away from them toward the door. "I'm just going to . . ."

"Stay," Chet said, standing once again. This time he was holding a gun. While I was focusing on A. J., he'd gotten his gun from his now unzipped duffle bag.

My hands instinctively flew above my shoulders. Now the hairs on the back of my neck were practically jumping off my skin.

He pushed the chair so it rolled over to where A. J. was sitting. "Go sit over there," he said.

A. J. flinched again when the barrel of the gun passed his way. This wasn't what I had thought at all.

"A-Are you holding A. J. hostage?" I stuttered.

"No. I just wanted to tell him my brother's story. This isn't Jeremy's fault. I-I'm sorry about this." He referred to the gun. "But I can't you let you go now. You'll just go to the police."

"Listen, we're not going to say anything you don't want us to," A. J. assured him.

"I trust you, A. J. You've always been loyal to me. But Willa? Please, sit."

"Okay." I started toward the chair. "If I sit down, will you stop pointing that at us?" I said.

He didn't agree, but I did as I was told anyway. When I sat down, I looked at A. J. next to me. Why didn't I notice how pale he was when I first came in? The curls that hung over his forehead were damp. A red pin of light shone through his fingers. He was holding a mini voice recorder in his hand.

"Are you still recording?" Chet asked him.

"Yes." A. J. lifted the recorder so Chet could see the red light was still on. "You were telling me about your childhood with your half brother before your mom married a third time."

Chet nodded. "That's right. That's when things changed. Gerard had a lot of money. He was way too controlling, but my mom had never had money before. We both hated him, but Jeremy became rebellious. He started skipping school and running with a bad crowd. He was my older brother and I looked up to him, but he even pushed me aside. Gerard decided Jeremy needed to be sent away to military school for his senior year to straighten him out. That's when Jeremy ran away and never came back home.

"I had two years until I graduated, then when I went to college, I started looking for him on my own. I found him a year later, but he was strung out. I tried to help him, but he disappeared again. When I graduated college and started working for the tech company, I was making big bank. Most of my friends were buying sports cars and homes, but I was living with two roommates and saving whatever money I could. The only thing I splurged on was my boat, but that was for us. Jeremy loved the water. I was always looking for him. I thought if I could find him, I could help him. We could take off in my boat and find our way through life together.

Chet wheeled a third chair over from his desk to use for himself. He held the gun on his lap, pointed to the side. He still had a firm grip on it, however, while he continued. "He ended up finding me. He had gotten clean and was working for Phoebe. I was so proud of him. He seemed really good. We didn't get to see each other much. He made excuses, but looking back, she was isolating him to keep him under her thumb. She seemed to control his every move, almost like an abusive girlfriend. I could tell he was in love with her, but she was his boss. He insisted he was happy, and since he was clean and sober, I had to believe him. I was burnt out from my job and I didn't care about the money—it was only for him and he didn't need it. So I quit my job and came up here to live the simple life. I thought I'd get to see him more now that I wasn't so busy, but he was wrapped up in his life with Phoebe. She'd crashed and burned and he was trying to find a way to get her out of it. He made it sound like it was his whole life. I remember being worried for him. Then I started seeing her name in the tabloids again, like she'd made a comeback. I thought everything was fine until he called and told me she fired him. He was so loyal to her—he'd stayed with her at her lowest to build her back up, but she didn't want to be associated with him anymore in case anyone found out about his past drug use. He wasn't ashamed of it so he never hid his past. She should've been proud of him that he pulled himself out of homelessness and substance abuse, but instead she used it against him."

He stood quickly causing the chair to roll. A. J. and I flinched, but he didn't seem to notice. He went on, "I told him to come to Yarrow Glen and live with me. He was too upset. He said he loved her. Then we lost contact again. The next time I heard from him was a few weeks ago. He'd relapsed, just like I was afraid he'd do, but he was back in rehab. I was really proud of him for getting help again. I told him so. But I was still so angry at her. It was her fault. She drove him to relapse."

He gestured to A. J. "You can turn that thing off now. I want Jeremy's story recorded, not mine."

"Sure, Chet. Whatever you say." A. J. clicked the button and showed him the red light was off.

What would Chet do now? I knew we had to keep him talking.

"Was it all planned before she even came to Yarrow Glen?" I said. I didn't want to use the word *murder.*

"Nothing was planned." He leaned against the cluttered table. "All I did was send her his photo. I wanted her to remember him and what she'd done to him. She shouldn't have cast him aside like yesterday's trash. Then I found out she was coming here. I thought about confronting her, but I didn't know how. When I came into your shop that day, I really was just looking for Ginger. When I saw Phoebe, I didn't know what to do. I pretended I didn't know her. I had no idea she knew Ginger."

"Ginger never talked about her?"

"Ginger never said a word about her. But I saw the way Phoebe treated her assistant when I was in your shop. I just knew she treated Jeremy that way. It sickened me. I followed them to where she was staying. I realized it was the house I had stayed in to dog sit a few years ago. Thomas was with her, so I didn't stick around.

"When I met Ginger at The Cellar that night, I asked her about Phoebe. She told me Phoebe had laughed at her idea of opening a vegan café, then she ended up stealing some of her grandmother's recipes for her first cookbook. Phoebe claiming to be vegan was just another slap in the face to Ginger. And Phoebe thought they were still friends, after all that. It only confirmed for me how horrible Phoebe was and that she was to blame for Jeremy's relapse.

"I was the one who put the note in your pocket when

you left your jacket at the table," Chet said to A. J. "You'd talked about her and I could tell you knew she wasn't a new and improved version of herself. I told you how to find her because I wanted you to catch her off guard and interview her so you could tell everyone what a fake she was. It was pure luck that she was eating Mac's Barbeque that night. It was meant to be. The house and the barbeque—she was meant to be found out for the fraud that she was."

He continued to speak to A. J. "When you showed me the photos, I knew you'd taken them, but I couldn't tell you I knew. I was stoked. I thought those photos would be enough revenge for me. Then the more I thought about it, the more I was afraid she'd find a way to get out of it just like she got out of it the last time people found out what she was really like. So I went to her house on Saturday. Archie was leaving, so I drove past and found a spot to hide my car by the bushes."

"How did you get in?" I asked.

"At the gate, I told her I was Jeremy's brother and that he knew a way to help her. She still didn't open it, so I reminded her that I was Ginger's boyfriend and Ginger wanted to help too. She must've been feeling desperate because she let me in."

He paced the floor. I didn't take my eye off the gun.

"As soon as she opened the door, she threw her arms around me," Chet continued. "She was drunk and in a flimsy bathrobe. She said none of this would've happened if she'd kept Jeremy. She said so many good things about him, I started to think maybe I was wrong about her. Maybe she did love him, too, but he'd gotten back into drugs and that's why she made him go. I haven't known my brother well since we were kids. She got me to thinking I was wrong about her. She said it was kismet that I was there because he'd just sent her a photo of himself in the mail. She didn't know I was the one who sent it. She went upstairs to get it and told me to come up too.

"I told her that he was in rehab, that he'd relapsed. I figured she'd want to help him out. But as soon as I told her, she said she wanted me to take his place, said she needed someone smart to get her out of this bind. I told her I couldn't do that to Jeremy.

"That's when she changed her tactic. She took her glass of tequila and went into the tub and asked me to join her in the bath. Can you believe it? She didn't care what she had done to him. She didn't even ask how he was doing! All she cared about was herself. I told her no way, that I just wanted his picture back. As soon as I rejected her, her attitude really changed. She said she'd told Archie to throw it out. She laughed when she said it."

Chet's mouth tightened and so did his fist. I continued to stare at the hand holding the gun, hoping it wouldn't tense enough to squeeze the trigger.

"I don't even remember what happened after that, I was so infuriated," Chet continued. "The next thing I knew, I snapped awake and somehow I was in her bathroom and my shirt was wet. Phoebe was underwater, dead. I was drying off as best I could when I heard her phone ding. Thomas was outside at the gate, buzzing to get in. It was lucky for me, otherwise, I think I would've forgotten that I'd been on camera when she let me in. The password was the number of the address, so it wasn't hard to remember. I still can't believe my old password worked, otherwise I would've had to hack her phone, which would've taken longer."

"Like you hacked A. J.'s car to mess with his brakes?" I guessed.

"Yeah, I wasn't texting Ginger in the car. Sorry about that, dude," he said to A. J. I guess he wasn't sorry to me. He rolled his chair back to the center of the floor and sat down again. "I didn't know Willa would pull the emergency brake. I was just about to slow the car down myself when it went into a spin. I wanted to take the heat off of you since I knew you took the pictures. I figured if it looked like you were threatened, nobody would suspect you anymore. I thought if you were in the car, too, Willa, it might scare you off. It was just supposed to be thirty seconds without brakes and then I was going to figure a way for one of you to find the note."

"I understand, bro. I appreciate it," A. J. said.

I took my gaze off the gun to look at A. J. The perspiration above his lip told me he was just placating Chet. He hand was still tensely gripped around the recorder.

Chet pushed his hair behind his ear. The lull in his story gave me a moment to wonder how I was going to get out of this. I knew no one would think to come to the *Gazette* to look for Chet. For now, I had to keep him talking.

"So what happened after you—" I stopped myself again from using the word *murder*. "After you deleted your video from the surveillance camera?"

"I looked through the trash to find the picture of Jeremy. I wanted it now more than ever so no one would connect us to her murder. I waited for Thomas to leave, then I left and used the old app on my phone to delete the surveillance video showing me leaving. I left the door unlocked and her phone there to implicate Thomas. I thought the police would arrest him and that would be that. But it all unraveled when you got involved, Willa." He leaned over and zipped his duffle bag back up, but he kept the gun in his hand.

A. J. and I looked at each other. The story was done. What did that mean for us?

"The police know it's you, Chet," I said.

"Why do you think I told you Jeremy's story? If something happens to me, I want everyone to know Phoebe deserved her fate, but Jeremy didn't ask me to do it. He had nothing to do with this."

"Will you turn yourself in?"

"I've got a boat that's been sitting for too long." Chet stood. "I need to get to it, but I need a head start."

"You can count on me," A. J. replied immediately.

"Loyalty means everything to me, and you've been a loyal friend, A. J." Chet said. "I think Willa's going to need to come with me, though. Just for insurance."

"Oh, I don't think that's necessary," I said. "I'll just stay here with A. J."

"I won't hurt you unless the police come for me. This way I know A. J. will stay quiet too. If anything happens to me, A. J., you know what to do."

"Jeremy's story is right here, safe with me." A. J. lifted his hand with the recorder in it, then retracted it in an instant. It was too late. The red light shone through his fingers.

Chet stared at it. He approached A. J., gun in hand. A. J. leaned as far back in his chair as he could. Chet grabbed the recorder from him. "You turned it back on!"

"N-No, I didn't—" A. J. stuttered.

Chet clicked the buttons and played the last part back. Part of his confession played back to us.

"It was a mistake!" A. J. yelled. "I swear. We can delete it."

"I thought I could trust you."

"You can!"

"I can't. I can't trust either of you." He walked back to his duffle bag as he swung the gun from one to the other of us. "I can't chance bringing both of you with me. Now I have no choice."

Suddenly the door burst open and Buttercup bounded in, barking. Startled, Chet turned. I leapt out of my wheeled desk chair and pushed it at him as hard as I could. It struck him, unbalancing him so he toppled over his duffel bag to the ground. The recorder and gun flew out of his grasp and careened across the floor. He crawled toward the gun, but A. J. and I raced over to him, leveling ourselves on top of him.

"What's going on?" Thomas stood dumbfounded by the door.

"Thomas, help us hold him down!" I yelled.

He ran over and sat on top of Chet with his knee between Chet's shoulder blades while A. J. held Chet's arms behind him. I retrieved the gun that I hoped I wouldn't need to use. Buttercup raced back and forth between us.

Deandra charged in, another surprise. She hadn't been in the building when I came in. "What's going on?"

"Call the police," I said. "We've got Phoebe Winston's murderer."

EPILOGUE

The flames of the bonfire were mesmerizing as they danced around the firepit, changing shape and color. The aromas of the food trucks carried beyond the patrons who were lined up to buy their warm cider donuts, buttery popcorn, and hot and cold apple cider. Most of Yarrow Glen and a good many tourists stuck around to enjoy the final hours of Yarrow Glen's successful harvest fair. Needless to say, Guernsey didn't win the scarecrow contest, but she did have the place of honor at the front of our float. However, Archie stole most of the attention walking behind in his cheese costume.

Between the dancing flames, I saw a handsome face I recognized. Detective Heath and I caught each other's eye. He came around the bonfire.

"Hello, Detective." I wanted to remind myself of the *detective* part.

A smile at my formal greeting played on his lips. "Willa," he greeted simply.

"It's a nice surprise to see you here." It really was and I couldn't keep myself from smiling.

"Why a surprise?" He sounded amused at my question.

"You don't strike me as the festival type."

"And what is the 'festival type'?"

"Oh, I don't know. Somebody who doesn't wear a suit to a harvest fair?" I teased.

Heath shrugged one shoulder, as if to say he couldn't disagree. "I walked over from the station."

"You don't get to take a Saturday off? You just closed a murder investigation."

"Mounds of paperwork."

"Is the case wrapped up then? No loose ends?"

"Chet admitted to the confession A. J. recorded. There were also some fingerprints in the house we hadn't been able to identify that we discovered were his now that we have him in custody and were able to get his prints."

"Why doesn't it ever feel as good as it should? I feel sad for Chet and for his brother."

"Catching the bad guys doesn't make everything right, but it's the right thing."

I nodded.

"We would've gotten the information eventually, you know, without any of you putting yourselves in danger," he said, using his height to his advantage to look down at me sternly.

"Is that your way of thanking me?"

He shook his head slowly, but the smile that had been threatening his lips appeared. "All right. You did a good job. Okay?"

"*We* did a good job. I think we make a good team, don't you?"

He tilted his head, noncommittally.

"I heard Shep found the teenagers yesterday who were responsible for vandalizing the floats," I said.

"He hears everything in town and finally got a tip. He's been waiting for the right moment to catch them in the act."

"What's going to happen to them?" Now that the stress of the murder was over and the parade was a success, the juvenile stunt didn't seem all that serious.

"They just need something to fill their free time so they'll stay out of trouble. In lieu of charges being filed, they're now members of the Good Neighbor committee. You'll be seeing them around town helping with events, planting flowers, and sweeping sidewalks."

"I can't imagine Lou's going to let them sweep in front of his market."

"I hope he doesn't give them a hard time. After all, he had similar issues with throwing things into dumpsters that weren't his. Maybe he'll surprise us and become a mentor to one of them," Heath said optimistically.

"I'm always open to being pleasantly surprised."

"Detective!" Roman, in jeans and a casual sweater, joined us with the warm drinks he'd gone to get for us. He gave me one paper cup and held the other out for Heath. "Hot apple cider? I can get another."

"No, thanks. You two enjoy." Heath briefly locked eyes with me. I'd been pulled in by those eyes before, but this time he didn't seem to want to push me away. His disappointed smile before he sauntered off made me believe it wasn't all in my head, and left me rattled.

"Cheers," Roman said, snapping me out of my silly thoughts. We tapped our cups and sipped the warm drink.

"It's no apple-pie mead, but it'll do," I said as the spicy cinnamon beverage warmed my throat on its way down.

"I'm discontinuing that flavor. Bad vibes." He stared into his paper cup.

"I'm sorry about the partnership. I know you were excited to expand."

"I don't seem to pick very good people to go into business with, do I?"

"Maybe it's the universe's way of telling you that you can do it on your own."

His crooked smile dimpled his cheek. "I'm glad I'm better at picking friends than business partners." He wrapped an arm around me, and I leaned into his embrace.

We heard friendly greetings before catching sight of a glowing headless skeleton approaching from the darkness, which turned out to be Baz in a glow-in-the-dark skeleton hoodie and sweats. He was flanked by Mrs. Schultz and Ginger as they joined us near the bonfire. Baz must've been pleased Ginger had decided to stick around, especially since he had to talk her into participating in the parade earlier—she was still trying to make sense of the revelation about Chet.

"It looked like your pumpkin-carving station was a big hit. I've seen so many incredible jack-o'-lanterns tonight," I said. I knew what a talented woodworker Baz was, so I shouldn't have been surprised that he could make masterpieces out of pumpkins and help others do so too.

"People seemed to enjoy it, thanks to my two fantastic assistants," Baz replied, pointing one thumb at Mrs. Schultz and the other at Ginger.

"All I did was make sure nobody gouged themselves with those sharp tools. I prefer my Halloween gore to remain fake," Mrs. Schultz said. Also dressed for the occasion, her cardigan was adorned with full moons and broom-riding witches, and her scarf with cute black cats. "Ginger and Basil are the artists."

"I'm glad he talked me into staying," Ginger said, smiling at Baz.

She looked like the protagonist of one of those wholesome Hallmark movies with her rosy cheeks and perfect autumnal outfit—low suede boots over leggings with a fitted auburn pullover that was the same color as her hair. I kept my fingers crossed that it was a romance and Baz would eventually be the love interest.

"It was fun, and we raised some money for the farm-animal sanctuary," she continued.

"Congratulations." Roman lifted his cup in cheers.

"I wasn't sure which charity to choose before we got started, so Ginger suggested it." Baz reciprocated her smile.

"I know the people who run it. They do good work," she said.

Although there were good vibes all around, I still felt some awkwardness with Ginger. I didn't want to make the same mistake with her as I had with Heath—waiting too late to apologize. "Listen, Ginger, I owe you an apology. I'm sorry I suspected you in Phoebe's death."

This only magnified the awkwardness until she spoke. "I just don't want people to think I had anything to do with it because of Chet."

"Of course not. None of us think that."

The others echoed my assurances.

"You and I didn't really know each other, so I can't hold it against you that you'd suspect me. Apology accepted," she said.

"Thanks for being so gracious. I know Baz, though, and he didn't suspect you for a second. I should've listened to him more."

"Wait, what was that?" Baz put a hand to his ear and leaned in with exaggeration, so I'd repeat my confession.

I pushed him away, laughing. He accidentally backed into Thomas, who was holding Buttercup.

"Thomas, what are you still doing in town? I thought you'd leave the minute you were free to go," I said.

"I heard this sleepy town was finally doing something fun, so I thought I should stick around for it. It's not so bad."

He surveyed the park. Our shop tents closed at dusk, but the festive atmosphere of the fair was only heightened by the darkness. The walkway that curved through the lawn was lined with lanterns illuminated in the shapes of leaves, acorns, and pumpkins. Glowing orange lights and handkerchief ghosts hung from the trees dotting the park. Our scarecrows, positioned near the hay bales, now looked spooky under spotlights.

Baz, Mrs. Schultz, and I gave Buttercup ear scrunches. "Are you keeping him?" I asked Thomas.

"Yup. It's just the two of us now."

"Are you okay with that, Baz?"

"Yeah. It would've been too hard anyway to bring him to all my jobs." Then he turned to Buttercup. "We had a good time while it lasted, didn't we, Bruiser?" He put his face up to the dog, and Buttercup licked him on the nose—one last goodbye kiss. "I talked to Thomas earlier. He promised to take good care of him. Right, Doolittle?"

"We're buds now," Thomas said about him and Buttercup. Buttercup's kisses turned to Thomas. "And I'll have plenty of time for him. Phoebe's publisher called and offered me a contract to write a book about my experience working with her."

"Wow. You've agreed?" I said, surprised. "Will it be a tell-all?"

"I want people to know the good side of her, too, but now that she's gone, it's like her spell on me has been broken. I see things in a new light, especially after what I found out about how she treated Jeremy. I'm going to go see him in rehab. Maybe he can be a part of the book too. I want to support him."

"I bet he'll appreciate that," Mrs. Schultz said.

"I'm glad Baz literally ran into you so that I could thank you again. I never asked you—why did you come to the *Gazette* that night?" I asked him now.

"Buttercup and I were across the street at Let's Talk Tacos, like you suggested. Deandra was there too. I saw you go into the *Gazette* building. When we were done eating, I was going give Buttercup back to you. I couldn't keep him at the inn and Deandra said you were probably upstairs with A. J. It was pure serendipity."

"It was lucky, for sure. I think you and Buttercup were meant to be together."

"I hope I do all right. I'm not used to being on my own. I'm usually the wind beneath someone else's wings," he said.

"You're going to do fine on your own, Thomas," I said.

"You were the one who led everyone in the right direction. You're a hero," Mrs. Schultz told him.

"Wow, thanks." It could've been the light playing on his lenses, but behind his glasses, his eyes were a little misty.

Archie arrived, having shed his cheese costume and found Hope.

"Here you all are! You should've come with us on the Haunted Woods Ghost Tour," he said to us.

"It was so scary! The best!" Hope agreed, still clinging to Archie's arm. She had bright orange streaks through her short hair this time. Her long nails were painted orange and embellished with haunted-house nail art.

Thomas suddenly ducked behind Archie, not a great hiding spot given how thin Archie was.

Archie peeked over his shoulder at Thomas. "It's on the walking trail. There's nothing to be scared of here."

"I'm hiding from A. J. I just saw him over there. He's been hounding me for a story, but I'm saving it for my book. I'm gonna go. Take care, guys."

With goodbyes from us and extra kisses for Buttercup, Thomas slunk away.

"This harvest fair was a great idea," Baz declared.

"Our floats were a big hit," Archie said.

I was happy to see his effervescent personality back in full force.

I had followed Mrs. Schultz's motto and changed into a red cable-knit pullover for the evening to match my desired mood, but this time my emotions needed no convincing. The warmth I felt wasn't just from the bonfire and apple cider. My heart was warm with love for my friends and community. When A. J. published the story in the *Gazette* two days ago, neighbors who I'd only pass on the street or see occasionally in my shop, came by to make sure Mrs. Schultz and I were okay. I didn't mind that A.J. embellished the story to make himself the hero of the hour—I didn't need any more attention than I was already getting. I just wanted things to be back to normal. Now that we had pulled off a successful harvest fair, my friends were safe and happy, Heath and I were in a good place, and Roman and I were becoming closer, I finally felt like everything was going in the right direction. Even my stress-induced cheese cravings had dissipated.

"Roman!" A voice called from the darkness. A woman in a tight sweater dress and wedge heels came swishing over to us and hugged Roman. It was only after they'd released their embrace that I realized it was Angela, the former hostess of Apricot Grille.

"You guys know Gia, right?" Roman said to us.

Gia? I couldn't help but notice her arm had lingered around Roman's waist longer than necessary after the hug.

She introduced herself to the others while ignoring me. "I'm Angela. My friends call me Gia."

"Sure, from Apricot Grille," Baz said, nodding hello. He and I had caught Angela and her manager Derrick last spring making out in the restaurant's dumpster area.

"I'm not there anymore. I just found a much better job," she said. Her burgundy matte lips parted in a wide smile.

"Gia's replacing Chet. She'll be working with me at the meadery," Roman said with a smile to match hers.

As everyone wished them well, I plastered on a smile of my own. I reminded myself that life was good, although I couldn't deny a sudden craving for a hunk of soothing Curds & Whey cheese.

RECIPES

Bavarian Beer Cheese (Obatzda)

We celebrated autumn by bringing the best parts of Oktoberfest to Curds & Whey with this intensely flavored classic Bavarian spreadable cheese dip.

Start to finish time: Approximately 10 minutes (plus 3 hours chill time)

Serves: 8–12

Ingredients:
- 8 ounces Camembert, room temperature
- 6 ounces Romadur, Brie, or a spreadable cheese/cream cheese, room temperature
- 3 tablespoons butter, softened
- 4 tablespoons wheat beer or German beer
- 1¼ teaspoons sweet Hungarian paprika (or whatever paprika you have)
- ½ teaspoon ground caraway
- ½ cup onion, minced
- ¼ cup chives, finely chopped

Instructions:
Note: If you don't have a food processor or want a chunkier dip, you can mash ingredients together with a fork.

1. In a food processor, add roughly cubed cheeses and butter. Pulse until they are mashed together and fairly smooth.
2. Add beer and paprika. Pulse until combined.
3. Transfer dip into a bowl. Add ground caraway and mix.
4. Cover and store in refrigerator for three hours so flavors can meld.

5. While bringing to room temperature, mince onions and finely chop chives.
6. When ready to serve, mix in onions and top with chives. Serve with soft pretzels, hard pretzels, or salted pretzel bread.

The dip stays well for three days, refrigerated, without onions. Do not add the onions to any portion you plan to keep stored until you're ready to serve it.

Cheesy Apple Pockets

These savory autumn pastries kissed with dollops of smoked Gouda were a hit with Roman.

Start to finish time: 35 minutes (plus 40 minutes to thaw pastry)

Yields: 48 small pockets

Ingredients:
- 1 large Granny Smith apple (about 1½ cups, finely chopped)
- ¼ cup fresh chives, finely chopped
- 2 tablespoons sugar
- 3 ounces smoked Gouda cheese
- 1 package (2 sheets) puff pastry, thawed

Instructions:
1. Preheat oven to 400 degrees.
2. Peel, core, and finely chop apple into small chunks.
3. Mix apple chunks with chives and sugar in a bowl until coated.
4. Cut smoked Gouda into forty-eight ½-inch cubes.
5. On a lightly floured surface, roll thawed pastry sheet into a 16"×12" rectangle. Repeat with second sheet.
6. Cut each pastry sheet into twelve squares. (A pastry cutter or pizza cutter works best for this.) Then cut each square in half diagonally to make triangles. You'll have forty-eight triangles in all.
7. Put about ½ teaspoon of apple-chive mixture into each square.
8. Add one cube of Gouda to each.
9. Brush tips of pastry with water and fold them over the filling so they meet at the corners, first the two bottom halves of the triangle, and then the top— like an envelope. Press to seal. (If serving at home

and not transporting them, like I did, you can also keep the envelope open by not securing the third corner. This makes for a pretty presentation.)

10. Place the pastries on two baking sheets and bake for 15 minutes or until pastries are golden brown. Let cool on wire racks before serving or transporting.

Jalapeño Popper Grilled Cheese

This grilled cheese sandwich with an added kick helped "kick" some information out of one of our suspects. This vegetarian version can easily be made vegan by substituting vegan cheeses.

Start to finish time: Approximately 30 minutes
Serves: 4

Ingredients:
- 6 fresh jalapeños, seeded
- 1 tablespoon olive oil
- 8 slices hearty bread, like country white, sourdough, or ciabatta
- Butter for grilling
- 1 cup sharp cheddar cheese
- 1 cup garlic and herb cream cheese, room temperature

Instructions:
1. Preheat oven to 400 degrees.
2. Stem and cut jalapeños in half. Remove seeds. (Wash hands afterward.) Toss with olive oil.
3. On a baking sheet lined with parchment paper, place jalapeño halves skin-side up. Bake for 10–15 minutes until jalapeños start to blacken and blister.
4. Remove blackened jalapeños from oven. While hot, place in resealable plastic bag for 5 minutes to loosen skin. Tear skin off jalapeños and slice.
5. Butter four bread slices on one side. Place butter-side down on a sheet of wax paper.
6. Shred cheddar cheese. Put half of the cheese on these four bread slices. Slightly press into bread.
7. Put jalapeño skins on top of the cheddar cheese. Add remainder of cheese.

8. Slather cream cheese on the other four (non-buttered) bread slices.
9. Close sandwiches. Butter tops of bread.
10. Transfer to a pan. Grill both sides on medium heat until golden.